THE
CARLOS
CONTRACT

THE CARLOS CONTRACT

A Novel of
International Terrorism

DAVID ATLEE PHILLIPS

Macmillan Publishing Co., Inc.

NEW YORK

Macmillan Publishing Co., Inc.
866 Third Avenue, New York, N.Y. 10022
Collier Macmillan Canada, Ltd.

Library of Congress Cataloging in Publication Data
Phillips, David Atlee.
  The Carlos contract.
    1. Carlos, 1949–   —Fiction. I. Title.
PZ4.P5546Car [PS3566.H477] 813'.5'4   78–14378
ISBN 0–02–596110–1

First Printing 1978

Printed in the United States of America

For Gina

". . . One of my profoundest sorrows has been the experience that, thanks to the discipline of the hood, I learned to read much from the human eye alone and now, without the hood, to recognize the eye of violence in the streets, shops, parks, even on the television screens of my own and other ostensibly terrorist-free countries."

> —*Sir Geoffrey Jackson,* Surviving the Long Night, *the story of his captivity for eight months in a "peoples' prison" after being kidnapped by Tuparmaro terrorists in Uruguay.*

Carlos exists. He is a Venezuelan named Ilyich Rameriz-Sanchez, and he is the world's most audacious terrorist. The other characters in this novel are fictional.

While the story is imaginary, the events and counter-intelligence methods described are authentic, as I knew them during twenty-five years as an intelligence officer in eight foreign countries. Everything in this book was suggested by something that did occur, or could have, in the real life arena of espionage and secret operations.

THE
CARLOS
CONTRACT

1.

William McLendon tugged at his ear lobe, as he often did when distracted or disturbed, while he listened to the recorded weather report. The metallic voice droned out a ninety percent chance of rain which, even given the penchant of Washington's forecasters for covering all bets, meant the cancellation of his afternoon tennis match.

He dropped the telephone into its cradle, rose from his wooden office chair, and went to the window. The spires of the National Cathedral were shadows in the overcast sky. On Wisconsin Avenue two students from nearby St. Albans School clasped their caps as the wind scattered the last of November's leaves and swirled scraps of the *Washington Post* around the bus stop where the boys were waiting. McLendon patted the bulge under his belt buckle and promised himself to join a club with indoor courts where he could continue his thrice-weekly matches during the winter months.

The rap at the door was businesslike. McLendon walked through the unoccupied secretary's office and opened the door.

"Well, this is a surprise, Cook." He had not seen the bantam-like bureaucrat for two years, but unfortunately Willard Cook remained unchanged. He was a short, puffy man with theatrically silver hair and an air of pomposity. He wore a dapper but too-tight silk suit, a yellow shirt with ostentatious links clipping the French cuffs, and loafers with ornate buckles.

"Greetings, Mack." The handshake was loose and perfunctory. "You're looking great. Retirement must suit you." Cook waved toward a tall man standing patiently behind him. "This is Allen Symser."

Mack acknowledged the introduction, led the two visitors into his office, motioned them into chairs, and idly speculated on where Cook's fingernails were manicured. Certainly not in the austere barbershop in the basement at Langley headquarters.

"You probably don't smoke these," Mack said, offering his cigarettes first to Cook, who nodded negatively, then to Symser.

"I haven't seen any for more than thirty years," Symser said, quickly inspecting the pack of Gauloises, hesitating, then returning it to Mack. Symser was a slender, relaxed man. He wore an expensively-casual jacket, grey slacks, and ankle-high boots. And some sort of old-school tie, Mack guessed. He wondered whether Symser had been introduced to the French cigarettes during World War II. Probably not. Mack had first been offered one of the cigarettes by an American criminal in Marseilles. A fledgling OSS operative, Mack had found it useful in 1942 to work with the Mafia to thwart German efforts to sabotage the French port.

Symser smiled pleasantly. "Good of you to see me on such short notice, Mr. McLendon."

"Not at all," Mack said. "I'm not the busiest lawyer in town." He lit his Gauloise with a cheap, disposable lighter. "I gather you are not from the Agency."

"No, Mr. McLendon. I'm in charge of international operations for Scott-Wagner Petroleum. At the moment I'm on a special assignment." Symser leaned forward and peered past Mack. "That's a striking lithograph. I find it unusual to see a Siqueiros on the office wall of an ex-CIA man. Wasn't Siqueiros a communist?"

"Secretary-general of the Mexican party," Mack confirmed. "Fifteen years ago I saw one of his large canvases in the window of a gallery in Mexico City. Didn't recognize the painter, but I decided I just had to own that painting. I went inside and priced it. The gallery owner told me that if I were a Mexican citizen he would be pleased to sell it for $75,000, but that the oils of Siqueiros, and those of Rivera and Orozco, were considered part of the national patrimony and not to be sold to foreigners. So I settled for the lithograph."

Willard Cook cleared his throat. "Mack, Allen is here not only as a representative of Scott-Wagner but a number of other firms which do business overseas. You can speak freely with him. He has all the clearances the Company allows non-staffers. And . . ." Cook cleared his throat again, "you should know that I arranged for all your own clearances to be reinstated."

"Thanks," Mack said, dryly.

"One thing must be clear," Symser said. "I'm here in a private capacity for private firms to explore the feasibility of a private arrangement with you."

"But not so private that you came alone," Mack said. "As I recall, Scott-Wagner had a businesslike relationship with the Agency some years ago. Your Dallas office provided deep cover for some of our people overseas."

"That's right," Symser agreed, "but in 1975 that changed. Neither our stockholders nor Congress looks kindly on that type of relationship now. My only contact with CIA in recent times has been to ask Will to help me find someone not now connected with the government who can be useful to us on a contractual basis. We need a person with very special talents. Will and his associates tell me you are the man."

"The Agency recommended me as a *lawyer*?" Mack eyed Cook warily.

The telephone interrupted. Mack spoke briefly, agreeing the tennis game should be postponed and promising to call back when the weather cleared. Then Mack leaned back in the antique office chair. He pulled at his ear.

"What do you want, Mr. Symser? I'm only a sometime lawyer, hanging out my shingle because I had a degree when I went into OSS. I'm not much more than a wills-for-friends man. I have a comfortable pension. I'd rather spend my time doing some things and traveling to see some places I missed during my thirty years as a spook. Except for the tennis that's about it. What is your proposal?"

Cook cleared his throat again. "I've told Allen that you were the best street man in the outfit."

5

"And Will tells me that's what I'm looking for," Symser said. "A street man." Tantalized, he watched Mack blow a smoke ring. "May I have one of those, after all?" When Mack lit the cigarette, Symser inhaled gratefully.

"The dozen companies I represent have substantial investments and operations in thirty countries around the world. We have American executives in some places, and local managers in others. In the past two years four of our Americans have been assassinated and several kidnapped. One was kidnapped *twice*. We paid almost fifteen million dollars in ransom in one case."

"Argentina?" Mack asked.

"Yes. And it's not been much better with our indigenous executives. Beyond our concern for their personal safety, there's a financial problem. The cost of protection is becoming unacceptable: guards, follow-cars, alarm systems, ballooning insurance rates. One of our companies is being sued in a Detroit court by the family of an American technician ambushed by terrorists in the Middle East. The family is claiming that our protection was inadequate."

"Iran?"

"Yes." Symser looked at Cook. "It seems Mr. McLendon *does* know what's going on."

"I read newspapers," Mack said.

"We want to reduce our risk and cost factors," Symser said. "Will you help us?"

"No," Mack said, shaking his head. "You need the services of one of the companies specializing in personnel or plant security. Try Wackenhut. I'm not interested, even as a consultant."

Cook cleared his throat again, officiously. "Let Allen finish, Mack."

"We already use commercial firms for industrial protection," Symser said, "and each of our companies has its own security staff. But they aren't getting the job done. We're aware that violence against American corporations abroad is not going to go away, at least in the Third World countries. But there is an extra dimension to our problem: we find the attacks against us are now being orchestrated, with one man leading the effort, one single bastard responsible for most of the killings and abductions. He is costing us millions. We want you to help us reduce that expense."

"Who?" Mack asked.

"We don't know. But Will says the Agency does."

Mack turned to Cook and repeated his question.

The CIA officer cleared his throat again, hesitated, and then said, "Carlos."

"The Venezuelan terrorist?" Mack whistled softly. "You *do* have a problem, Mr. Symser. But even Carlos can't operate alone. He needs a support apparat to handle the money, logistics, and safe haven between operations. Over and above that, he needs some *éminence grise* who can command resources and open doors for him in a hurry with no questions asked." Again, Mack turned to Cook. "Who gives Carlos that support?"

"That we don't know," Cook said. "We suspect Quaddafi. He has a history of financing nuts with Libyan money if they are willing to attack American interests, especially the oil companies. Or it could be Amin or one of the other African groups. Maybe even the Sovs or the Cubans. We just don't know."

"And you don't have any sources inside Carlos's group?"

"Not even on the edges," Cook said. "We were pretty much on top of him when he was still a smalltime extremist in Caracas, but since then we've picked up only fragments from other services. We know that he is a young man, speaks several languages fluently, takes ridiculous chances and gets away with them. He has worked with most of the crackpot groups of Europe and the Middle East, but now he has developed his own organization. We haven't been able to penetrate it. Most of what we know about Carlos we read in the newspapers."

"He kidnapped the OPEC ministers in Vienna?"

"That," Cook said, "and killed two French counterintelligence people in Paris, laid seige to the French Embassy in the

7

Hague, pulled off two bazooka attacks against El Al planes . . . and so on. Altogether, Carlos has carried off more successful terrorist ops than anyone we know."

"What do you expect *me* to do about Carlos?" Mack asked Symser.

"Put him out of business," Symser said, speaking evenly.

Mack rose from his chair and went to the window. The rain had begun. A van splashed through the wet street. Mack smiled; the logo of one of the corporations most likely to be among those which had dispatched Symser was blazoned across the truck. Tough guys these business people, Mack mused, especially when it comes to trimming costs.

Cook cleared his throat again.

"Do you want a cough drop?" Mack asked the question without turning from the window. Of all the people in the Agency, why had the prissy Cook, whom he had disliked for twenty years, been sent?

"What about it, Mr. McLendon?"

"No," Mack said. He turned to Symser. "I don't like the odds. If I go after Carlos the chances are that I will become certifiably dead. He is a target for an organization, not a lone, retired ex-operative. A battalion of spies wouldn't be able to ferret out Carlos and neutralize him without an information data base. Without intelligence, *hard* intelligence, there's no way. I don't know whether Will mentioned it, Mr. Symser, but my parting with CIA wasn't exactly amicable. Will and some of his friends thought of me as a maverick, and I doubt they will be inclined to provide the kind of intelligence I would need to smoke out Carlos. I'm not even sure the Agency is capable, these days, of acquiring the hard product I would require."

"We're doing all right," Cook said defensively. "But you *would* have to work alone, for a number of reasons."

"Don't you bother to list your reasons," Mack said, "and I won't list mine."

Cook's face flushed. "I'll damned well tell you—"

Symser cut him short. "That's enough, Will." He addressed Mack. "But that's just what we insist on—that you work alone, without CIA collaboration. We can't afford to be associated with CIA, nor CIA with us, in any type of venture, even of this sort, after all the ruckus about ITT and the Agency in Chile. I have the authority to make a commitment now: whatever you need for expenses, and a suitable fee for your services."

"What will I do with the money, Mr. Symser? Ask Halston to design a shroud?" Mack lit another Gauloise. "I can't accept. Without information support from the Agency, I wouldn't even know where to begin. I know some fine former CIA and military operatives who might be willing to help me, but it would be farting against thunder to go after Carlos without intelligence. The terrorist target is the toughest target in espionage. Without CIA help I couldn't do it."

Symser shrugged, and rose from his chair.

"Wait." Cook touched Symser's shoulder. "Allen, allow me to speak to Mack for a moment. Alone."

"Very well." Symser extracted a cigarette from Mack's pack, lit it, and went to the secretary's office. Cook closed the door.

"Mack, I have a message from the Director." Cook's voice was low-key, conciliatory. "The Director told me to say he would consider it a personal favor if you take on Symser's assignment."

"The Director?" Mack laughed. "Hell, I've never even met the new Director."

"I know. But he believes you're the best man, perhaps the only man, to snare Carlos. He's reviewed your file. The Soviet case in Vienna. The Fifth of May Commando you wrapped up in Bogota. The STMAYBUD op against the Chinese. All of them."

"Did he read my final fitness report?"

"Now, Mack." Cook's tone was soothing. "There were some difficulties between you and the Agency, sure there were."

"Nothing," Mack said, "that couldn't have been resolved in ten or twenty years."

"The fact remains that you are the best counterterrorist specialist the Company ever had."

"I've had some luck," Mack admitted. "And there's no point

in denying that I've been bored recently. This case would be challenging." Then, looking at Cook, "So offer me a contract. I'll travel, work with the fellows in the stations abroad, and we might get lucky again."

"We can't do that, Mack."

"Why not? The Agency calls back retirees all the time for one-shot operations."

"Your case is . . . tricky. How would the new Senate intelligence committee react if they found you were on our payroll again?"

"Don't tell them."

"We have to tell them," Cook said, sighing. "We tell Congress everything now. Every covert action has to be run through the Senate committee—and through six others as well, three in each chamber. If the word got around that the legendary Mack McLendon was aboard again, Congress would tear us apart."

"Legendary?" Mack snorted. "My ass hurts."

"You know it would leak to the press. All those stories about Mack the Knife would be resurrected."

"Don't believe those ridiculous stories."

"They still come up at the Farm when the trainees belly up to the bar." Cook hesitated. "Aren't they true? What about the story that you cut off the ear of the Lebanese who jumped you in Damascus?"

"Of course not. It's a blivet."

"A what?"

"Two pounds of shit in a one pound sack," Mack said. "We had a knife fight and I accidentally notched one of his ears."

"Cowboy stuff. That was always your problem, Mack. How many other notches in other ears?"

"None."

"That's not what I've heard," Cook said. "But you know as well as I do there were other problems. An Agency regulation wasn't really considered on the books until you had broken it."

"Never broke an Agency regulation in my life," Mack said. "Just bent them when necessary."

"Things aren't the same in the outfit," Cook said. "No more

rough stuff. No more cowboys. No more being Matt Dillon in old Dodge City."

"I know," Mack said. "When they tried to make that kind of bureaucrat out of me in 1975 I told them thanks, but I was too old to learn how to be Rebecca of Sunnybrook Farm."

"Mack?" Cook glanced about the office furtively. "What are the chances this place is bugged?"

"Minimal," Mack said. "Who the hell would care?"

"I'm going to be straight with you and tell you why you've got to help us." Cook opened his collar, loosened his tie.

My, Mack thought, it must be serious.

"Carlos is murdering our station chiefs."

Mack drew in his breath, then exhaled slowly.

"Who? Dick Welch in Athens?"

"We still don't know who got Dick," Cook responded, "but that's when it began. For years, ambassadors and consuls and military attachés were targets and CIA people were immune, but not any longer."

"I read Chuck Leonard's obit in the *Post*," Mack said. "It said he died overseas of a heart attack."

"He was poisoned. One Sunday morning he went to the local golf course for a little relaxation. They found him stretched out stiff on the floor just outside the locker room. Someone had slipped a needle-sharp thumbtack through the soles of his golf shoes. Something new and something fast. He couldn't have lasted more than a few seconds—only put on one shoe."

"How do you know it was Carlos?"

"He claimed credit. A few days after Chuck died a letter mailed in Bonn reached the CIA box, the address that's in the phone book. Carlos said he had killed Chuck, and that there would be others."

"Were there?"

"Bob Cartwell, in Kuala Lumpur. Someone pretending to be a Marine guard from the embassy telephoned him at home to say there was a flash message to be answered. When Bob asked to speak to the communicator, he was told the radio man was busy receiving a second cable. Bob lived on the side of a steep hill outside town and went bombing down the road to answer what he thought were two urgent messages. On a hairpin curve his car hit a thirty-foot stretch of highway that had been smeared with grease. He went over the edge and rolled two hundred yards. They had to use torches to get his body out of his car."

Mack grimaced. "That fellow who carves the commemorative stars in the marble plaque at Langley headquarters must be working overtime."

"Then just two weeks ago Don Robertson died in Buenos Aires," Cook added. "He was deep, deep in the embassy woodwork, and had only been there a few weeks. We didn't believe anyone outside knew he was Agency, or even suspected he was Chief of Station there. He was gunned down outside his house coming home from work one night. Eleven slugs."

"Carlos again?"

"Another letter. This time posted in Panama."

"I won't say anything to Symser," Mack said, "but who is Carlos working for?"

"I tell you we don't know." Cook dabbed perspiration from his forehead with a monogramed handkerchief. "Maybe he's accumulated enough capital to go into business on his own. Remember, one of Symser's clients paid somebody more than fourteen million bucks. Whatever the case, we're worried. So far we've been able to keep word of the murders bottled up in the Agency, but sooner or later the news will get out. When it finally leaks, other terrorists and assorted nuts might try to emulate Carlos. If that happens, CIA people will be so busy with security there'll be no time for ops overseas. Morale will go down the drain. Wives and kids will be penned up, jumpy, and you can imagine the other problems. Hell, it's worse than the investigations. We have to stop him."

"Are you getting anything on Carlos from other services? The Brits? Israel's Mossad?"

"They're pretty leery about dealing with us these days," Cook explained. "They're afraid of the Freedom of Information Act, afraid their information might surface in this country."

"I knew Welch and Cartwell," Mack said, "but not Robertson."

"A comer. Youngest GS-fourteen in the Clandestine Service. What about it, Mack? Will you help?"

"Are you sure about Symser?"

"Absolutely," Cook said. "He has the authority and the money to support you right down the line."

"But not the intelligence I need," Mack said. He went to his desk, sat in the wooden chair, and uncovered his old Underwood. He slipped a paper in the typewriter and began to type:

Director of Central Intelligence
Washington, D.C. 20505

Sir,
Pursuant to the Freedom of Information Act, as amended in February 1975, I request any information in your files concerning "Carlos," whose true name is Ilyich Rameriz-Sanchez, a Venezuelan citizen.

William McLendon

Mack pulled the paper from the typewriter and handed it to Cook. "Thanks for the idea. You always were a good staff man. I need everything you have. Now, and for as long as I am on the assignment. Tell the new Director that's a demand."

"You're crazy, Mack. He'll never agree. We have fifty lawyers working on FOI now. God knows, we don't want to set the precedent of opening up the files to ex-CIA people."

"My request is perfectly legitimate," Mack said. "My rights as a citizen. The Agency has the authority to declassify its own information, and there's no reason not to do so for its own benefit, and for American citizens in legitimate business overseas. How many thousands of pages have you passed out to kooks who clobber you with it in magazines? At least I can promise to protect the sources. If you have any flak from Congress or the press you can say you're simply complying with the law. Tell Symser the same thing."

"The seventh floor will never buy it," Cook said.

"Then find yourself another boy," Mack said. "One more condition. I understand that I'm not to expect operational help or support from CIA people. But I will need an FOI case officer who can meet me, even travel with me, if necessary. And I'm not talking about one of those lawyers. I want someone who has ops experience, who can cut through the red tape and dig into the files quickly. Available on a full-time basis. Is Skip Wilson in town?"

"Yes," Cook replied. "Are you sure you want Skip?"

"I'm sure."

"I'll ask."

"Insist!" Mack went to the door, and opened it. "Come in, Mr. Symser. Let's talk." He handed Symser a notepad. "You should take a few notes."

Mack waited until Symser was seated, and his gold pen poised.

"How many of your people are aware you've come to me? How many know my name?"

"Only my chief, Crassweiler, Chairman of the Board of Scott-Wagner. For now," Symser added.

"Forever," Mack said. "Keep it to yourself and Crassweiler. Tell any others they'll just have to trust you, without knowing my identity. If I find that my name has leaked to even one other person, the contract is null and void. Do you understand that I'm serious?"

"I understand," Symser said. "And I believe the principals will agree."

"I must also ask that you give me the list of companies underwriting the operation."

"That I can do now." Symser rapidly named the sponsors. The final corporate giant was an internationally known telecommunications company.

Mack smiled. He had been right about the passing van. "Okay," he said, "except for the last one. Scratch it. The others will have to make up the monetary difference. I won't be linked to a firm already being probed by a grand jury."

"What else?"

"Draft a contract," Mack said. "Unless you type, make it handwritten on one page. No secretaries. One copy for me. My customary fee is $250 a day, but for this venture I'll ask $1,000. For one hundred days. Then we'll see."

14

"Accepted," Symser said. "You do understand that for IRS purposes the payments will be described as legal fees?"

"Weekly deposits into my account for expenses." Mack opened his desk drawer, removed a checkbook, and ripped a deposit slip from the back. "This is the account, until I open another exclusively for our operation. I'll need an initial deposit of $50,000 and will expect you to check and bring the balance back to that level every week or so. There'll be a great deal of travel, first class, among other expenses. I'll provide an accounting at the termination of the contract, but none of the names on the receipts will be true names."

"False signatures on receipts?" Symser frowned.

"I am convinced," Mack said, "that the aircraft company in your consortium will have had some experience along those lines."

Cook chuckled. Symser smiled thinly.

"If we sign the contract," Mack continued, "I'll be giving you a list of several friends who will be joining me. I'm sure they can be prevailed upon to accept a term life insurance policy from you for the duration of the operation. Say, $125,000 each."

"Done," Symser said. "What does 'if' mean?"

"I'll let you know first thing in the morning if we have a deal. Where are you staying?"

"I'm at the Madison. But as far as I am concerned I can draft the contract now and make the deposit this afternoon."

"No." Mack looked at Cook. "My decision depends on Willard and the Company. While I'll agree to operate independently, I must have some basic information. I'll know tonight."

"I can't promise an answer so quickly," Cook said. "You know how the bureaucracy works."

"It works damned fast at Langley when it has to," Mack said. "Go to the seventh floor, genuflect, and tell the Director I expect to see Skip Wilson tonight. Dinner at The Angler's Inn at eight. If Skip shows I'll do business with Mr. Symser. If not, forget it."

Symser stood. "A final question. Since $100,000 is not chicken feed, my principals will want to know exactly what

15

they might expect. What is your definition of putting Carlos out of business?"

Mack stroked an ear lobe. "That, as the result of my operation, Carlos will be incapacitated. In prison." Mack looked directly at Symser. "Or in the ground."

This time it was Symser who cleared his throat, not Cook.

His visitors gone, Mack covered the typewriter, dumped the ashtrays, and flipped the triple lock on the office door as he left. He rode the elevator to his fifth-floor apartment.

Mack hesitated, as he often did when entering his apartment, to contemplate the floor-to-ceiling bookshelves and the collection of paintings he had accumulated over the years from the countries where he had served. The apartment was a little untidy, and Mack spent a few minutes putting it in order. Then he changed to a sweat suit and went out on the small balcony where he usually exercised; it was still drizzling. He returned to the apartment for his daily push-ups. When he finished the mandatory fifty, he marvelled at his discipline, particularly after so many years of loathing every minute of the exercise.

Mack showered, squirmed into an old jumpsuit, and entered his kitchenette to boil two eggs. That and a scoop of cottage cheese would be his lunch. Having lived alone for almost ten years—after the divorce and his only child's departure for college—Mack had learned that his penchant for cocktail-hour relaxation and rich evening meals at Le Provençal or The Company Inkwell precluded breakfast, and permitted only the most meager luncheon. He made two telephone calls during the four and a half minutes the eggs boiled: to reschedule his tennis match for the next morning (weather permitting), and to make a reservation for two at The Angler's Inn.

As he lingered over lunch, Mack experienced a palpable second-thought shudder. Why had he agreed to sign a contract on Carlos? Such hasty bravado might lead to the writing of his own death warrant. Mack was resigned to the fact that he would have to attend at least one funeral, but why seek out that inevitable ceremony? Over the years in the Company he had gained a reputation as a fearless operator, but in fact he had been frightened for his life many times, and once had actually lost control of his sphincter. Jesus! What would his colleagues have thought if they had suspected that? And he had never become inured to the pain of looking at death when he saw it in the grey face of a friend.

And what *about* his friends—Clyde Warner, for instance? Clyde and Mack had worked together on several high-risk operations, and Clyde would be the first person Mack would ask to join him in this new operation. Clyde had resigned from the Agency five years before Mack had retired. He owned a prosperous consulting firm in Washington now, had a lovely wife, and three kids in college. Could Mack expect him to agree to participate in such a foolhardy adventure?

In addition to questioning the wisdom of involving friends, Mack questioned his own actual ability to outwit Carlos. Had his professional talents and determination atrophied? Would he be a fool to enter the arena again?

And, more importantly, did he still have the gift of perceiving when grandmother was on the roof?

Mack had once been given a memorable bit of advice by a senior CIA officer and veteran Latin American hand: "An important part of intelligence work is sensing, before you have hard proof, that a critical development will occur. Call it professional intuition, the conviction that a number of pieces, when eventually assembled into enough of the entire puzzle, will constitute a revelation that is vital. I always try to think of it in terms of knowing when grandmother is on the roof."

"Of *what?*" Mack had asked.

The older officer had then launched into a story which he identified as Brazilian folklore, a "Portuguese story" somewhat on the order of yesterday's Irish and today's Polish jokes.

A Portuguese man living in Brazil, Mack's mentor had said, received a cable from his cousin in Portugal, announcing the death of the family cat, a pet the immigrant had been especially fond of. "Our beloved cat," the message said, "fell from our roof to her death in the street below."

The immigrant wrote to his cousin in Lisbon: "Do not send

such a message again. I am a sensitive person; I can't stand shocks. Should such a thing happen again consider my temperament and let me know gently, in stages. For example, you should have sent a message saying, 'The cat went up on the roof.' Then, a few days later another, saying, 'The cat went to the edge of the roof.' Then, finally, a letter with the bad news: 'The cat fell off the roof and died.'"

Some months later the immigrant in Brazil received another cable from his cousin. This time it read: "Grandmother just went up on the roof."

"So that's what you must look for," Mack's friend had told him. "That one new piece of information, perhaps a single line in a report, some awareness which gives you a funny feeling at the back of the neck—the suspicion which suddenly becomes a conviction that something important is in motion, that grandmother is on the roof."

Mack rinsed his dishes in the small sink. With or without grandmother, he told himself, he would need good intelligence. He wondered if the Agency would accept his demands for information on Carlos and for Skip's designation as his liaison officer. Even so, locating and confronting Carlos would be a tricky operation—"hairy" in the intelligence jargon. The Venezuelan had staged a dozen audacious operations for political movements in Europe and the Middle East. Was he now planning new, even more dramatic, ones? Or, had he become a freelancer simply for the money he could extract from Symser's business colleagues? And why a vendetta against CIA? Why was he killing station chiefs? Whatever the answers to such questions might be, one thing was certain: it would be only a matter of time before Carlos would be aware that Mack was on his trail. Then the mission would be hairy indeed.

It would take some luck. Mack recalled that baseball manager Branch Rickey was once asked how he had been so lucky in producing pennant-winning teams. Rickey had explained that it was easy: he contracted the best players available, worked their asses off, then waited until he was lucky.

Mack knew he would need a team, and he would have to assemble it quickly. Members of the old breed, with language and area expertise as well as guts, who had, for one reason or another, left the business.

And Skip. Mack enjoyed the quicksilver anticipation. It would be exciting as hell to be in action again.

Especially if Skip were on the team.

The waiter was a Latin American, probably an Ecuadorian, despite the reasonably convincing French-accented English he affected. Too bad; The Angler's Inn had become pretentious.

"Martini, straight up," Mack said. "A few drops of brandy, no vermouth. And a Jack Daniels on the rocks, with a twist. Bring them both now."

Mack looked at his watch: it was two minutes before the hour. Probably Skip had arrived early and was waiting in the parking lot so as to be on time, a habit derived from years of experience when a meeting had to be aborted if the timing was not precise.

A fire crackled in the huge hearth. Mack sat on one of the several stuffed sofas in the dimly-lit lounge; each sofa faced a low table illuminated by a candle in a hurricane lamp. A young woman and a much older man wearing riding clothes whispered and nuzzled in the corner, while another couple, hand in hand, ascended the ship's circular stairway to the dining room.

Janet Wilson entered and walked past the fireplace toward Mack. Her full-length leather coat hung open, revealing the easy movement of her firm stride. She wore a cashmere sweater and black slacks. Mack's breath quickened. He stood to take her coat, draping it over the end of the sofa.

"Hi, Skip. Long time." He looked first at the small Haitian amulet which she wore on an almost invisible chain, then raised his eyes to find Skip challenging his gaze as she sank into the low sofa. She crossed her legs, slowly, while staring at Mack without speaking.

Mack fell into thought. Who would suspect that this woman

—with her fine body, high cheekbones, golden hair trapping the fire's light—was one of the best in the business?

The waiter served their drinks. Skip shook her head at Mack's proffered Gauloise. Finally she spoke.

"You son of a bitch."

"Now, Skip," Mack said, "that's a gamy salutation after such a long time. Why?"

Skip lifted her glass, testing the drink.

"Because you were waiting for me here, at the same place, even the same table. Because you were arrogant enough to order my drink on the assumption that after three years I still drink bourbon on ice. Because I was called into the Director's office this afternoon and given this new, dubious assignment."

"Welcome aboard, Skip." Mack lifted his glass, smiling tentatively. "I'll need help."

"Why me?" Skip asked. "For your information, you managed to scuttle the assignment I've been wanting for twenty years. They yanked me from the COS course. I expected to be overseas by the end of the month, my first COS job."

"The Office of Equal Opportunity is alive and thriving at Langley," Mack said. "A distaff Chief of Station. That's new."

"New, but not a first."

"What were the Director's marching orders?" Mack asked.

"That I'm to be your FOI connection," Skip replied. "Pulled out of the COS course for this . . . staff job."

"What else?"

"He confirmed what I've known for a long time—that you are a lunatic, that you are contemplating suicide by going head to head against Carlos."

"And that you will pass me everything the Agency has on him?"

"It's not much," Skip said. "The file is thick, but the bits and pieces don't make much of a picture. Just what Willard told you today: that Carlos has his own squad now, and he writes us faithfully when he kills one of our chiefs. The Director also reiterated that I'm not to participate operationally. I only serve as a channel between the Agency and you; so

20

we will be clean if there's a flap and the Senate intelligence committee calls us to testify."

"Not us," Mack said. "I don't have to talk to anyone, not even a Congressional committee. I'm a private citizen with a lawyer-client relationship to protect. Do you have a psychological profile on Carlos?"

"I don't know."

"You don't *know?*" Mack arched an eyebrow. "In the old days you always knew everything about your operations."

"May I remind you that I've been on this one for less than three hours," Skip said. "I did try and check with the shrinks but it was too late; they go home early. And I had other things to do, including breaking a dinner engagement."

"What kind of poison killed Chuck Leonard? Shellfish toxin?"

"Very funny." Skip sipped her drink again, this time appreciatively. "A cyanide base, mixed with a simple chemist's extract from rat poison, a common brand available in vast quantities at any exterminator's. The techs are working on it."

"And the weapon used on Robertson?"

"Ingram nine millimeter submachine gun, thirty-eight caliber." Skip touched her hair absently, an ineluctably feminine gesture. "Made by an outfit in Powder Springs, Georgia. Thirty-two clip cartridge, effective at one hundred meters single-shot, and more if sprayed at the full automatic setting."

"And," Mack added, "designed for use with a silencer, in fact out of balance without it. Concealable inside a suit coat. Practically no recoil. No purpose other than killing by stealth."

Skip nodded.

"If I wanted to change the subject rather abruptly," Mack said, "I would say that it's good to see you again and that you continue to be a lovely woman."

"*Un poca pasada,*" Skip said. She touched her hair again.

"Not at all over the hill," Mack said. He reached forward and fondled the ebony amulet where it hung between her breasts, taut under the cashmere. She pushed his hand away.

"Please don't." Suddenly Skip's eyes were rimmed with silver. She spoke softly, near tears. "Please don't touch me and please let me out of this assignment. I want to go back to the COS course. Any one of a dozen people could handle the job. Don't involve me."

Mack thought. "No, Skip. I need you, for professional reasons. And it's been too long. Remember the week in Port-au-Prince? Why can't we begin again?"

"Yes, I remember." Skip dabbed at her eyes with a cocktail napkin. "I remember it well, and with pleasure. It was exciting and beautiful and I'm glad we had it. But no more."

"Why?"

"You know why."

"Webb?"

"Of course."

"How many years since you've seen him?" Mack asked.

"Fifteen in January."

"That's a long time."

"Another ten years to go," Skip said. "Unless he gets time off for good behavior or there's some sort of political deal."

"Not likely with Fidel," Mack said. "Castro's not much for commuting sentences, especially for CIA agents convicted of espionage in Havana after the Bay of Pigs. How often do you hear from him?"

"Half a dozen times a year, when they allow him to write or when he is able to smuggle a note out of *La Cabana.*"

"Nothing has worked?"

"Nothing. The Agency's attempted a number of gambits: all sorts of offers made indirectly, things they thought Castro couldn't turn down. If Webb were in a Soviet prison there would have been some sort of exchange by now."

"I knew Webb even before you married him," Mack said. "I remember him as an understanding kind of guy."

"That's irrelevant," Skip said. "If he can survive in *La Cabana*, I can survive in a cold bed. And I have, too . . . except for that week we had in Haiti."

"All right." Mack snuffed his cigarette. "Strictly business then."

"What do you expect from me?" Skip asked.

"Absorb everything the Agency has on Carlos. Then be at my

place day after tomorrow, at eight. We'll have a Chinese dinner reunion."

Skip shook her head.

"Please, Skip," Mack said. "I need your help. I'm going to try to put a team together. Some of the retired old-timers, and younger fellows who quit early. But I know now it won't be easy. I wanted Clyde Warner to come aboard more than anyone else; he knows Europe and the Middle East, has the languages he needs, and he and I carried off some tough ones when we were working together. But before coming here tonight I stopped off at his place to discuss it, and he told me to get lost. He said he wasn't about to risk everything he has now—his family, his business—on such a dubious scheme. I'll have to find others to help: Frank Coughlin, maybe Hyphenated-Jake and Emilio Gonzalez, if I can find him. I understand Lucy has retired and is running a computer service downtown. She could be useful. We'll have a strategy session, then start turning over some flat rocks."

"Mack, are you really committed to this?" Skip asked. "Don't you realize that the risk factor is just out of sight. Carlos wouldn't have lasted this long without superb support and his own intelligence network. Within a week he'll know you're sniffing after him, and he'll cut you to pieces."

"Maybe," Mack said. "But he's murdering friends of mine. Maybe I can cut him down to size."

"Still the street man," Skip said, "still the tough guy. Mack the Knife."

"That foolishness." Mack touched his ear.

"Yes, that foolishness."

"We'll see," Mack said. "Let's order and have dinner upstairs. Then we'll come back to the fire and have some rum."

"Rum? After dinner?"

"Remember the Barbancourt Five Star in Port-au-Prince? We sipped it instead of brandy all that week."

"They won't have it here," Skip said.

"They do," Mack said. "I brought along a bottle for the bartender. The corkage will be outrageous."

"I suppose I'll be sorry," Skip said, "if Carlos destroys you."

23

"So then you'll be at the reunion?"

"Yes," Skip said. "I'm a little crazy, too."

After the dinner and more drinks by the fire, Skip made a call from the pay phone while Mack settled with the waiter. He spoke to him in Spanish, and found that he had been wrong; the waiter was Uruguayan, not Ecuadorian.

So now Skip was in it with him. Mack felt queasy. Why the hell had he listened to Cook? Rooting around the international terrorist nether world was the Company's responsibility, not his. His loyalties were no longer with the Company, but with himself; with Tom, off at school; with friends he was about to involve. Why hadn't he looked ahead and considered all the factors?

Had he decided to do it for the money? A thousand bucks a day was enticing.

Mack walked with Skip to her car in the parking lot alongside the canal. They stood together for a moment in the cool rain.

"I have more Barbancourt at the apartment," Mack said.

"No," Skip said. "Thanks, but no thanks."

Mack drove slowly, with after-drink caution, down MacArthur Boulevard toward Washington's center. What a shame, he thought, that Skip is going home to a cold bed. And so was he.

Headlights flickered off and on behind him. Skip was signaling. Had she changed her mind? He stopped, and Skip pulled up beside Mack's old Cougar.

"Hey, James Bond," she laughed, "better take your heap in to be fixed. Your muffler is about to fall off."

2.

Symser turned down the volume on the morning television news when the telephone rang in his room at the Madison. "Yes?"

"Bill McLendon here, Mr. Symser. I accept. You may make that deposit now."

"I'll be there when the bank opens."

"Later today," Mack said, "I'll open another account and rent a post office box. I'll let you know. Where will you be?"

"In my Los Angeles office, at least for the next three weeks."

"Rent a post office box at your end for our exclusive use. Then scout around your home and office, list the numbers of a half dozen pay phones which are accessible day and night, and give each of them a code designation like Alpha, Bravo, Charlie, and so on. Send the numbers and post office address to me. Also our contract. I'll sign your copy and return it to you."

"Mr. McLendon, I have no objection to playing cloak-and-dagger, but is it likely that anyone will read our mail and listen to our telephone conversations in this country?"

"Highly unlikely now. But during the next few weeks the chances will increase. My first priority will be locating Carlos's support apparat, and once he realizes I'm on his trail his first move will be to try to find my sponsor."

"My!" Symser laughed weakly. "You make it sound as if I might become personally involved in this."

"Not," Mack said, "if we are careful. I'll do my best to keep you out of it—and I remind you that my name, and the identities of my associates, are not to be revealed to anyone other than Crassweiler and whoever is necessary in lining up our insurance policies."

25

"I understand."

"When I telephone you at your office or home I'll use your code indicators to tell you which of the public telephones to go to for our conversation."

"You really are serious about all this?"

"Mr. Symser, when I first went off to the university my father told me to be happy. His only other parting remark was this: he had observed that most successful people were reasonably clever and very, very polite. When I started working in secret operations I soon found that the important thing was to be reasonably clever and very, very *careful*. You'll hear from me soon."

Francis Coughlin tilted his patrician profile. His eyes narrowed behind the bifocals: he looked like an elderly physician listening to a patient's heartbeat. "Mack, there's something loose under your car."

"I know," Mack said. "Muffler. Remind me to have it fixed."

Mack gunned the old Cougar up the ramp toward Rosslyn and the Virginia end of ancient Key Bridge. As he crossed the Potomac, he could see rain clouds rolling over Georgetown University's towers and the lean, expensive houses clinging to the Prospect Street cliff. Mack turned on to the Whitehurst Freeway, heading downtown through the Georgetown area.

"Where are we going, Mack?"

"To visit a friend, Frank, and to persuade her to join a team I'm trying to put together for a risky project. I hope you will work with us, too. I'll be traveling frequently for the next few weeks." Mack lit a Gauloise. "I'm going to ask you to hold down the office."

"A desk job?" Frank was taken aback. "I'm no good at a desk."

Mack stopped at a light and prepared to turn off K Street toward Dupont Circle. He smiled at his friend. "Francis, you are a man of almost unique talents, but it's been a long time since you've been on the street."

Frank snorted. "Too damned old is what you mean." He removed his bifocals and polished the lenses, as he always did when irritated. "Civil service doesn't require government employees to quit until they're seventy. Didn't you read about the three judges ruling that mandatory retirement at sixty for foreign service officers is unconstitutional? How can the State Department and the Company dump people like us now? Why, if that decision is upheld I can insist on going back to work."

Mack smiled. "For a few months, maybe. With the problems it's having now, all the Agency needs is to have a bunch of old farts like you and me padding around the halls at Langley."

"You," Frank said, "are a young fart. But why shouldn't I go back? My brain's not addled. My fingers are nimble and, if I say so myself, I'm holding together pretty well. The other day I visited a friend in Foggy Bottom and a woman stopped me to ask if I were Ellsworth Bunker. He's still working—and *he's* over eighty!"

"Francis, how did a nice boy like you wander from the Ivy League into the business of being safecracker, forger and expert in surreptitious entry?"

"Drifted into it," Frank replied. "After the war when I came aboard with the Agency from OSS, someone read in my file that I had been a cartoonist on the *Harvard Crimson*. They were scurrying all around old K building, the reflecting pool, and the Lincoln Memorial looking for someone to fabricate some documents. My supervisor asked me to do it on the rather risky premise that anyone who could draw could imitate the signature of an East German communist. He was right . . . in my case."

Frank admired a nubile young girl as she sashayed in front of the Cougar; he blinked appreciatively.

Mack, despite his query, was familiar with Frank's Agency career, and how the impromptu forger had eventually become one of the most dependable odd-job experts in the business. He had been sent to work at a half dozen factories around the country to learn how tumblers were designed and safes constructed around them. Over the years he had studied locks and picks until he could open doors in a jiffy, flaps and seals until he could open and close letters and packages with his eyes shut. Then Frank had studied the advanced course on phony documents: ink, paper, paste, and type. For more than two decades he was the operative CIA would dispatch overseas for tricky second-story operations, or when anything had to be taken apart, photographed, and reassembled so cleverly that the owner would not realize his property had been compromised. Frank's exploits were legendary in the Agency, especially at the Farm—the CIA training school in Virginia several hours' drive from Langley—where students were enthralled when instructors recounted the exciting details of his many successful operations.

Mack also recalled that one of Frank's operations had resulted in disaster, but he enjoyed hearing Frank tell the story of the flap, and asked him about it.

"Yes," Frank said, "I had some real trouble back in fifty-seven. It was an entry into communist party headquarters in Vienna. I was to get in, photograph the files, and get out. A fairly routine job. I had no problem jumping the wall, climbing to the roof, lowering myself through a window into the top-floor office of the Party chief, and finishing the job before midnight. But I decided the safest way to decamp was to wait until morning and amble out when people started entering the building. So I poked around the office to kill time and found a well-stocked bar with a bottle of Dutch gin, a brand I had become genuinely fond of while working with the Resistance in Amsterdam. There was a tremendous photograph of the Party chief hanging behind the desk. So I relaxed in a stuffed chair, sipped the gin straight, and occasionally toasted the man whose taste in liquor I appreciated so much. The more gin I drank, the more I became fascinated by the man's portrait. He was a clean-shaven type but it occurred to me that with a proper mustache he would look exactly like Joe Stalin. I guess I was a little drunk, because I just couldn't resist the urge to pencil a great big flowing mustache onto the photograph. By God, I was right! He was a dead ringer

28

for Old Joe! Of course I had to have another drink to *that.* Then I fell asleep, woke later than I had planned, and beat it without being spotted. No one would ever have known that I had copied those documents except . . .″

"Except," Mack said seriously, "you forgot about the mustache?"

"Unfortunately," Frank said. "Of course I had had every intention of erasing it before departing. How could I have forgotten such a thing? When the communist leader opened his office the next morning he knew he had been had because his portrait had grown a mustache overnight."

"I don't believe a word of it," Mack said.

"It's true. When I got back, Allen Dulles almost threw me out. Only time in my life I ever heard him use abusive language. He refused to use me on another operation for almost two years—until he was convinced by my vows that I would never have another drink. And I haven't." Frank glanced down as Mack snuffed out his Gauloise. "Or a cigarette, either, for that matter."

Mack was still smiling when he stopped the car in front of an old townhouse converted into offices. In the lot next door a dozen men in sweat suits were tossing a football back and forth to a group of teenagers.

Frank asked, "Mack, where are we?"

"Remember Lucy Stevenson?"

"Certainly," Frank said. "For years Lucy and I exhibited together at the Agency's annual rose show."

"She's retired now," Mack said. He pointed to the second floor of the building. "Running a computer service. I hope she'll agree to join me, and you, in the operation."

"What's the operation, Mack?" Frank was leery. "Are you planning something that will get us all in trouble?"

"Carlos, the international terrorist, has been murdering CIA station chiefs. Bob Cartwell, and at least two others. I'm going to try to stop him killing any more."

"Bob? Why, the three of us worked together on the Solkowski defection in Hamburg in sixty-two."

"Are you with me?"

"Under those circumstances, yes. And not just at a desk. I can still operate."

"It looks like we'll have to work overseas, and it might be pretty tough."

"You may be twenty years younger," Frank said, "but I have a question for you. Who was leading five games to three this morning when the first set was rained out?"

"We'll see," Mack said. "Now let's recruit Lucy."

"My son's with those boys playing football out there," Lucy said, pointing through the window of her office. "He's the only one in the neighborhood who knows I was with the Company. Watch your talk if he comes in here with his friends. They think I spent the last twenty years working at the Pentagon."

"Does it make that much difference," Mack asked, "now that you're retired?"

"I don't want to be hassled. Half the folks down here are convinced the CIA had something to do with shooting Martin Luther King and the other half don't believe it only because they think the FBI acted alone. The climate is simply not conducive to objective discussions about the intelligence community, so be discreet with shoptalk."

Lucy Stevenson had gained weight since Mack had last seen her at Langley, but he still rated her as an unusually handsome woman. She was obviously delighted to see old friends and relished the opportunity to exchange gossip about former colleagues. Such gossip is always the first order of business when former intelligence people get together. For the participants, it's a sort of ritualistic flashing of credentials, a demonstration of their good standing in that closed society. She served coffee in Styrofoam cups while they chatted. When the social exchange was exhausted, Lucy walked to a dull grey machine the size of two breadbaskets and patted it affectionately. "Gentlemen, this is Butterfly, the sweetest little computer this side of Langley."

"Very expensive I understand," Frank said.

"I lease it," Lucy explained. "The problem is to find enough clients to pay the cost and then some."

"I can offer you a contract," Mack said, lighting a cigarette, "a contract which will keep Butterfly aloft for at least three months."

"Oh dear me!" Lucy put her hands on her hips, looking first at Mack and then at Frank. "I think highly of both of you," she said, "and it's good to see you. But, let me make it clear that I'm out of the spy business for good. I learned enough about those big computers at Langley to make this little one hum industriously and, I hope, profitably. Aunt Lucy has a good thing going, and I don't want to spoil it by becoming tainted by the intelligence connection. Not these days."

Mack nodded thoughtfully for a few seconds and then said, "Lucy, I know you remember the Carlos case. Well, I've taken on the job of finding Carlos."

Lucy's eyes widened. "You're working again?"

"My own operation entirely, except for some biographical info and other traces from the Agency. We will be acquiring other data on our own during the next few weeks, and I need you and Butterfly to keep track of it. When you were working you probably knew more about Carlos than anyone else in the Agency."

"More than I really cared to know about that maniac. But how did you get into this?"

Mack elaborated: his meeting with Cook and Symser, the agreement that Skip would act as liaison for information, the terms of the contract—and Carlos's campaign against American companies as well as his vendetta against Agency station chiefs.

"Who will be working with us?" Frank asked.

" 'El Indio,' for one," Mack said. "Otherwise known as Emilio Gonzalez. Best dark alley operator I ever worked with in the military. He retired recently when the Pentagon abolished his task force created to handle really sensitive intelligence operations. I'm also going to try to locate Clarence Clements. Maybe you know him. He's a colorful old-timer, a former Tucson sheriff, with a background in OSS and border patrol.

In the sixties he trained counterinsurgency forces in three or four Latin American countries under the A.I.D. public safety program."

"Carlos is only twenty-nine," Lucy said. "The team you're putting together sounds—forgive me, Frank—a touch geriatric for the assignment."

Mack nodded. "You're right, Lucy. I need a couple of real street men. There'll be some hairy chores overseas. Clyde Warner would have been just right, but he turned me down flat. He made a valid point: the Agency won't be around to help us if we get into scrapes, and certainly won't go behind the scenes to ask liaison services to spring us if we find ourselves in jail somewhere. I was thinking of asking Jacob Klupperman. Remember Hyphenated-Jake? He speaks several languages with native fluency, is full of piss and vinegar leavened with guile, and was without question the best street man in the Agency when he quit in 1975. He told me he was fed up with the investigations and headlines in Washington. But, even worse, he claimed the Soviets and Cubans were laughing at him when he tried to recruit and convince them the Agency could still keep agent reports and identities secret."

"I don't know him," Frank said. "Where does the 'hyphenated' come from?"

"Jake is a Jewish boy from New York," Lucy explained, "and he looks it. He used to give the operational fellows fits because he insisted on using the cover of society types with hyphenated aliases. I remember he once worked under the assumed name of Talbot-Jones." Lucy turned to Mack. "There's another young hotshot who left the Agency. Perhaps you should talk to him. Do you know Perry Allison?"

"Name rings a bell, that's all," Mack said.

"Rich young kid," Lucy said. "Left the outfit in 1971 because his father became ill and needed Perry to run the family business, a petroleum investment fund called the Allison Trust. In 1973, Carlos spent a month in Venezuela and the Agency decided to try to recruit him to report on European terrorists. The computers coughed up a card indicating that

32

Perry was the right man to give Carlos the pitch. Perry had grown up with his family in an American oil community in Maricaibo where he was born; he attended high school in Caracas, knew Venezuela, and spoke fluent Spanish. Perry agreed to come back on a short-term contract to make the pitch. He spent three weeks at headquarters digging into the files on Carlos, and so he knows him well, at least up through seventy-three. He managed to talk with Carlos in Caracas, but Carlos turned the pitch down cold."

"I don't know, Lucy." Mack stroked his ear. "I mean I don't know him."

"I can vouch for him," Lucy said. "He shouldn't be hard to find. He's known as an international jet setter, and his name is in the gossip columns all the time. Even so, he's a profes—"

There was a sudden crash and window glass erupted into the office.

Mack reached out for Lucy and dropped to the floor, pulling her down with him.

"What in heaven's name?" Lucy was bewildered.

On the floor, a few inches in front of Mack and Lucy, a football bounced back and forth, quivered, and was still. Mack eyed the football grimly, and helped Lucy to her feet.

It's early in the operation, Mack told himself, for me to become paranoid. In the seconds following the crash of glass he had entertained the notion that someone—Carlos?—had become aware of his intentions and was trying to kill him.

"Sorry, Lucy," Mack said.

"Junior's football!" Lucy exclaimed. She stepped carefully through the broken shards, then shouted out the window. "Junior! Get yourself up here right now and see what you've done!" She turned to Mack and Frank. "I swear, I don't know what I'm going to do with that boy!"

Junior appeared in the office door, his head hanging and a sheepish grin on his face. Junior was wearing a sweat suit and was, Mack calculated, about thirty. He was at least six feet five inches tall, and probably weighed close to 240. Junior went to his mother and put his arm around her.

"Mom, I'm really sorry." Junior's voice was in the bass range. "One of the kids is just learning to kick." He turned to the visitors. "Hope no one was hurt."

"We're okay," Frank said.

"I'll sweep this up, Mom."

"Never you mind," Lucy said. "But soon as you finish that football game out there, get down to the hardware store and buy a pane of glass so it won't rain in here tonight." She introduced the visitors. "I used to work with Mr. McLendon and Mr. Coughlin, son."

Junior shook hands with Mack and Frank. "My name is Albert."

Junior picked up the football, smiled at Frank and Mack, and was gone.

"Junior is a big boy," Mack said.

"Come here." Lucy beckoned them to the window where they could see the scrimmage being resumed upon Junior's return. "Junior is a football coach at Miller High. Those men with him are working on a volunteer youth program. All those kids are high-school dropouts, and Junior and his friends are trying to 'big brother' them back to school. It's a good thing they're doing." Lucy's eyes twinkled. "He's a fine man."

Mack and Frank began to pick up pieces of broken glass.

"Leave that alone," Lucy said. "I'll take care of it. Now, where were we?"

"Perry Allison," Mack mused. "Maybe I'd better talk to him. What about you, Lucy? Will you help? The first ops meeting convenes tomorrow night at eight at my place. Will you be there?"

"When I left that pickle factory," Lucy said, "I promised myself I'd never think about it again. But when Carlos thinks he can get away with killing our people, it makes me stubborn." She smiled at Mack. "I'll be there."

"Hyphenated-Jake?"

"Yes? Who is this voice from the past?"

"Bill McLendon. I'm calling from Washington."

"Mack? Well, how the hell are you?"

34

"Doing tolerably well, Hyphenated," Mack said. "What are you doing these days?"

"Pursuing royalty," Jake replied. "It's like you would never dream. The lovely Jewish princesses swarm down from New York by the planeload, determined to enjoy the sun but frightened they will be lost in the lonely crowds on Miami Beach. I provide solace. Sort of a prince consort."

"I've always respected your talents," Mack said, "and admired your energy. I'm sure you're providing stellar service."

"What's up, Mack?"

"I have an operation starting," Mack replied. "Will you be able to join me for three months or so?"

"You working for the Agency again?" Jake asked.

"Only obliquely," Mack said. "But, nonetheless, there's liable to be some real action, the kind you thrive on."

"I do happen to be available," Jake said. "I'm going to run for Congress next year, but my campaign won't get under way for six months."

"Run for Congress?" Mack was incredulous. "How the hell is a thirty-five-year-old ex-CIA man going to win an election?"

"I'm a legal resident of Dade Country," Jake explained. "I've been working in local politics here and I can't find any difference between that and the spy business: you have to lie constantly in order to survive, and if you want to get anything done you have to cultivate your friends and castigate your enemies. It's just like espionage and covert action."

"But who will vote for a CIA type?"

"Look at the facts, Mack. My district is sixty percent Jewish, twenty percent Cuban refugee, and five percent Italian. I'll make lox-and-bagel speeches in Yiddish for the Jews, advocate the overthrow of Fidel Castro in Havana-accented Spanish to the Cubans, and tell ribald stories in Roman dialect to the Italians. How can I lose?"

"With that approach," Mack said, "I don't see how you can. In the meantime, will you fly to Washington tomorrow?"

"I don't know, Mack. I feel a certain sense of responsibility for the princesses. And I'm not sure I want to have anything to do with the Agency again. Every time I pick up a newspaper there seems to be another headline indicating the outfit is self-destructing. Did you hear they're thinking of having guided tours of Langley for the tourists?"

"I assure you this is not an Agency operation. And it's important. There'll be action and travel. How would you like to see Rome again, all expenses paid and first class all the way?"

"First class?" Jake chuckled. "*Now* I believe you. It can't be an Agency op if first class travel is allowed."

"The pay will be good," Mack added. "You will have something for your election coffers which I understand can become gigantic maws once a campaign gets under way."

"Okay, Mack," Jake said. "When and where?"

"My place on Wisconsin Avenue. Tomorrow night. Have a pencil and paper?"

Hyphenated-Jake sighed, and thought of the poor, languishing princesses.

"I telephoned for a reservation. Gonzalez. Frontier 343 to Dallas, then American non stop to Dulles."

The clerk looked up. The man standing at the counter looked like an Aztec chieftain in a sports coat; there was a military decoration on the lapel.

"Yes, Colonel. I was just writing up your ticket."

"You know me?"

The clerk smiled. "Of course. Who in Las Cruces doesn't? There's no hurry; the flight will be ten minutes late from Phoenix."

As he waited for the clerk to write out the ticket, Emilio Zapata Gonzalez—Colonel, USA, retired—turned, leaned against the counter, and looked out at the landscape beyond the airport tarmac. He was content. Through the tinted glass he could see the low hills, scrub and cactus bathed in the twilight glow he had remembered so many times in the service when thinking of New Mexico and his family. He smiled at Mary, who waited on a leather sofa near the exit gate; five of the children were with her, watching a cowboy movie on the television set. Emilio considered himself a successful man.

36

Achievement had not been easy for the son of a Mexican beet-picker and his Cherokee Indian wife. Now, after a military career which he had ended with eagles on his uniform shoulders, he and Mary owned two apartment buildings and there was money in the bank for each child's education. The extra pay from his Vietnam and Laos tours, and years of carefully husbanded travel money had been invested shrewdly in real estate. Of his eight children, six were boys: pretty damned *macho!*

"Gate one," the clerk said, handing the ticket to Emilio. "Have a good trip, Colonel."

Emilio sat beside Mary, placing his hand over hers.

After a moment Mary said, "I thought that we were finished with these good-byes when I don't know where you are going or for how long."

"A few weeks, honey. You'll see."

"Yes, I'll see. Is the McLendon who telephoned the one we knew in Madrid?"

"Yes. He was the station chief when we were there."

"Are you going to be working with the CIA?"

"Not a chance. I wouldn't associate with the bums. Mack promised this was an independent mission."

"Where? What will you be doing?"

Emilio shrugged.

"I know. None of my business. Do you really have to go?"

"Yes," the Colonel said. "I have to go."

"What you mean is that you want to go. You're so excited you can hardly wait for that plane to arrive."

"A little skittish," Emilio admitted. "I may never have another chance. And Mack said there would be some money in it. Maybe we can manage the down-payment on that motel near the lake. When the new road is finished, that should be good business."

"What if I don't let you go?" Mary asked. She clasped his hand between her two hands. "What if I just don't let loose of your hand?"

Emilio glanced down at Mary's hands, so small on each side of his own.

"Emilio Gonzalez," he said softly, "loves Mary Gonzalez."
They sat together quietly, bodies touching. Mary tightened her grip on her husband's hand when she saw the speck in the sky growing larger until there was a silver reflection from its wings. The jet banked in the light of the sunset and began its descent.

Two things appeared to Mary Gonzalez to be absolutely inevitable: the lovely sunset would surely be gone in about five minutes, and soon Emilio, too, would be gone.

Mack fastened the seat belt in the smoking section of the Eastern Airlines shuttle from Washington to New York, opened the slim, paper volume entitled *Terrorism in Latin America* by Ernst Halperin, and began to read. Perhaps the expert could shed some light on why the son of a Venezuelan millionaire had become the world's most notorious terrorist.

When La Guardia was in view, Mack closed his book and pondered how he would approach Perry Allison. Because of the young man's encounter with Carlos in Venezuela, Mack would attempt to elicit as much information as he could, but would be wary of telling Allison too much. Mack, who had grown up in Kansas City and attended the state university, had always been cautious in his initial relations with CIA officers who came out of the Ivy League. He decided he would wait and see before trusting Allison, an Ivy Leaguer who had become an international socialite. Play it by ear.

In New York, Mack paid the taxi driver, entered the glass-and-steel office building, checked the list of occupants, and took the elevator to the twenty-fourth floor.

Perry Allison was civil but cool. "I'm really rather occupied this morning. When you called I was about to say that I didn't have time to see you—until I realized I was talking to Mack the Knife. Agency people have called me before, but mostly security types checking out applicants. I presume you have something else in mind. Cigarette?" Perry offered a silver box.

"Thanks, I'll have one of these." As he lit his Gauloise Mack admired the severely modern office, steel and chrome with exotic plants growing to the high ceiling. Through the window he could see the United Nations building framed in a skyscraper alley. Perry Allison appeared to be very much at home in the luxurious setting. He was a strikingly handsome man: tall, lithe, and, Mack guessed, not more than thirty-four. Except for his jutting, hirsute eyebrows, his countenance was male-model perfect; his clothing was elegant and his manner easy and confident.

"We never really met," Perry said, "but you lectured to my class when I was a student at the Farm, and I was a fly on the wall a couple of years later when you briefed an ambassador about to be assigned to the Middle East. I thought about that recently when he was assassinated in Beirut."

"So did I," Mack said. "He was a nice guy."

"What brings you here, Mack, if I may call you that?"

"Sure," Mack said. "I hope you will help me."

"Providing cover is out," Perry said. "Much as I would like to, it's just too chancy being associated with the Agency these days. I can't put any of your people on my payroll."

"I retired two years ago. This is private."

"If you're looking for a job," Perry said, "I just might have one. The Allison Trust depends on good, hard information most of which is top secret in OPEC files or available from clerks in private companies who can be persuaded to pass it to us. We call it industrial espionage, but it's really no different from the garden variety spying you're used to. So I would guess that Mack the Knife could help in that department."

Mack grimaced. "Mack is okay, but you overdo it with the 'Knife' bit! I'm not looking for work. I'm just doing some research. It involves someone you once met and pitched for the Agency."

"That could have been anyone of a half dozen people," Perry said. "Who?"

"Ilyich Rameriz-Sanchez."

Perry started. "Carlos?"

Mack nodded.

"Fascinating," Perry said. "Carlos certainly graduated into the big time after I met him in Caracas. I didn't miss a single news broadcast a couple of years ago when he kidnapped the OPEC ministers in Vienna. Where is he now?"

"I don't know," Mack said. "But I want to find him. I hope you can give me something to get started on."

"I'll tell you what I can," Perry said, "but that's not much. The Agency asked me to fly down to Caracas in the summer of 1973 to try to recruit him. The people he had been working with in Paris had been killed by Israeli goon squads and Carlos went to Venezuela to cool off. The target-study people figured he might be frightened and looking for new friends. There had been a number of reports that he was disenchanted with the Russians after they booted him out of the Patrice Lumumba school in Moscow. It seems that Carlos had joined some African students in a rock throwing riot at the school and the Soviets didn't tolerate that sort of juvenile delinquency. Anyway, the chief of the Venezuelan service owed the Agency a favor, and so he arranged a meeting for me with Carlos in Venezuela. When Carlos realized I was from American intelligence, he was pleasant as hell about the whole thing; he said he was honored that the CIA considered him important enough to approach. But he wasn't having any of it. We talked for over an hour, but he told me to kiss off. That was about it. I wrote a long report which should be available somewhere at Langley."

Mack recalled the report. "During that hour you were with him, did you get any feel for his motivation? Did he say anything to suggest why a rich kid would become involved with Arab terrorists in Europe?"

"There was no question about his ideological motivation," Perry said. "His father. Carlos mentioned him a half dozen times, dwelling on the fact that Rameriz-Sanchez senior was simultaneously a convinced communist and a successful, wealthy lawyer. Carlos was emulating his father: he saw no contradiction between swinging in London and Paris social circles on the one hand and operating safehouses or smuggling weapons for the Arabs on the other. But I suspect the motivation went beyond ideology. He liked what he was doing because it was fun. He liked the excitement, the danger. He mentioned once the young women he recruited as safehouse keepers and couriers and how *macho* they considered him for operating under the nose of the British and French authorities. He certainly fancied himself a cock-of-the-walk revolutionary more than a dedicated anarchist. In fact, in my final report I suggested that the customary inducements shouldn't be offered in any future recruitment pitch. Carlos wasn't fazed one whit when I intimated that we would give him money, or when I threatened him with blackmail. I made it clear that should he refuse our offer we were prepared to reveal to the Mossad his involvement in the Commando Boudia. Later, my suggestion to the Agency was that any future approach should be one in which he was offered an even more exciting and thrilling life style. That assessment turned out to be right, because when he returned to Paris he took up violence fulltime. I understand he's personally killed several people."

"More than several," Mack said. "And the word now is that he has recruited his own gang of dedicated terrorists."

Mack paused. Obviously, Perry could provide valuable insights into whatever motives made Carlos run; he decided he would tell Perry more.

"Carlos and his cohorts have murdered three CIA station chiefs, among others," Mack said.

Perry inhaled rapidly. "I can't believe that."

"Believe it," Mack said. "Chuck Leonard, Bob Cartwell, and Don Robertson."

"My God! Cartwell was my first boss. He had a bunch of kids."

"Five," Mack confirmed. "It would be helpful if you would take the time to dredge up everything you can remember about Carlos. Maybe talk into a tape recorder for a couple of hours. Anything he said to you in Caracas, everything you remember from the time you studied his files."

Perry looked at Mack, skeptically. "You're still working for the outfit, aren't you?"

"It's not really important," Mack said, "but I'm not. My research is sponsored by American firms because Carlos has been causing problems for them. They don't know about Cartwell and the other two assassinations."

Perry whistled softly. "Sure, I'll do what I can. I'm going to Europe and the Middle East tomorrow for a few days. I'll try to remember everything I can during the trip, and I'll send you something when I return. How can I contact you?"

Mack handed Perry a card with his office and home numbers and addresses.

When Mack told him that he was returning to Washington, Perry called the office driver and instructed him to take Mack to La Guardia. He escorted Mack to the elevator and, shaking hands, reiterated his promise to provide as much information on Carlos as he could remember.

On the return shuttle Mack jotted down notes on the points he would want to make at the meeting in his apartment that evening. Frank Coughlin, Lucy Stevenson, and Skip Wilson would be there, as well as Emilio Gonzalez and Hyphenated-Jake, both of whom had agreed to participate in the operation during his telephone conversations with them. There had been no reply to the telegram Mack had sent to Clarence Clements.

When Mack opened the door of his office he found a telegram from Clem, indicating that he would be on hand for the reunion at eight that night.

Mack removed his fur-lined raincoat and was hanging it up when the telephone rang.

"Mack, this is Perry."

"Yes?"

"I've been thinking about our talk," Perry said. "And what I've been thinking is that Mack the Knife never spent his time with the outfit doing research, and it's highly unlikely that he's doing it now. Do you have a contract on Carlos? If so, I would like to do more than talk into a tape recorder. Is there anything I can do for you on my trip? I'll be in Europe and, for a couple of days, in Lebanon."

Mack hesitated. Lucy had said that Perry had been an imaginative operative during his brief CIA career. He certainly had the language and area knowledge necessary for the job, and the use of the Allison Trust cover for him and perhaps other members of the crew would certainly be useful.

"Yes, Perry," Mack said after a moment. "But the operation is going to be risky. Carlos has graduated from the fun and games category. If you should meet him again it might not be a pleasant encounter."

"I'm bored with Daddy's business," Perry said, "and I'd like to do something on behalf of Bob Cartwell."

Mack looked at his watch. "There will be a briefing in my office four hours from now. Could you catch the shuttle in time to join us?"

"Tonight? Mack, I have a date tonight with an absolutely smashing blond." There was a pause. "Fortunately, though, she's an understanding woman. I'll be there. The Trust has a plane and I fly it. I'll be there."

"First rate," Mack said. "See you at eight. You have the address of my apartment. Welcome aboard."

Mack dropped the telephone into its cradle. Good. His team was complete.

Business was slow; the young bartender looked up from a book. Two couples were drinking in the booths but the bar itself had been deserted until the curious-looking man entered. He wore a Western hat, a string tie, a plaid suit, and a bracelet and very large ring, both Navajo jewelry.

"Hi, pardner. How far are we from the 3600 block of Wisconsin Avenue?"

"Just a couple of blocks," the bartender said. He closed his book, marking the place with a swizzle stick.

"Plenty of time, then. I'll have a large shot of bourbon, with three drops of water."

"Three drops?"

"Yup." The visitor pushed aside a bar stool. "I'll just stand. Flew in a while ago from California, and my butt's flat from sittin'. Good flight, though, better than the redeye special. First time I flew across the country was right after they started the flights back in the twenties and it took four days of puddle jumping."

Clarence Clements set his watch back three hours. A few minutes after seven in the evening, Washington time. He was due at Mack's apartment at eight.

"Three drops," the bartender said, placing the drink on the bar, "of water."

"Thanks, son. Call me Clem." Clem sipped the bourbon, then smacked his lips. "Not too good, but not too bad. Must be Schenley's."

"We don't identify our house brands," the bartender said without irony.

"Don't have to," Clem said. "That's Schenley's all right. You see, son, I grew up in the Southwest and learned about liquor early on. First drink I ever had—I was about eleven—was a shot of Kentucky barley mash moonshine called Whistle Belly Vengeance. Since then I've made a point to learn about liquor and I've developed a fine taste. We couldn't afford anything better then. You might say I began my life in poverty. Why, we were so poor my mother sewed rubber pockets in my pants so I could steal hot soup from the school lunchroom and smuggle it home to the family."

Clem drained his glass.

"I'll have another, son. This time with two drops of water."

"Two drops?"

"That's right," Clem said. "Got no complaints now. Life's treated me pretty fair. I live out in California in a place called Leisure World. You know what that is, son?"

"It's where, uh, older people live, isn't it?" He presented the second drink to Clem. "Two drops of water."

"Exactly. Like me. Mighty fine place, nearly all retired people and we get along and have a good time. I worked for the United States government for thirty-seven years, son."

The bartender found himself enjoying Clem's banter. He had heard so many bad jokes from sodden barflies during the afternoon that it was a relief to hear Clem's cascade of anecdotes about his past. The bartender had grown up overseas with a foreign service family and was working on his masters degree in political science at American University. He understood Clem's references to his colorful career as a border patrolman for the U.S. Customs Service, during the war a commando in the famed 101 Burma Detachment for OSS, as the sheriff of Tucson, and as an A.I.D. public safety officer engaged in counterguerrilla training in Latin America. The yarns were embroidered, but consistently credible. The bartender decided, however, that during his next study session at the Library of Congress, he would check out Clem's claim that he was the United States pistol-shooting champion for three straight years during the 1930s.

Clem looked at his watch. "Time for one more. Another bourbon, please, with one drop."

"One drop of water?"

The bartender challenged Clem with his eyes as he placed the third drink before him. "One drop."

Clem and the bartender chatted until the third drink was finished. Then Clem paid his bill and started out the door.

"Just a minute," the bartender said. "I hate myself for it, but I'll ask. Why?"

"Why what?"

"Three drops of water in the first drink, two in the second, one in the third?"

"Oh, that." Clem beamed. "I told you I was from Leisure World where the old folks live. I've got to the point in life where I can hold my liquor pretty well—but I'm so old I have a little trouble holding my water."

Clem was pleased with himself as he strode down the street toward Mack's place. It was rewarding to make a special effort and have everything work out the way it should.

"Thanks for coming," Mack said. It was almost eight-thirty. Skip Wilson was hanging a sheet over a large Haitian oil painting. Perry Allison, the last of the group to arrive, was mixing a drink; the others sat about the living room of the apartment. A slide projector on a coffee table was aimed at the sheet Skip was arranging as a screen.

"We're here," Mack continued, "because we all agree that a man called Carlos must be found and, one way or another, neutralized. Skip Wilson will provide information from CIA, but the operation will be ours. That means each of you might be called on for some risky international reconnoitering. If at all possible we want to wrap up not only Carlos, but his band of terrorists as well. When Carlos realizes we are after him, the entire operation will turn hairy. In recent years Carlos has murdered a dozen people, and he won't hesitate to kill again. You'll be paid well, and covered by plenty of insurance. That's about as far as the promises go." Mack turned to Janet Wilson. "Skip, what do we know about Carlos?"

"Carlos was born in Caracas in 1949." Skip consulted a notepad as she spoke. "His father is a lawyer, a millionaire—and a staunch communist. Obviously he admired Lenin: Carlos's true first name is Ilyich, and his brothers are Vladimir and Lenin Rameriz-Sanchez. The Sanchez, of course, is the matronymic, the mother's family name. Dr. Rameriz and his wife separated after the birth of their third child; she is a devout Catholic and refuses to be divorced. Nevertheless the family relationship remains close and the father has supported his wife and three boys generously. The sons attended good schools or were tutored as they traveled around the world with their mother. When he was nine Carlos lived in Mexico. Then the mother took the boys to Jamaica where they could learn English, and later to Florida where they became fluent in the language. In 1961 they returned to Venezuela. During the next five years Carlos absorbed Marxist philosophy from his father and participated, with some other students, in his first political protest: a melee of rock throwing directed against the regime of Perez-Jeminez, who was then the rightist dictator of Venezuela. In 1966, when Carlos was almost seventeen, the three boys and their mother moved to London, where they remained for the next eight years. The father continued to support them, and used his connections to obtain a scholarship for Carlos and his brother Lenin at Patrice Lumumba University in Moscow. In 1968, Carlos and his brother were expelled from the university and from the Soviet Union for rowdyism, and they returned to London."

"Skip," Frank Coughlin interrupted, "is it possible that Carlos was recruited by the KGB at Lumumba, as so many of its students have been, with the expulsion merely serving as a cover?"

"Could be," she said. "But there's no hard information in the file to prove that." Skip looked at Lucy Stevenson, who nodded her head in confirmation.

"Carlos was then twenty-two," Skip said, "and this is what he looked like." Skip flipped on the projector. The image was a head-and-shoulders photograph of a handsome, dark-haired young man with full lips and, for such a young person, slightly heavy jowls. He wore a dark shirt, open at the collar. "This was taken just after Carlos returned from Moscow; he later used it on a Kuwaiti driver's license."

"Looks a little prissy to me," Emilio said.

"In fact," Skip said, "he had become quite a lady's man." She changed the picture. Carlos stood in a cocktail party group, his arm around a young girl, and an older woman standing beside him. He wore a dapper suit and stylish accessories. "Carlos taught Spanish to young English girls during the day and appeared regularly on the diplomatic cocktail party circuit evenings. This was taken at the home of the Venezuelan military attaché. Don't know who the girl is, but the woman nearby is his mother, Elba. During this period Carlos gained something of a reputation as a playboy. He even joined a posh London dinner club. He never attempted to conceal his Marxist sympathies, however, and cultivated friendships with left-of-center diplomats and exiles. Carlos is cultured, and in addition to his Spanish speaks perfect English, fluent French and serviceable Russian. His background of international travel and acquaintances and his father's impeccable Marxist-socialist credentials made Carlos the inevitable choice of some underground group. He didn't hesitate when he was approached and recruited by the PFLP in 1971, and sent to their camp in Lebanon for training."

Hyphenated-Jake: "PFLP?"

"The Popular Front for the Liberation of Palestine, the Marxist-Leninist resistance movement founded by Dr. George Habash, and headquartered in Aden. Carlos refused to attend the political indoctrination classes at the camp, but he was an ace student in the bombs and weapons course. He learned how to use—" Skip looked down at her notes, "—the Kalashnikov AKN-forty-seven rifle, the modified version with a folding stock which can be hidden under a coat; the Czech Skorpion machine pistol; the Russian Tokarev and Makarovs automatic pistols and the Egyptian version known as the Tokagypt. He was also introduced to the Czech M-fifty-two pistol, which he liked and later used for assassinations. He was checked out on all NATO-country small arms, one test consisting of taking apart and putting together again an Israeli Uzi submachine gun—in total darkness. He became expert in the use of the Dragunov sniper's rifle."

"A howitzer in drag," Clem interjected. "It weighs a ton, has a telescopic sight, a cheek-piece on the butt, and can pick off a man at three hundred yards!"

"Carlos also learned how to handle plastic explosives and gelignite," Skip continued, "and several kinds of grenades ranging from the Soviet RKG-three percussion antitank model, so heavy that it has a tiny parachute to insure that the right end hits the target, to the miniscule Dutch V-forty fragmentation type which weighs only a hundred grams."

She paused, shuffled some notes, and then continued. "All this weapons training would come in handy later. Meanwhile Carlos was assigned to nonviolent chores upon his return to Europe. He was the number-five man in a small but highly efficient support apparatus in Paris called the Commando Boudia. Mohammed Boudia was an Algerian actor of genuine talent who taught Carlos how to protect himself by assuming false identities, using disguise and deception techniques; Boudia himself had undergone plastic surgery. Carlos thrived on the role playing. During the next two years he traveled in and out of a dozen countries under five aliases. He had passports, all false, which identified him as a Chilean engineer called Adolfo Jose Muller; as Glen H. Gebhard and Charles Clarke, both Americans from New York; and as a Peruvian economist with the name of Carlos Andres Martinez-Torres. Most of Carlos's work was strictly support: communications, obtaining false documents for the activists in the Boudia Commando, and finding safehouses for them in Paris and London. Carlos was particularly proficient in the safehouse department. His modus operandi was simple, almost foolproof: he seduced young female students, usually Latin Americans, with no history of involvement with the radical left or terrorists, and recruited them as safehouse keepers."

"Carlos is no slouch," Hyphenated-Jake commented wryly, "in any department."

"Then," Skip said, "two events occurred in which Carlos was not directly involved but which were to have a profound influence on his future. The first was at the Lod Airport in Tel Aviv."

Click. The grim picture made Lucy wince.

"In May of 1972 three JRA—Japanese Red Army—terrorists massacred twenty-six people and injured almost eighty. You will recall that members of that terrorist group found sanctuary in the PFLP training camp after their network was smashed in Japan. The Israelis were not amused."

Click. The second slide was also familiar: a ski-hooded man in a window, cradling a rifle in the hook of his elbow.

"September of 1972," Skip said, "when Black September terrorists murdered eleven Israeli athletes at the Munich Olympics."

"And that," Lucy said, "is when the Israelis began to play hardball."

"Yes," Skip said. "WOG teams. The Wrath of God. Mossad, the Israeli secret service, also known as Shin Beth, set up a clandestine unit which dispatched teams of ex-commandos and ex-paratroopers, men *and* women, throughout Europe. They were supported by Mossad agents, but their operations were completely separate from those of Mossad so that long-term Israeli intelligence assets would not be compromised. The mission of the WOG teams was simple: to assassinate the leaders of the various anti-Jewish terrorist groups in Europe who had been responsible for the Lod Airport and Munich killings. One team in Sweden botched their assignment and was apprehended. But most of them were chillingly efficient, especially the unit sent to Paris to attack the Commando Boudia—so successful, in fact, that Carlos suddenly found he he was being rapidly promoted to fill vacancies in the Commando's leadership. First on the hit list was a Syrian journalist, Khodr Kannou, gunned down in front of his Paris apartment. Carlos became the fourth in the chain of command. Then, in April of 1973, the WOG team planted a bomb in the car of Dr. Basil al-Kubaisi, a Lebanese university professor who had recently arrived in Paris to work with the PFLP. Carlos was then number three. In December they killed Boudia's deputy, Mahmud Hamchari, publically known as Arrafat's PLO spokesman in Paris. This time they used a telephone bomb."

Emilio: "A telephone bomb?"

"Hamchari was in bed with his girl friend. During the day a WOG agent had entered the apartment and hidden an explosive near the telephone. That night he telephoned and, once he knew Hamchari was holding the instrument, sent an electrical charge through the telephone line to the detonator which set off the charge. Hamchari's girl friend survived."

"The bomb didn't work?" Emilio asked.

"It worked on Hamchari," Skip said. "To be precise, it blew his head off."

Hyphenated-Jake whistled.

"Carlos found himself second in command," Skip said. "But, understandably, the Commando Boudia was in disarray. At this point CIA decided to attempt to recruit Carlos. Perry can tell you about that."

"Yes," Perry said. "The CIA station in Paris had been under pressure from Langley to develop sources in the French terrorist movements. The Israelis and the French had penetrations in most of them, but *that* kind of information they weren't passing on to Washington. The station picked up one access agent who reported on Carlos—one of his girl friends who learned a lot from pillow talk. Carlos wasn't so indiscreet that he re-

50

vealed operational details, but she did find out that he was frightened for damned good reasons. His colleagues were being methodically eliminated by the WOG's. The Paris COS instructed one of his street men to try a cold pitch on Carlos by approaching him unexpectedly and making a two-part proposition: first, money and, secondly, the suggestion that CIA could try to persuade the Mossad to have their WOG team leave him alone. If Carlos turned that down, the alternate plan was to threaten to expose him to Mossad. That would place him alongside Boudia himself on the WOG team hit parade."

"You spooks," Emilio said, "are really nice fellows."

Perry shrugged. "But the plan fell through because Mohammed Boudia decided to suspend operations until the heat was off from the WOG team. He instructed Carlos to leave France for a month until things cooled down. Carlos visited his mother in London, then flew to Caracas to see his father. The Paris station knew about the trip from their agent who saw Carlos off at the airport. Headquarters decided to shift the approach to Caracas, where it would be easier to get to Carlos. Figuring I was the guy for the job because of my Venezuelan background, they called me in New York and asked if I would come back to work long enough for the pitch. The chief of the Venezuelan service arranged the meeting by telling Carlos I was a leftist journalist who wanted to write an article defending the Arabs in the Middle East situation. Carlos trusted the Venezuelan security chief enough to meet me on the top of a mountain near Caracas in an abandoned tourist hotel. When I revealed that I was from CIA, Carlos burst out laughing; he was delighted to be considered so important. We talked for about an hour. When it became obvious that he was not about to buy the original pitch (that he work for money and a promise of immunity from the Israelis), I tried the blackmail idea: we would identify him to the Mossad and he would become a prime target of the WOG teams. Gutsy guy, Carlos. He told me to stuff it. That was the end of that, and I flew back."

"At the time Perry was seeing Carlos in Caracas," Skip said, "the WOG team in Paris located Boudia. They placed a bomb of some kind in his car and Mohammed was blown to smithereens. That left only one man in charge of the Commando Boudia: a Lebanese, Michael Waheb Moukarbal, who had been a courier between Boudia and Dr. Habash in Aden. But Moukarbal's situation was so precarious that he was ordered to go into hiding after sending a cable to Carlos instructing him to return to take over the Commando. Carlos flew back to Paris. He recruited new activists, tightened security, and began to operate in a thoroughly professional way. He used cut-outs to handle his former support agents. When the Paris station, for instance, tried to have their female agent get close to Carlos again, he refused to meet her and saw to it that information about him and his movements was held to a 'need-to-know.' He abandoned all his previous phony identities and documents. He probably had plastic surgery, as Boudia had, because witnesses never again described him as having full jowls. He certainly lost weight, changed the color of his hair, and often wore a mustache or beard when engaged in an operation."

"The files show that Carlos was always anti-Semitic," Skip continued, "which probably explains why he agreed to work with Arab terrorists in the first place. By now he had developed an intense hatred of the Israelis and the WOG teams that had decimated the Commando Boudia. He began his counterattack against the Jews. In December 1973 he broke into the home of Edward Sieff, a prominent London Zionist, and shot him pointblank in the face, but Sieff, miraculously, survived. In January 1974 an Israeli bank was bombed in London, probably by Carlos. That summer a Japanese Red Army courier was arrested at Orly in Paris. Carlos sent a terrorist team to take over the French Embassy in The Hague and demanded the release of the courier. When the authorities began to stall in the negotiations Carlos decided they needed a little prodding. From an interior balcony of *Le Drug Store* in Paris he dropped an M-twenty-six grenade into the crowd below, killing two and wounding over thirty."

Click. The picture was much like the one which had shown the shattered bodies in the Lod airport.

"This fellow is a real nut," Frank said.

"The courier was released," Skip said, "and the terrorists in Holland were allowed to leave the country. The next month, January of 1975, Carlos and two fellow terrorists used a rocket launcher against an El Al plane as it taxied on the runway at Orly with 135 passengers aboard, mostly Americans. They missed, hit a Yugoslav jet instead, and escaped. Then Carlos proved just how audacious he had become: six days later, despite newspaper publicity that the security force at Orly had been increased to 750, he sent a three-man team back to the airport to try the same trick. A gunfight ensued, and a number of hostages were taken. The terrorists were allowed, after several days of negotiation, to fly to Baghdad."

"Later," Skip went on, "for reasons which are not clear, Carlos's colleague, Moukarbal, became an informer for the French police. He led three of them to an apartment in Paris where Carlos was holed up. The policemen were armed, but Carlos shot and killed two of them *and* Moukarbal, and wounded the third police officer."

"That's good shootin'," Clem said. "Really good."

"Nothing was heard from Carlos for four months." Skip said. "Then in December he pulled off the most remarkable terrorist op in history. Carlos headed a six-person team, including a young German girl, and took over OPEC headquarters in Vienna. They killed three people, with Carlos himself pumping five bullets into one victim. They were driven by bus to a waiting plane, then flown out of the country."

Click.

"This is the most recent file photograph of Carlos," Skip said. "It's a blurred front view of a Vienna bus transporting Carlos and his OPEC captives to the airport. The sign above the driver's seat, in German, reads 'Special Trip.' As you can see, the windows are curtained, but that's Carlos in the front seat on the right of the driver. Unfortunately you can't really make out his facial features. It's probably not an accident that he is dressed to look like Ché Guevara—beret, long hair and beard, dark glasses. In the bus, and later on the DC-nine which flew out of Austria, Carlos had forty-two hostages, including twelve oil ministers from as many countries. After landing at and taking off from several Middle East airfields, Carlos finally released the last of his hostages, the ministers from Saudi Arabia and Iran. He had received, by then, a coded message indicating that a ransom had been deposited in Switzerland. Our best information is that the ransom was twenty-five million dollars. How much went into PFLP coffers in Aden and how much Carlos kept for himself we don't know. But Carlos now knew how lucrative terrorism could be. For the past three years he seems to have been operating independently against American companies, particularly the ones Symser represents. And, of course, he has assassinated three CIA station chiefs."

"Skip," Frank asked, "is Carlos a crusader, a criminal, or just crazy?"

Skip turned off the projector. Mack flipped the light switch on the wall.

"There's a psychological profile," she said, "which asks the same question but doesn't come up with an answer. If he is crazy it hasn't interfered with his planning or the execution of his operations. If you classify him a criminal, he's probably the richest one in the world. Certainly he sees himself as a crusader, perhaps emulating Ché Guevara, if one can attach any significance to his appearance in the Vienna photograph."

"I once met Ché," Emilio said. "He was a revolutionary and a guerrilla strategist, but for all that a gentle man and not a killer. He would have never dropped a grenade on a crowd in a Paris restaurant."

"The psychological profile does contain one flat prediction," Skip said. "Carlos won't rest on his OPEC laurels but sooner or later will attempt something even more dramatic and sensational. He considers himself a worldwide personality now. During the flight from Vienna he went down the aisle of the plane signing autographs like a movie star. At age twenty-nine he's not about to retire."

"Unless we can force him into retirement," Mack said. "For that we need a great deal of information. For the next few weeks we'll use a vacuum cleaner technique. We'll travel, contact old friends and sources, develop and recruit some new ones. We need to know about his capabilities, especially his support apparat. He might have money deposited in Swiss banks, but somewhere he must have a trusted agent handling his operational funds, large sums in different denominations and currencies, collectable on demand. He won't be keeping that money in banks which are closed on holidays and weekends! We need to know about his personnel. Which of his old chums has he picked up and who are his new recruits?"

"A few months after the OPEC op," Skip said, "there was a report that Carlos was boasting of having put together a group of twenty, a sort of super WOG team."

"Then we need to know his intentions," Mack said. "If he's not satisfied with harrassing American businesses and killing CIA chiefs, what spectacular new operation does he plan as a means of getting back into the headlines so that he can sign autographs again?"

"I realize," Lucy said, looking about the room, "that we have, collectively, about two hundred years of intelligence experience, but it seems to me we're a pitifully small band to make this a successful mission."

"That could be, Lucy," Mack said. Then to all of them, "Final call at the bar; then we'll have something to eat."

The telephone rang. Frank reached for it.

"Careful," Hyphenated-Jake said. "Remember the telephone bomb."

"Not funny," Perry said, mixing himself a drink at the bar.

"Yes?" Frank extended the instrument to Mack. "It's for you, Mack."

Mack took the telephone from Frank. "Yes? This is Bill Mc-Lendon." Holding one hand over his ear so that he could hear above the swelling hum of conversation, Mack turned his back to his guests. Emilio and Clem talked together animatedly, agreeing that their paths had crossed in the past but unable to remember when and where. Hyphenated-Jake served drinks at the bar while the others discussed Skip's briefing on Carlos.

Mack, his hand now over the telephone mouthpiece, turned

to the others. "Quiet!" The urgency of Mack's command stilled the conversation immediately. Mack spoke into the telephone.

"*¿Pero, como sé que esta no es una broma?*"

Lucy and Frank exchanged quizzical glances. Perry, Clem, Emilio, Skip, and Hyphenated-Jake spoke Spanish; they moved closer to Mack.

"*¿Y porqué esta llamando?*" Mack asked. After a few more exchanges in Spanish Mack said, "If that's true, we can speak in English."

There was total quiet as they stared, enthralled, at Mack.

"So do I," Mack said finally. "Until then." Mack lowered the telephone into its cradle. He looked about the room at his guests, slowly, his eyes narrow as he shifted his gaze from one to the other. Then he walked to the bar and poured brandy into a snifter. He did not speak until he had tasted the dark liquid.

"The call was from Europe," Mack said evenly, "from a man who identified himself as Carlos."

There was a stunned silence. Frank's voice quavered when he asked, "Shall I try to trace the call?"

"Useless," Mack said. "He said he was calling from the public booths at the Bonn airport. Whether that's true or not is irrelevant. He could have been calling from just around the corner."

"What did he say, Mack?" Mack noticed that Skip was wearing the Haitian amulet again. My God, thought Mack, why have I involved this lovely woman, and my other friends, in this mess?

"He said he considered it an honor to challenge such a worthy adversary as Mack the Knife." Mack stroked his ear absently. "That he looked forward to our first meeting."

"This must be some sort of hoax," Hyphenated-Jake suggested.

"No," Mack said. "It's typical, unadulterated Carlos audacity. Somehow he's learned what we're up to, and he's thrown down his glove."

"Now the big pot is in the little pot," Lucy said. "And I don't know how we're going to get it out."

56

"Yes," Mack said. "We've been had. Skip, how many people at the Agency know about this meeting tonight?"

"The Director," Skip said, "and about a dozen more."

Emilio's face was dark. "You people have always boasted that you've never been penetrated by the opposition. Well, it looks as if you have—by the Soviets or the Cubans or Carlos."

"There's Symser," Mack said. "He knew about the meeting. Carlos might have recruited someone working in his office. Who else? Have any of you told anyone that you were coming here tonight, and that Carlos was our target?"

"I did," Clem said, lowering his head and staring at his boots. "Told my wife."

Mack wet the tip of his finger in the brandy, then ran it around the rim of the snifter until it produced a hum. He hated even to consider another possibility. He looked up and saw that the others were exchanging anxious glances.

Mack raised his cognac. "Happy hunting. You'll be given your assignments first thing tomorrow morning."

3.

"Yes, this is Allen Symser."

"Good morning," Mack said. "Sorry to call so early, but I'm leaving the country this morning, and wanted to give you a progress report. Hope I didn't wake you."

"As a matter of fact," Symser complained, "you did. It was six A.M. here when you called my home. I'm in an all-night drugstore now, feeling foolish that I'm still wearing bedroom slippers."

"I'll be brief," Mack said. "Yesterday I mailed you the number of a Washington post office box which you may use, but my office and apartment telephone numbers have been compromised. Don't use them again. A colleague will let you know when we have new numbers, probably later today."

"Then we're still playing cloak-and-dagger?"

"We're still being careful, Mr. Symser. My team is together. Their names and enough information for insurance purposes will be in the letter. There's a new bank account, too. My friends and I will be scratching around overseas for the next week or so. I'll call you when I return. Just wanted you to know we're in business. And I want to ask you a question."

"Yes?"

"Have you identified me, by name, to anyone?"

"Only to my chairman, Crassweiler. Why do you ask?"

"Because Carlos already knows that I have a contract on him."

Symser gasped. "How is that possible?"

"Carlos is talented," Mack said, "but not clairvoyant. Someone told him."

"Who?"

"I don't know, but I'm certainly curious."

"Very well," Symser said, his voice strained. "I'll stand by until I hear from you. And I promise not to complain the next time you wake me up and ask me to go out to a pay phone. But I still find it difficult to believe that telephone calls are being monitored in the United States after all those investigations."

"I seriously doubt," Mack said, "that any government agency would be listening to us, at least not without the authorization of the attorney general. But there are a number of locations which the Congress did not investigate. The next time you are in Washington stroll down Sixteenth Street and count the radio antennas on the top of the Soviet Embassy. Some are for communications, but others eavesdrop on American telephones. These systems exist not only in Washington but at the United Nations mission in New York and at Soviet consulates around the country. Other nations, and even private organizations, could do the same thing without too much difficulty."

"Disturbing," Symser said. "I suppose there must be a Russian consulate here in Los Angeles. How is it possible that they could sort out our numbers from the millions of telephone calls every day?"

"Computers," Mack explained. "Nearly all telephone messages in this country are beamed by microwave and can be intercepted and fed into computers which will record conversations on selected numbers and discard all others."

"Then you believe the Soviets have something to do with Carlos?"

"Possibly, but I doubt it. In any event, once the KGB learns of our interest in Carlos they will want to monitor developments in the case."

"How would the KGB learn of what we're doing?"

"Because," Mack said, "I intend to tell them. Good-bye, Mr. Symser."

The Concorde, ascending like a giant prehistoric bird, headed east over the umber and winter-green fields, and suburban communities of Virginia and Maryland. It was Mack's first flight on the supersonic jet. His breath quickened when he saw the green digital read-out on the cabin indicator (meaning they had passed into Mach I), and felt the forward nudge of the aircraft as it passed the sound barrier and sped toward London at 57,000 feet. When the stewardess served the first drink the plane was well over the Atlantic.

An imposing and talkative woman, an unopened Agatha Christie paperback on her lap, sat next to Mack. She told Mack of her excitement over flying the Concorde to London as the guest of her son who worked with an American company in England. Mack opened his briefcase and made it obvious that he meant to work.

He reviewed a memorandum of instruction, copies of which he had given to Emilio, Clem, Perry, and Hyphenated-Jake. During the next ten days they, and Mack, would be traveling to nine countries. Communications would be difficult, and each had to know what to do and how to re-establish contact.

The instructions Mack was reading were identical to the ones given the others except that the cities he would visit and the persons he would see were not inserted—even Frank and Lucy did not have that information. The rest of his crew had been given names, contact instructions and intelligence requirements: Perry would be visiting Bonn and Beirut; Emilio, Vienna and Madrid; Hyphenated-Jake, Paris and Rome; and Clem, Mexico City.

OPERATION CARLOS, PHASE ONE

We must identify and locate Carlos's support chief, and establish what government or group, if any, is sponsoring him.

Now that we know that Carlos is aware of our intentions, our tradecraft must be tight. This will be a 'need-to-know' operation. None of you is to know where the others are traveling, or whom they will be contacting. Do not share your information, but pass everything to Lucy when you return. Frank will be my deputy.

While our first priority is to find Carlos, we must also identify his fellow conspirators. Most will probably be PFLP terrorists Carlos has worked with before. But the Commando Boudia supported and supplied arms to other groups, and Carlos may have recruited activists from the Japanese Red Army, the German Second of June Movement and its various Baader-Meinhof splinter organizations, the Turkish People's Army, and the Italian Red Brigades. With his Venezuelan background, Carlos has undoubtedly recruited members of Latin American insurgent groups in exile, especially the Uruguayan Tuparmaros. We must identify those in Carlos's current cadre, and determine where they are.

By the time you return to Washington, Frank will have rented a safehouse which will be our headquarters. Do not telephone or visit my office or apartment. In the classified ad section of the *Washington Star* you will find a furnished-rooms-for-rent item: "Room available for quiet person willing to take care of landlady's six cats during her absence." Lucy or Frank will answer and tell you how to find the safehouse.

You are to visit the following cities:

The following persons are good sources, if you can persuade them to give you information, or to tell you where to seek it:

This is written on water-soluble paper. Dispose of it before landing at your first destination. Good luck.

Mack folded the paper. He dunked it in the half-filled martini glass before him and watched it disappear in a matter of seconds.

Despite the epicurean menu, Mack did not feel like eating. He advised the stewardess, slipped off his shoes, and tilted his seat to the reclining position. He glanced at his neighbor; she was absorbed in her Agatha Christie.

Mack closed his eyes, but could not sleep. How the hell did Carlos know about the operation?

"Yah?" The emaciated man who opened the door peered at Perry through square spectacles.

"Professor Baumgardner?"

"Yah."

"I'm Charles Miller," Perry said. "From Brandom Circle Publishers."

"Come in then, Mr. Miller. I have been waiting for you."

The professor escorted Perry into what had been a parlor but was now a studio, cluttered with files, boxes of paper, stacks of newspapers, and books piled on improvised shelves. Perry waited while the professor cleared a chair and then sat without taking off his coat. It must be, Perry thought, sixty degrees in this house.

"You please forgive the untidiness. Since my wife died I find I am not a good housekeeper."

"I'm sorry," Perry said.

"Yes, she died eleven years ago." The professor cleared a space so that he could sit on a love seat which otherwise served as a repository for perhaps two hundred books. "Well, welcome to Bonn, Mr. Miller. I have been waiting with some curiosity since your call. What brings you to this scholar's den so far from New York?"

"I have been told," Perry said, "that you are writing a book on the Baader-Meinhof terrorist movement. I would like to talk to you about acquiring the American publishing rights."

"American rights?" The professor surveyed his threadbare quarters. "As you see, I am not a wealthy man. The pension of a professor emeritus in criminology from the University of Muenster is a pittance. I would welcome your dollars, but I do not even know that my work will be printed here in Germany. Why should America be interested?"

"There is considerable interest," Perry said, "in the origins of the Baader-Meinhof group, especially in the motivation of the young people who have turned to violence."

"As a sociological phenomenon it is intriguing. Ulrike Meinhof hanged herself while in custody in 1976, and Andreas Baader committed suicide in prison in 1977 after his comrades were foiled in Mogadishu. But the movement is far from dead. The latest splinter group is called 'The Red Morning' and almost half its membership is composed of young women who have recently taken to carrying a bouquet of red roses to the homes of their victims before kidnapping or murdering them. But I do not write of these things in a sensational manner, Mr. Miller. Publishers here seem to be interested only in the sensational. My work is to be a scholarly dissertation, I must warn you."

"Brandom Circle is a serious house, Professor. Perhaps

what you are writing is what we are looking for. Have you done research on the German terrorists as individuals?"

"Of course." The professor indicated a shelf of files. "I have dossiers on all the principal activists."

"When do you expect to finish?" Perry asked.

"Two, maybe three years."

"I see." Perry prepared to light a cigarette, but put away the pack when he saw no ashtrays in the room. "I am curious, Professor Baumgardner. How have you been able to accumulate data on these individuals?"

"From public records, from the press, and after many interviews. And . . . confidentially, I have very good sources in the government. A professor of criminology makes friends among policemen." The professor touched his lips with one finger. "And then my real secret—you promise not to tell?"

"I promise," Perry said.

"My nephew works for the federal police here in Bonn. He has been most helpful in providing a certain, uh, access to the government's files. Confidential reports, birth certificates, photographs. This is not to be repeated, of course."

"Of course," Perry said. "Any commitment I make must be justified when I return to New York. But I feel inclined to give you an advance which would guarantee Brandom Circle first option on your completed work. Would you be kind enough to allow me to inspect your files, and to read that part of the manuscript which is completed?"

"Why not?" The professor shrugged. "But again I must warn you not to expect sensationalism. I am rapidly approaching a mundane conclusion, Mr. Miller. Other terrorist movements have had their origins and justifications in political causes. German terrorists seem only to find our remarkably stable and prosperous system tedious. Their affliction is ennui. They are nihilists, nothing more."

"Are you saying that the Baader-Meinhof kind of terrorists have turned to murder and violence just because they are bored?"

"Precisely, Mr. Miller."

"I wonder," Perry said.

63

Standing in the hotel window, Mack surveyed the London skyline. Since his last visit the panorama of old buildings and cathedral towers had suffered by the addition of modern incongruities, glass office buildings which Sir Christopher Wren might have admired, but would surely have constructed elsewhere.

Mack went to the telephone and, consulting a pocket notebook, began to dial. The number he marked was not the same as the one written in his notepad: from each even-numbered digit Mack subtracted one, and added two to each odd-numbered digit.

"Good morning." The secretary's voice was cheerful.

"This is William McLendon. May I speak to Mr. Rollins?"

"Would you have a given name for Mr. Rollins?"

"Mitchell."

"Just hold on for a moment, please."

Several moments passed as Mack waited. The call was being transferred to another building, or Mitch was being summoned to the cover telephone from an office at some distance.

"Is that William McLendon there?"

"Yes, Mitch, this is Mack."

"Of course. I don't want to appear rude, but would you just refresh my memory? You are the William McLendon from Washington?"

"Yes, Mitch." Mack tolerated the query, understanding that Mitch was simply going through the proper drill. "The Mack you played tennis with at Kenwood and lunched with at Jean Pierre's. The last time I had dinner at your place in Cleveland Park, Elinor served salmon."

"Indeed. Splendid fish, wasn't it?" Mitch's accent was very public school. "It's marvelous to hear your voice. You're not calling from outside the U.K., are you?"

"No, Mitch. When you gave me this number three years ago you said it was not to be called from abroad. I'm here in London."

"Elinor's in the country and there's a guest room in the flat here. Stay with me tonight and tomorrow we'll go down.

64

Elinor just happens to have a salmon, fresh from Scotland."

"Thanks, Mitch, but I will only be here for a day or so, and I've checked into a hotel. I flew in on the Concorde from Dulles."

"First rate. That should help our balance of payments. What's your hotel, Mack?"

"The Holiday Inn."

"The Holiday Inn?" A pause. "Oh, dear."

"An unexpected trip," Mack said, "and the Connaught was completely booked, as was Brown's."

"Indeed," Mitch said. "Undoubtedly crammed to the eaves with Arabs. Look here, I have a luncheon date with an office chap but it can easily be cancelled. Shall we?"

"Great."

"I'll see you there. Oneish. Bye-bye."

"Hold it, Mitch! Where is there?"

"The club, of course. You remember?"

"Yes," Mack said, "the Travelers."

"Indeed. Oneish."

Mack knew that most Englishmen are punctual; British intelligence officers, no exception to the rule, are precise when arriving for a social engagement. Mack and Mitch met in the club foyer at the stroke of one.

"You're looking marvelously well," Mitch said. "Come right along to the bar."

Mitch ordered a sherry and Mack asked for a martini on the rocks, with brandy in lieu of vermouth. The bar attendant was aghast.

"Yes, Angus," Mitch said. "Really heap the glass with ice, will you? That's a fine fellow."

Mitch turned to Mack. "Now tell me what brings you to London. I understand you retired some time ago. Long before your time was due, wasn't it?"

"Yes. But I'm working again."

"If you've returned to the Agency," Mitch said, "we should be doing this through your chap at the embassy. Protocol, you know."

"That's not necessary. I'm on my own."

65

The waiter served the drinks, and departed in silence.

"Cheers," Mitch toasted.

"Cheers."

"Before anything, Mack, tell me about the quite extraordinary events occurring in Washington."

"What's that, Mitch?"

"The disembowelment by headline of your intelligence services. Extraordinary. Dear as it is, we've budgeted for the airmail editions of the *New York Times* and the *Washington Post* to be delivered to our offices. Can't wait for our chaps over there to pouch the clippings. Until we deported him we had your Mr. Agee in London revealing the names of your agents in press conferences, and I understand that now other Americans do the same thing in Washington. Certainly you have laws to prohibit that sort of thing?"

"Not enforceable ones," Mack said.

"Extraordinary. I don't see how you can possibly run secret operations without secrets. Haven't you something like our Official Secrets Act and Q Notices to journalists? I have heard all sorts of explanations of why this situation developed. I'd be interested in *your* theory, Mack."

"Simple," Mack said. "Vietnam and Watergate."

Mitch shrugged. "I can assure you that the developments in Washington are causing anxiety in our own front office. Our parliamentarians are beginning to emulate your congressmen, poking around in all sorts of cubbyholes. And, quite frankly, my chief is becoming increasingly hesitant to approve passage of our documents to your people. It's your—what do you call it?—Freedom of Secrets Act?"

"Freedom of Information Act, Mitch."

"Whatever. There was the most bizarre story in the *Post* not long ago. It seems a fellow wrote your Department of Justice demanding that he be provided with the FBI's classified training manual. He was sent almost a thousand pages describing how the Bureau agents go about apprehending criminals. Do you know what the fellow's occupation was? He was an inmate of the federal penitentiary in the state of

Illinois—serving a thirty-year-sentence for bank robbery and narcotics violations! Now I find that absolutely *ex*traordinary!"

Mitch slapped the table, causing the crystal to tinkle. Disapproving club members turned to stare.

Mack smiled. "Yes, I remember the story. But the prisoner didn't actually receive the manual. When the package arrived it was inspected, and the warden refused to let him have it."

"Bully for the warden," Mitch said, "for violating the fellow's civil rights."

"If you can help me," Mack said, "you can assure your chief he won't have to worry about such things. Any information you pass to me will be used on behalf of a client. I will not reveal my source to him and I will claim a lawyer-client relationship as far as anyone else might be concerned. Your chief will remember me; in fact, we once had lunch together here. Do you believe he will approve?"

"Highly unusual. But then," Mitch paused, "my chief is an unusual man. He might well do so."

Mack explained his mission to the MI-6 officer. Mitch's face tightened when Mack related the circumstances of Carlos's campaign against CIA station chiefs, and his record of three murders.

"That is a bit extreme, isn't it?" Mitch asked. "And good reason for us to help if we can. How?"

"I need any personality data you have on Carlos and others you suspect might be working with him now. Anything, however trivial. I'm working with several associates and we need as many bits and pieces as we can obtain to make some sort of picture emerge when we put them together."

"That falls in my territory," Mitch said. "I'm in counterintelligence for the nonce."

"CI?"

"Don't use that condescending tone. CI is a very respectable branch of our service—despite all that egg on our vests from Philby and Blake. There's an odd chap in our shop who is an absolute wizard on terrorists. Does nothing else. We call him Mr. Rubbers because he is so enthralled with his work that on rainy mornings he often forgets to remove his galoshes and sits at his desk all day wearing them."

"May I meet Mr. Rubbers?"

"I doubt that, Mack. But if the chief approves I'll ask Mr. Rubbers to do a paper for you. He's absolutely ecstatic when anyone pays any attention to him, and bonkers with joy when given a crash assignment."

"Carlos lived in London, off and on, for almost eight years," Mack said. "You should have a great deal of information about his MO, his contacts. If Mr. Rubbers could provide an extract from the files I would be grateful."

"Much of that is MI-five's department," Mitch said. "Internal. But they are very good about giving us drop copies of their memos. What else?"

"I need to know if Carlos is acting independently, with his own support network, or is still connected with the PFLP or another of the international organizations. My chances of ferreting intelligence out of Dr. Habash's well-guarded headquarters in Aden are poor. Your service has always been good in the Middle East. Is Habash still funding Carlos or is one of the Arab splinter groups? Quaddafi?"

"If the chief approves, we just might be useful on that score. As you say, the Middle East is where we do as well as anywhere." Mitch pulled his pocketwatch from his vest. "The chief is due back at the office threeish. We'll have time for lunch and then I'll give you the Cook's tour of some of Carlos's London haunts while I return you to . . . your Holiday Inn."

"I can spare only a few moments, signor . . . ?"

"Smith-Forsythe," Hyphenated-Jake said, "Julius Smith-Forsythe."

"Yes." Luigi Alessandroni motioned to a chair, then sank into his own, sighing in a gesture of exhaustion. "Only a few minutes. You see, I am the busiest man in Rome! Are you aware that with the possible exception of Northern Ireland there is more political terrorism in Italy than anywhere else in Europe? We are in a state of anarchy. The streets are not safe, not even for Aldo Moro, five times our prime minister, who was abducted and murdered!" Alessandroni waved with a limp hand at a chart on the wall of the dingy office in the Interior Ministry. "This year there have been more than fifty major terrorist incidents. Politically motivated mayhem." Alessandroni let his hand fall on his chest. "And I am charged with stemming the bloody tide, with too few investigators, the local police intimidated, the courts moving with the speed of a glacier. . . . And now the terrorists are shooting their victims in the legs. Insane! Yes, their latest tactic is to shatter the knees of anyone—journalists, television commentators, priests—perceived as disagreeing with their ideology."

"Quite bizarre," Hyphenated-Jake said, edging his fluent Italian with a British accent. "Who is behind it?"

"The Red Brigades," Alessandroni said. "Young Marxists so violence-prone that they have been repudiated even by the communist party here. University students, many of them. And even the women are joining them. It is crazy! What am I to do? Too much is expected of me! I tell you signor. . . ." He hesitated, then abandoned the attempt to repeat his visitor's name, ". . . I am the most overworked and underpaid official in all of Italy."

Hyphenated-Jake contemplated his next move. Alessandroni could be had. Men who consider themselves overworked or underpaid or put upon in any way by their system become informants, even traitors, if manipulated adroitly. In the case of Alessandroni, Hyphenated-Jake decided, scruple would not be an obstacle. He needed some pretense to allow him to establish a rapport with the harried bureaucrat, and a face-saving device to camouflage the passage of money. Then it would be a case of buying the company store to obtain access to the information on the Red Brigades in Alessandroni's files.

"You are kind to take the time to see me," Hyphenated-Jake said, unction in his tone. "I am a barrister. My firm in London has dispatched me to find the heirs to the estate of one Humberto Alessandroni. He died recently, leaving no will, and no family in England."

"Alessandroni?" Shedding his weariness, Alessandroni leaned forward attentively. "Do you have reason to believe I am an heir? I believe that one of my grandmother's brothers was named Humberto, and he immigrated somewhere. I forget."

"I fear that is probably not the case," Hyphenated-Jake said, "but I wish to explore every avenue. This Alessandroni family is from the Turin area. A chap at our embassy made the quite sound recommendation that I would do well to contact you, an Alessandroni with investigative experience and local contracts, to assist me in my search. Whatever the result, I would, of course, want to recompense you for your valuable time."

"Busy as I am," Alessandroni said, "I feel I have a duty to help you if I can."

It was sometime later when Hyphenated-Jake enjoyed a final cappuccino behind the window of a restaurant on the Via Venuto. Mack would be pleased; it had been a quick, easy recruitment. Alessandroni had delivered a thick package of documents (photographs, police reports, copies of birth certificates) and had promised future cooperation. He had not questioned Hyphenated-Jake's motives when the British barrister abruptly became interested in data on Italy's terrorists. The purloined documents, Alessandroni made clear, were a gift passed on in a spirit of patriotism. He did accept, however, the thick envelope stuffed with lira in payment for his cursory advice on how Smith-Forsythe, Esquire, might go about checking out the Turin branch of the Alessandroni family tree. Hyphenated-Jake noted that the patriot counted the bills discreetly but carefully before leaving.

As the waiter pocketed his tip Hyphenated-Jake looked at his watch: time to go to the airport for the flight to Paris.

The waiter was distracted by a beautiful woman striding through the crowd of pedestrians on the sidewalk. Despite the cold, the lovely Roman woman had tossed her stylish coat over one shoulder. The men looked on admiringly as she passed.

"What magnificent movement!" the waiter exclaimed.

"Like two monkeys," Hyphenated-Jake grinned, straining forward for the last glimpse, "fighting in a sack."

Mack savored the luncheon of partridge and fine, moist Stilton served with hard crackers. When they had finished, he walked with Mitch to his car and squeezed into the small Austin. They had only gone a few blocks when Mitch nodded at the façade of a narrow building.

"Churchill's," Mitch said. "First landmark on the Carlos tour. Really a quite stylish dinner club in its time. Mr. Rubbers often remarks on the intriguing fact that Carlos was once a member in good standing. Played a gentlemanly game of poker and drank nothing but Napoleon brandy. Highly unusual, you must admit, Mack, for a graduate of one of our better clubs to become the world's most famous terrorist."

"We had Patty Hearst," Mack said. "Who would ever have predicted that the daughter of a multimillionaire would learn to brandish a machine gun?"

"Indeed," Mitch said, "but the circumstances were hardly similar." They had driven only a few more minutes when Mitch stopped the car, allowing the motor to run. He pointed out a Georgian mansion across a narrow street. Mack glanced at the street signs on the nearby corner: Queen's Grove, St. John's Wood.

"The residence of Joseph Edward Sieff, president of one of our larger store chains, Marks and Spencers, and a prominent Zionist. The street here was shadowy on the penultimate day of 1973, as our Mr. Edward Heath had lowered the street lights because of a miners' strike. Carlos rang the bell and the door was opened by the butler. Sieff was shaving, and Carlos forced the butler at gunpoint to lead the way to the bath. Carlos rapped on the door and, when Sieff opened it, shot the businessman in his lathered face from a distance of not more than ten inches. But Sieff survived, as the bullet struck his teeth and was deflected just short of the vital area of the brain. His wife saved his life by being quick-witted enough to turn him onto his stomach so that he wouldn't drown in his own blood. Plucky woman—an American, by the by. Carlos escaped, of course."

"He learned to be more efficient," Mack said. "The following year he killed two police officers and one of his former colleagues in Paris. One gun, without reloading. How can you be sure the assailant who shot Sieff was Carlos?"

"Apparently there was no question. Mr. Rubbers will know. I do recall that the PFLP claimed the credit at a press conference in Lebanon. Odd the way the world turns: the Arabs said the attack was in retaliation because Sieff had entertained a visiting right-wing Israeli politician named Begin."

"The same?" Mack asked.

"The same," Mitch said. "He was renowned as a terrorist himself, long before he became prime minister."

They drove again through the London streets.

"Carlos established a number of safehouses in this part of the city," Mitch said, "each with its bird to mind the nest."

Mack chuckled.

"Do you remember," Mitch asked, "when your new Director Schlesinger visited London in 1973? Our fellows were quite amused when he announced that he wanted his weekend free of socializing because he intended to go bird watching. We all assumed he intended to ogle the human birds in Picadilly Circus, but he really did mean bird watching of the feathered variety."

"I've heard the story. And you say it's true?"

"Indeed." Mitch stopped the car. "This is Lawrence Lane, just off Cheapside. And that is the Israeli Bank of Hapoalin, a trade union establishment. Just one month after Sieff was shot, a young man described as in his mid-twenties tossed a homemade bomb through the window. Mr. Rubbers believes it was almost certainly Carlos. Extensive damage, but only one person was hurt."

"Again," Mack said, "Carlos learned from experience. Later the same year he chose to use an M-26 grenade in Paris. A lot of people were hurt, and two killed."

"Quite," Mitch said. "Carlos really is a nasty sort, isn't he?"

He pulled the car into the traffic. "I fear that's about the extent of my knowledge of Ilyich Rameriz-Sanchez, also known as Carlos. But I will drop you now, consult with the chief and, given his blessing, see to it that Mr. Rubbers gets hopping on your assignment."

"If at all possible," Mack said, "I would like to leave in the morning."

"I'll see what I can do. Mr. Rubbers would drool if asked to work all night. In any event, I'll pick you up at seven. We'll have a bite, an evening of theater, and tomorrow I'll drive you to Heathrow."

Mitch braked abruptly as a clanging siren cleared the traffic; a van of London policemen passed.

"Do you see those bobbies?" Mitch asked. "It was not so long ago that all our police wore those quaint round hats and none carried guns. Now they carry guns and wear crash helmets."

Emilio adjusted his weight carefully on the chair, which seemed the most substantial piece of furniture in the small parlor. The room was decorated on one wall with a lithograph of the Danube, and a vase of glass edelweiss sat atop a spinet piano. Through a curtained window Emilio could see the narrow street where, so the taxi driver had told him a few moments before, Richard Strauss had once lived.

Frau Fechner had gone to summon her husband. Police detective Gustav Fechner had been sent to the scene of the 1975 OPEC kidnapping in Vienna where Carlos and his terrorist team had held seventy-two hostages. He had been wounded in the shootout and, according to Lucy's notes, had headed subsequent investigations of the incident.

Emilio considered several options. Perhaps he would pose as a member of the Spanish police, or as an investigator from the Venezuelan service. Perhaps he would be more direct; a retired Austrian police officer might prefer an offer of money for his information.

Gustav Fechner rolled his wheelchair into the parlor. While

Emilio knew that the detective had been injured in the encounter with Carlos, he had not realized he had become an invalid. Emilio chose the more honest option. He stood.

"Herr Fechner," Emilio said, "I am Colonel Gonzalez, from the United States, and I need your assistance. I am investigating the case of Ilyich Rameriz-Sanchez with every intention that he will be arrested and punished. Will you help me?"

Fechner stroked the arms of his wheelchair. "Colonel, if I will not help you, then who will? Sit down."

Mack's travel alarm buzzed at six-thirty in his Rio hotel. His body ached as he lifted himself from the bed; he was jet-lag weary after the long flight from London. He showered, put on a bathing suit, draped a towel over his shoulders, stepped into beach sandals, and descended in the service elevator. He carried his billfold, hotel key, travel documents and Mr. Rubbers's report in a folded copy of *Jornal do Brasil*.

Copacabana Beach was a two-mile-long scimiter glowing in the early morning light as the sun rose over the escarpment of apartment buildings. Sugar Loaf loomed at one end of the beach. Mack crossed the avenue, which had been widened since his last visit to Rio de Janeiro. He walked for five minutes before arriving in front of the rococo building where Boris Seymonov lived.

The beach was already spotted with physical fitness buffs playing featherball or pickup soccer. Mack purchased a pungent Brazilian coffee from a barefoot vendor who poured the steaming liquid from his thermos into a plastic cup about the size of a standard jigger. Mack glanced at the headlines of the paper, and then began to read Mr. Rubbers's report, the one Mitch Rollins had delivered to him at the airport in London.

Mr. Rubbers must have worked all night. His extracts from the files on Carlos and on his contacts in England would be useful grist for Lucy's mill. On one point Mr. Rubbers was unequivocal: it was his professional opinion that Carlos was no longer operating under the aegis of Dr. Habash's PFLP or any of the Arab splinter groups. Unless Carlos was a controlled agent of the Soviets or the Cubans, Mr. Rubbers had

74

concluded, he was conducting his operations independently.

Mack had been waiting for an hour and a half and the sun was blazing when Boris Seymonov emerged from his apartment building. The tall Russian carried a beach towel, wore only a bathing suit and a black swimming cap, and pranced gingerly over the now burning sand. Watching as Boris plunged into the surf, Mack fidgeted for fifteen minutes while the Russian bobbed up and down in the heavy Atlantic swells. He found himself thinking of Skip Wilson, and how pleasant it would be to have her sitting beside him on the warm sand. Then his thoughts turned to the business at hand: what would Seymonov's reaction be when he recognized his whilom adversary, Mack McLendon? He changed his location when the swimmer stroked toward the shore. When the KGB officer shook off the final wave, picked up his towel and began drying himself, Mack was quietly waiting nearby.

"Good morning, Boris."

Seymonov smiled tentatively, pulled off his rubber cap, and squinted in the bright sunlight. "Who's that? I'm afraid I don't have my glasses."

"William McLendon," Mack said.

Seymonov stepped closer to Mack. His face flushed.

"McLendon?" The Russian looked up and down the beach. "Are you alone?"

"Yes, Boris."

"Is this a provocation?" Seymonov pointed a finger directly at Mack. "I hope you are not up to that old foolishness. I am not at all interested in becoming a traitor and working for the CIA!"

"You convinced me of that eight years ago in Mexico City," Mack said. "This is not a pitch, Boris. I just want to talk."

Mack summoned the coffee vendor, who poured a cup for Mack, then extended one to Seymonov. The Russian hesitated, then took the coffee and sat on the sand. Sipping the strong brew, Seymonov challenged Mack with his eyes. Seymonov was a large, muscular man with broad shoulders; his features were heavy, almost Mongolian.

"Very well, William." Seymonov spoke English with only a

trace of an accent. "We will have one very small coffee and one very brief conversation. What does the CIA want of me? I repeat, I am not for sale."

"My business with Boris Seymonov is personal," Mack said. "The CIA does not even know that I am here."

"Not even your chief in Brasilia?" Seymonov cast his eyes heavenward. "Permit me, William, to be skeptical. This is nonsense again. How many times do you think I will play the fool? Once yes, but not again. My comrades still make jokes about me and the foolishness in Mexico."

He lapsed into silence and winced slightly at the memory of his aborted vacation in Tasco. Beside he and his wife, there had been only one other foreign guest at the *pension*, an absent-minded but pleasant nuclear scientist named George Bellows from the space laboratories in California. What a tempting prize! He had telephoned his embassy in Mexico City and they had advised him a day later that George Bellows had been a college radical but had become involved in top secret research and development.

"But George Bellows was not George Bellows at all," Seymonov said aloud, crumpling his cup and throwing it on the sand. "He was William McLendon of the CIA, and he had planted himself in that *pension*, waiting for me!" Seymonov nodded slowly. "I must admit, William, it was a good—" he searched for the word in English "—what do you call that kind of operation?"

"A dangle," Mack said, smiling. He picked up Seymonov's cup and buried it, and his, in the sand. "I was dangled in front of you."

"Yes. You were the bait and I was the foolish fish which bit. Back in Mexico City there were those two weeks of spending time and money escorting you to the best restaurants, challenging you to drink too much, flattering you. All wasted. I believed I was pursuing 'George Bellows'—but no, McLendon was hunting me!"

"You and your wife were charming, and treated me well," Mack said. "How is Natasha?"

"My wife is well," Seymonov said, looking at his huge waterproof watch, "and will be alerting my office if I do not return to the apartment soon."

"I can imagine," Mack said. "Didn't a Russian ambassador disappear from this beach in 1961?"

"Sixty-two," Seymonov said. "Farther south, at another beach called the Baja de Tijuco. He swam out to sea early one morning and was never seen again. But don't change the subject. Just when I was ready to recruit Mr. George Bellows, *he* attempted to recruit *me* as a CIA agent! A dirty trick! You might at least have let me try first, under the circumstances."

"Boris, you sound like a looter who complains because another thief makes off with his swag. You and I have been international looters for a long time."

"It is true," Seymonov said, "that we are not Boy Scouts. But tell me, even if you are not with the CIA—which I do not for one minute believe—they must have told you where to find me."

"No," Mack said. "I looked you up in the library at the Department of State in Washington. They have diplomatic lists from all over the world. And, really, you're too burned to be sent overseas in anything other than diplomatic cover and too senior for minor posts. I went through the lists of Soviet representation in England, France, Germany, and Italy before finding you at the bottom of the Brazil list. How did you manage to escape the move to Brasilia when the others in your embassy had to move there?"

"Brasilia?" Seymonov shuddered. "And live in a grim compound, as we did in Mexico City? Never!" Seymonov tilted his head impishly. "In any event, the government may have gone to Brasilia but the culture remains in Rio."

"Yes, I noticed on the diplomatic list you are described as the cultural attaché at the consulate here." Mack smiled. "How is the cultural business in Brazil these days?"

"Thriving," Seymonov said. "See that, for instance."

A slender girl in a bikini strolled unhurriedly past the two men, her lithe body undulating. She did not avert her gaze when the American and the Russian admired her.

"Brazilian women," Seymonov said, "are the only amateurs

in the world who will look you straight in the eye when you flirt." He turned to Mack. "I was able to persuade my superiors that Natasha and I should remain in Rio. Fortunately I have a highly placed relative in Moscow who served as an advocate."

"Your uncle?" Mack queried. "Gregorio Ivanovitch Bula, in the Ministry of Foreign Trade?"

"You are being a show off, William. I know you must have studied my file diligently before the escapade in Mexico."

Mack smiled.

"Why were you waiting for me on the beach?" Seymonov asked. "Why not telephone, or ring my doorbell?"

"As you say, I know your file. I suspected that a man with your tastes would not waste the most beautifully adorned beach in the world." Mack nodded toward the bikini-clad girl, who had turned and was walking toward them again. "And I didn't know what kind of radar screen might have been erected around your home and office. I saw no reason to embarrass you in any way by becoming a blip on the screen."

"Thoughtful," Seymonov said, "if you are telling me the truth, and professional if you are up to foolishness. How could you be sure I was not traveling, perhaps on home leave in Moscow?"

"By telephoning your office from Europe," Mack said, "and pretending to be a Dutch journalist who wanted an appointment with you today. You can scratch that appointment from your calendar when you arrive at the office."

"Which must be soon," Seymonov said, looking at his watch again. "My wife will be setting all sorts of unnecessary wheels in motion if I do not return."

"May I see you later today?"

The Russian studied Mack's face. "William, I entertain a certain professional regard for you, and despite our roles as adversaries, some personal fondness. But you must understand that I have no choice but to report this encounter to my superiors immediately. Our service is much more . . . flexible . . . than in the past, but I would still find myself in hot water should it be learned that I have been talking with you."

"Don't report until I can see you again. Later this afternoon or tonight. It's important, and I ask it as a personal favor."

Seymonov laid his hand on Mack's shoulder. "William, you are asking me to take a risk. I cannot."

"You owe me one, Boris. An IOU. Do you understand what that means? I've had it in the bank since 1963, and now I want to collect. A personal debt."

"What do I owe you?" Seymonov asked, dubiously.

"You were dispatched by your chief in Mexico City on a mission to Costa Rica in 1963. Your assignment was to meet the hierarchy of the local communist party to plan strategy for an eventual re-establishment of diplomatic relations between San José and Moscow."

"Was I?"

"You were. You stayed at the El Sol Hotel, and your randy habits almost got you into trouble. In the hotel bar you met a young Cuban woman. She was attractive and, she told you, lonely. She did *not* tell you that she was a Miami whore. Even so, when you went to her room you had the foresight to inspect the premises. You found a camera mounted behind a wall-mirror, booted the girl in the ass, and avoided a nasty situation."

"Yes, William. That is an accurate account. I wondered then as I do now why the CIA should try such an infantile trick. You had already tested me in Mexico. Did you think I would react to that kind of blackmail, photographs of me in bed with a woman? Stupid. I would have simply advised my superiors and, perhaps, asked for extra copies for my private collection."

"It was not," Mack said, "a CIA operation. A rightist group in San José learned of your visit and set the trap to embarrass you, hoping the commotion would interfere with negotiations between the two governments. They didn't even know you were a KGB officer. As you say, it was childish. I wasn't particularly anxious to support the re-establishment of relations between Moscow and San José, but I couldn't believe that

79

pictures of Boris Seymonov making love to a Miami prostitute would make much difference one way or another. I remembered how pleasantly you and Natasha had treated me in Mexico, and decided to tip you off."

"You had a penetration of the rightist group?"

"Sure," Mack said. "So I sent an informal, out-of-channels message to our chief in Costa Rica, asking that he place a warning note in your hotel box."

"How do I know you are telling the truth, William?"

"The note was signed Guillermo," Mack said. "And it read something like this: 'Intelligence officers who sleep with strangers under uncontrolled conditions are seldom promoted.' "

"That's what it said!" Seymonov laughed loudly. "And you were right. It would have made me look foolish and I might well have not been promoted."

"Congratulations, Colonel," Mack said.

"And," Seymonov said, sobering, "Natasha would not have found it amusing. Natasha is a fine woman, but she is becoming testy as she grows older."

Seymonov stood, brushing the sand from his body.

"Very well, William. I do owe you. I will see you at five this afternoon."

"I'm staying at the Ouro Verde," Mack said.

"No," the Russian said. "As you have reminded me in the past, an intelligence officer who meets a hostile party in conditions not under his control is seeking trouble. A restaurant and bar called On The Rocks. You can find it easily on the top floor of an uncompleted building overlooking Lake Gavea. By nine in the evening it will be crowded with rich Brazilians and American tourists, but in the late afternoon it will be deserted. I will talk to you, but promise nothing. And I will report our contact to my superiors when we are finished."

"Fair enough," Mack said, rising to shake hands with the Russian. "And, Boris, during the day at your office check into your files and chat with your colleagues about Ilyich Rameriz-Sanchez."

"Carlos?" Seymonov pursed his lips. "Oho."

Another *carioca* walked languidly between them and the water line. She was about seventeen and wore the briefest bathing costume Mack had ever seen. Seymonov hummed a few bars of "The Girl from Ipenema."

"Quite a bikini," Mack said.

"Not a bikini," Seymonov said. "*A tanga.* Just as the Brazilian indians wore them before the white man came." Seymonov sighed. "The only chance you will ever have," he told Mack, "is if you hear I have been transferred to Brasilia, in spite of my uncle's efforts." Seymonov gazed again at the lovely girl. "In that case I will talk to you seriously about defecting to the West."

Frederico Espinosa was a ruggedly handsome man, Pancho Villa in a raw silk suit, with dark skin, a drooping mustache and a mane of grey hair. He had enjoyed the past half hour reminiscing with his old friend, Clarence Clements, with whom he had worked thirty years before on the Mexican side of the Rio Grande. Espinosa had retired from the Mexican customs service and now augmented his government pension by operating a private detective agency.

Getting down to business, Clem told Espinosa he was in Mexico on behalf of a wealthy Texan.

"Your friend from Texas, he is a rich man?"

"He sure is," Clem assured Espinosa. "Clever fellow. He bought American Tel and Tel when it was American Smoke Signal."

Espinosa laughed. "And how do I fit into his plans?"

"He's thinking of making a major investment here in Mexico City. Asked me to come down and check it out for him. He has the business side all figured out, but he's worried about terrorists."

"Terrorists?"

"Yup. He wants to send his favorite son-in-law down here to run the business. Doesn't want him to get into any trouble on the order of all those horror stories we've been reading in the newspapers."

"Horror stories?"

"All the kidnappings and murders of business people."

"It is true," Espinosa said, "that we have had a serious problem going back to about 1970. But recently things have been much quieter."

"How many policemen have been shot?"

"More than forty, counting the private guards. And your American consul in Guadalajara, and the father-in-law of our president were kidnapped. But I understand that kind of thing is about over. The leaders have been apprehended or killed. Some even say the groups responsible were not Marxists, as they claimed to be, but private groups financed by the right to give the government an excuse to annihilate the left."

"Sounds complicated," Clem said. "But I'd like to find out all I can." He took an envelope from his pocket and removed a thick stack of $100 bills. He counted out ten of them and shoved them across the desk to Espinosa. "Who are the terrorists, where are they, who's dead, and who's alive? How often do they go back and forth to Havana? Maybe you have a friend at the airport who can peek at the Cubana passenger lists? Maybe a friend who works on such matters in the government?"

"I have many friends," Espinosa said. "And if you will deal, say, two more of those cards with the face of Mr. Franklin on them, I will give you the name of one who can be of great help to you."

Clem counted out two more bills.

"Enrique Zayaz." Espinosa began to write on a card. "He can be found at this address just outside Puebla. Only forty-five minutes' drive. He is a former Marxist who has been in and out of prison a dozen times because of his activities against the government. Now he has recanted, is disenchanted with his friends, and will talk about them."

"If that's known," Clem asked, "isn't that dangerous?"

"Enrique only has a few years left at best. His heart is failing, and the medicos say he will not live long."

"I'll see him quick as you can say Jacobo Robinson," Clem promised.

82

The late afternoon heat shimmered over Rio de Janeiro as Mack's made-in-Brazil Volkswagen taxi catapulted through the tunnel from Copacabana to Ipenema Beach, then sped through a second tunnel to Le Blon. The driver alternately shouted or honked at other drivers, all of whom he seemed to regard as personal enemies. The cab turned inland, tires screeching, and skidded to a halt at the base of a tall, uncompleted building. As he paid the driver, Mack recalled the remark of a former CIA colleague who, when asked to name his most dangerous overseas assignment, said that without question it had been surviving the traffic in Rio de Janeiro.

Mack found a small, brass plate: "On The Rocks. Take Elevator to 16th Floor." The elevator was modern, carpeted and air-conditioned, but when Mack stepped out he found himself walking on a rough, concrete floor. There was a view in four directions, as neither partitions nor walls had been installed. A second elevator was located the length of a football field from the first; Mack rode it to the penthouse floor where a pretty girl met him and led the way into the bar.

Seymonov was waiting, seated with his back against the wall, a scotch cradled in his large hands. He wore a neatly tailored tan summer suit, a white shirt and tie, and rimless spectacles. The KGB officer looked like any benign tourist. He rose halfway out of his seat to greet Mack.

Mack and Seymonov were the only customers in the luxuriously decorated bar, and the service was prompt. Mack asked the waiter for a *caipparinga*.

"A what?" Seymonov asked. "According to your file you drink only martinis."

"Not in Rio at five in the afternoon when it's a hundred degrees in the shade. A *caipparinga* is made from the essence of sugar cane, poured over cut limes, ice, and sugar, all crushed together."

"How is it possible," Seymonov asked, "that a man on an expense account does not drink scotch?" When the waiter served Mack's drink, the American and the Russian toasted.

"Welcome to my capitalist rendezvous," Seymonov said.

"This building has been unfinished for many years; when the owners ran out of money the concessionaires put in the elevators and Brazilians think it chic. But you will note that the windows allow only a view of the beauties of Rio, and are designed so that you do not have to look at the slums. That might be distracting to other than socialist drinkers."

"Have you told anyone that we met this morning?"

"Yes. Natasha. She sends regards. She also advised me not to see you again."

"Boris, will you talk to me about Ilyich Rameriz-Sanchez?"

"My dear William, you must be unbalanced. That would be giving you material for blackmail more potent than snapshots of me in bed with a woman. How do I know that sometime in the future the CIA would not threaten to reveal my cooperation unless I talked more and more about other matters? I am not a child, William."

"Trust me. I will tell no one, not even my closest associates, that we have met. But Carlos and I are on a collision course, and I intend to survive. I need assistance from wherever I can find it. Carlos, or the people who work with him, have assassinated three CIA station chiefs, perhaps four."

Seymonov inhaled rapidly. "This is not more foolishness?"

"It is true, Boris."

"The Welch man in Athens?"

"That's not clear," Mack said. "But I am certain in the other three cases. I want you to report this to Moscow, and ask your superiors to help me in finding Carlos."

"Now I *know* you are demented." Seymonov held a forefinger near his temple, and made circles in the air. "Who else but a crazy man would make such a request? I am sorry to hear of the death of your colleagues, and I will admit that Carlos is a repulsive man. But he has done much for the Arab cause, especially that sector of it which my government . . . sympathizes with. Why should we help you destroy him?"

"Sooner or later," Mack said, "the press in the United States will have the story. There will be headlines, and public reaction. Your government will be suspect."

"Preposterous! Why should we return to those desperate days

84

of the Cold War? We know the rules of the game, and so do you. Why should we eliminate your station chiefs who would only be replaced? It would be better to abduct your diplomatic couriers, and snatch their pouches—but you would do the same thing."

"Of course I agree with you," Mack said. "And I am convinced that your service would not support Carlos in such a vendetta. But the American Congress might not agree, and your diplomatic efforts in Washington would suffer. There would be a public clamor if it were even hinted that the Soviet Union was Carlos's sponsor. The American CIA is not a popular institution these days, but our voters are basically conservative. There would even be pressure on our president."

"There would be no evidence," Seymonov said, stiffly.

"There is no evidence," Mack said, "that President Kennedy's assassination was the result of a conspiracy, but eighty-five percent of the public believe one existed. Do you think they will hesitate to believe the KGB is behind the killings of CIA chiefs? There is already a Russian connection: he went to your Patrice Lumumba school and has worked with others with whom you have been closely connected. If you are not blamed, the Cubans, thought to be acting on your instructions, would be. When the hostages in the French Embassy in Amsterdam were released after Carlos dropped a grenade on the crowd at *Le Drug Store,* the French Minister of Justice immediately expelled three Cuban diplomats from Paris. He said they were supporting Carlos."

"A reactionary bureaucrat," Seymonov said, "who had to blame someone but had no evidence."

"Could be," Mack said, "but if the American public even suspected Cuban or Soviet sponsorship of the deliberate murder of CIA men, it could be difficult for you in Washington. Think human rights, Boris. Tell your people in Moscow to think human rights. Wouldn't helping me put your government on the side of the angels?"

"You are a lunatic," Seymonov muttered. "You are asking me to persuade my government, and my service, to become your collaborator, if not agent, while you chase after an international nuisance named Carlos. Incredible! Why should we trust a CIA man, especially one who has been working against Soviet interests for some twenty-five years? Since 1953, in Iran at least."

"I was a very junior assistant when Mossedegh was overthrown."

"Yes," Seymonov said, "assisting what's-his-name, Teddy Roosevelt."

"Boris, Theodore Roosevelt was the twenty-sixth president of the United States. He died just after World War I."

"His offspring, then. And now are we to repay you for your role in Guatemala in 1954? You were not so junior an assistant then. Need I continue?"

"Boris, I want you to cable my request to Moscow. What can you lose? If I find Carlos, the truth will be known and the Kremlin will not be suspect. Even if I fail I can see to it that the record shows you cooperated in an attempt to thwart him. I have a number of friends in the press and the Congress who would be informed."

Suddenly Seymonov began to laugh. "I am having a delusion. This can't be happening! William McLendon, white knight on a white horse, his cloak and dagger flapping, riding to the defense of the Soviet Union! How shall we reward you for your service as an agent of influence—the Order of Lenin, or shall we strike a new medal?"

Seymonov laughed again, so uproariously that a young man and his girl friend entering the bar stared curiously. With a subsiding chuckle, Seymonov shook his head.

"Very well, William. I will forward your proposal. I can assure you there are times when our headquarters can use some levity. When your message is decoded there will be general merriment."

"What about you, Boris? Can you help me? Now?"

"Perhaps, William." Seymonov sobered. "During the day I did look at the file on Carlos. It is not much, as he never came to Brazil, and it ends abruptly after the kidnapping of the oil ministers in Vienna. The last entry is a form message, sent to all our centers around the world. It warns the people of our service that contact with Carlos or his collaborators is prohibited. I take that to mean he is not working for the Soviet Union."

"What are the chances, Boris, that your book message is a deception, meant to deceive even KGB officers in the field?"

"Possible." Seymonov shrugged. "But unlikely. And, I have one other little scrap for you. One of our men passed through Rio today en route to Brasilia. I asked him about Carlos. He knew no details, but said the cafeteria talk at our headquarters is that Carlos now maintains a team of twenty called Commando Carlos. If one of the unit is captured, or killed or injured, he is simultaneously replaced to bring the level back to twenty. Finally—and this is all I have for you—Moscow believes Carlos's next spectacular will be launched in the United States."

"Why? Why do they believe that, Boris?"

Seymonov hesitated. "Because the two most recent recruits in his Commando have been Puerto Ricans, members of the FALN, who have been blowing up your buildings in New York. They were trained in the Middle East, then sent back to the United States. That is all. I dared not be more inquisitive."

"Thanks, Boris. That is useful."

Seymonov tore a paper cocktail napkin into four pieces and dropped them in front of Mack. "So, William, my IOU is torn up and you are repaid. Anything else will have to be on instructions."

"Fair enough." Mack gave Seymonov a card; the printed telephone numbers had been scratched through, and new ones inserted in pencil. "I must return to Washington. You, or a colleague there, can reach me at these numbers."

"Before I go, William, will you reveal one CIA secret, as I have just done with my service's information?"

Mack was wary. "What kind of secret, Boris?"

"If you were to give me the plans of the cruise missile," Seymonov said, "I would be promoted instantly. But this is a personal request."

"What's the request?"

"How thick," Seymonov asked, "is my file at CIA Langley headquarters?"

Mack did not smile. He understood that it was a serious matter of professional curiosity.

"Your file is impressive, Boris." Mack held his thumb and forefinger about an inch apart. "That thick."

"Oh." The Russian was crestfallen. "That is not so much. The file on Mack the Knife is three volumes." Seymonov held his hands apart, the gesture fishermen use to indicate the size of the one that got away. "At least six inches. I am jealous."

It was close to three in the afternoon when Hyphenated-Jake and Inspector Piccard left the restaurant and walked a half block to the Champs Elysées, where Hyphenated-Jake signaled a taxi.

"*Non, non, non,*" the Inspector said. "We must walk. The luncheon was too rich. We must walk it away."

Inspector Piccard was a diminutive Frenchman. He wore a stubby black hat, a striped grey suit and a stiff, high collar. He patted his compact paunch appreciatively. "A fine repast. I have lived all of my life in Paris and that—my thanks to you—was the first time I have dined at the Tour d'Argent. Too dear. I observed surreptitiously when you paid. It was more than I earn in a week. I must thank you again M.—forgive me, I cannot remember your name."

"Leyland-Abbot," Hyphenated-Jake said. "Morris Leyland-Abbot."

"After such an exceptional duck," Inspector Piccard said, "I owe you the honesty to say what I think. And I think that if that is your real name I, in turn, am Charles de Gaulle. And further, if you are a television writer from New York, then I am Jeanne d'Arc, visiting Paris from Orléans."

"I fear you are a skeptic," Hyphenated-Jake sighed.

"Especially," the Inspector said, touching Hyphenated-Jake's elbow to guide him through the throng of pedestrians, "when you ask for information on a list of fifty names which could have only been compiled by an intelligence service. If you are from the CIA, why not approach my superiors directly, through normal channels?"

"I do not represent the American government. But it is true that I am engaged in intensive . . . er . . . research on Ilyich Rameriz-Sanchez and all who might have been connected with him. I would naturally seek out the man, renowned in all of Interpol, as the expert who knows most about him and his activities in Paris."

"I am not from Interpol," the Inspector said, "but from the DST—*la Direction de la Surveillance du Territoire,* and I believe you are well aware of that. It is my task to see to it that these fanatics shoot their guns and explode their bombs somewhere other than France. I recognize perhaps half of the names on your list, and there will be information in my files on most of the others. But a great deal of work is involved in preparing the summary you request. Moreover, the information belongs to the French government, and much of it classified."

"I will reward you," Hyphenated-Jake said.

"You are attempting to bribe me. I do not find that amusing."

"Not a bribe," Hyphenated-Jake said, "a reward." He extracted an envelope from his breast pocket. "Here are two round-trip airline tickets to New York, first-class, and a reservation certificate at a hotel where your expenses will be taken care of. But there is no money, consequently, there is no bribe."

"A fine line," Inspector Piccard remarked. "Two tickets?"

"One for Madame Piccard," Hyphenated-Jake said. "I am told your daughter works at the United Nations French Mission in New York."

"True. And in return I must—?"

"Prepare the report," Hyphenated-Jake said, dropping a calling card into the envelope before handing it to the inspector. "Then mail it to me at that address, within the next ten days. From New York."

"From New York?"

89

"Yes."

"What am I to deduce from this strange encounter?" The inspector studied the face of his American visitor. "First, you are, no matter what you say, from the CIA. Second, my government has decided that with the sievelike quality of your intelligence service these days it is not wise to pass you information of this kind. Accepting those conclusions as valid, I believe it is my duty to assist you, informally."

Inspector Piccard slipped the envelope into his pocket.

"Observe carefully," said Pedro Morantes, "when he serves the meat."

The waiter placed a tray on the table and, with a ceremonial flourish of the serving knife and fork, proceeded to divide the suckling pig into two portions, using the dull side of the knife to carve it. He refilled each wine glass and retreated.

"*Salud,*" Pedro toasted.

"*Salud,*" Emilio responded.

"This restaurant boasts that it has the finest pig in all of Spain. The waiters traditionally carve it with the dull edge of the knife to prove its tenderness."

The meat was succulent and moist under a carapace of crisp, brown skin. The friends ate in silence, devoting to the fine pork the attention it merited. Despite the excellence of the meal, Emilio experienced an uneasy rumbling in his stomach and a hangover pulsation at the base of his cranium. He had been gorging himself, at Pedro's insistence, with food and drink since he had arrived in Madrid the night before. He and Pedro had reenacted, between midnight and four in the morning, the wine and food tour they had taken together many times, ten years ago, when Emilio had been the assistant military attaché at the embassy. They had gone, on foot, from cantina to cantina, drinking a glass of wine and sampling the speciality of the bar at each stop—crayfish in one, mussels in another, clams, oysters, pork, chicken, skewers of beef in others—ending with a glass of raw, red wine for the road and a final *salud* as they stood ankle-deep in discarded shrimp shells.

Now, after only a few hours of sleep, they were having lunch in Segovia. Visible to Emilio through the restaurant window were the stone aqueduct, which still carried water to the town even though it dated back to the Roman era, and the turreted *alcazar*.

"Your wife Maria would be with you if your visit to Spain was for pleasure," Pedro said. "Do you have a mission?"

Emilio had not mentioned the reason for his trip to Spain until Pedro raised it—a matter of form—and was glad to get down to business.

"Yes, Pedro. I am working. Not exactly the same as before, but working. I am investigating the activities of Ilyich Rameriz-Sanchez, the terrorist known as Carlos."

"I have no reason to believe Carlos has been in Spain," Pedro said, "even though we have had our share of violence. Kidnappings, murders, policemen shot down in the streets. The Right clashing with the Left. You will recall the death of our premier, Carrero Blanco. It was a Basque operation."

"The street exploded under his car? A gigantic land mine that the terrorists triggered from a basement as he passed?"

"Exactly," Pedro said. "He was returning home from Mass. I had warned him not to establish such a regular Sunday morning pattern, but he paid no attention. He had a theory that Spanish terrorists would not conduct an operation on a Sunday." Pedro grimaced. "Sheer innocence." He poured more wine into Emilio's glass, pushing aside the colonel's hand with the neck of the bottle. "But I do not know that Carlos was connected with any of this."

"He may have recruited members of your Spanish groups for his own brigade," Emilio said. "And I know you have useful data on travelers to Cuba. I have a list of names. I need to know where each terrorist on the list is now. In jail? Abroad? Dead? Are you in a position to help me?"

"Yes," the Spaniard said. "I am number three in the service now. Perhaps I will be number two soon, even number one.

My superiors are older, and both were Franco men. They will not survive in the present climate. Fortunately, I was never a politician."

"Then you will help?"

"It is a forty-five-minute drive to my office in Madrid." Pedro snapped his fingers for the waiter. "You scratched my back many times in the past, Emilio. Let us go to my office and I will scratch yours, energetically."

"Chin higher," Dr. Karim instructed. "There, that's right." The physician inspected the screen of the fluoroscope. "This ancient device is almost useless. I should have x-rays, but there are no plates in all of Beirut. Medical supplies have been difficult to obtain since the war."

Perry smiled over the top of the fluoroscope. "You can stop checking my spinal column now, Dr. Karim. There is nothing wrong with my back."

"I don't understand. The desk clerk who called from the hotel said—"

"That an American businessman with a slipped disc needed an emergency examination," Perry interrupted. "I am the tourist, but my back does not ache. I want to talk to you." Perry stepped from behind the fluoroscope, picked up his shirt, and began to put it on.

"I am a busy man," Dr. Karim said, his face flushing with anger. "Get out. I have patients to attend."

"No," Perry said. "You will pay attention to me. You will tell your nurse that you must escort me back to my hotel. The other patients must return later. I will pretend great pain when we leave. You and I will talk elsewhere."

"I do not know who you are, or what you want. But if you do not leave this minute I will summon the police."

"No," Perry said. Turning to a mirror, he combed his stylishly cut hair. "For, if you do, the police and others will learn of your three occupations."

Dr. Karim drew a deep breath. "Three occupations?"

"You said you were a busy man," Perry said, putting on his jacket. "Indeed you are. You have your medical career, and two others. Your second occupation is to provide support to three Palestinian political organizations. Your situation is perfect for a cut-out. The couriers come and go from this examination room, where you give them instructions, funds, and travel documents. I wouldn't be surprised if one or more of those waiting outside is here for such nonmedical reasons."

"If so," the doctor warned, "between us we will prevent you from leaving. My diagnosis is that you are near death. One more body, even that of an American, will stir little interest when found floating in the Mediterranean."

"It is I who will do the threatening today, Dr. Karim." Perry removed a single piece of folded paper from his pocket and proffered it to the physician. "If I do not return safely to my hotel, and subsequently fly out of Lebanon without interference, a copy of that message will be delivered to six addresses here in Beirut—the three political groups for which you act as a cut-out, the chief of the government's secret service, the commander of the Syrian military, and the editor of *Al Hambra*. All will be titillated by the verifiable facts about your *third* occupation—your well-paid position as a CIA agent."

Dr. Karim turned white. He sank slowly into a chair, reading the letter.

"I don't understand. You are an American. If it is true that I am helping your CIA, why should you blackmail me like this?"

"I am an American who once worked for the CIA," Perry said, "and thus know of your connection. Now I need to ask you many questions. It will not harm you or the CIA if they are answered accurately. No one, not even your case officer, need know about our meeting. But if you do not cooperate with me I will expose you. In that event, I would guess that, as you say, there would soon be one more body floating in the bay."

Dr. Karim was defeated. For a moment he let his head sink into his hands. He sobbed, briefly. Then he looked up at Perry.

"I am a man who has betrayed his people. For a sordid reason. Money. I desperately need money—more than I can gather in this war-torn city—for reasons which have to do with my family, reasons which could not interest you. If I give you the information you want, will you pay me?"

"No."

"Nothing?"

"What is your fee?" Perry asked.

"My fee?"

"Your examination fee."

"Why, three hundred Lebanese pounds." Dr. Karim was still stunned. "About ten American dollars."

"Paid." Perry counted out the money for his examination, and dropped it in front of Dr. Karim. "Now that the finances are taken care of, doctor, it is time to take off your white coat and come with me."

Clem sang to himself happily as he drove the rented car down the highway to Puebla, past the Aztec pyramids at Teotihuacán, and into the pleasant valley. Two snow-covered mountains loomed on his right: Popocatepetl, known because of her sinuous outline as The Sleeping Lady, and her sister, Ixtacihuatl. Fifteen years before, Clem remembered, both peaks were visible from the streets of Mexico City, thirty miles away; now it was a rare occurrence when the city's ubiquitous industrial pollution cleared long enough to allow even a brief glimpse of the mountains.

At the village of Nueva Rosita, Clem turned off the highway and bounced along mud lanes, consulting the hand-drawn map Frederico Espinosa had given him, until he arrived at the unnumbered house where the former revolutionary, Enrique Zayaz, lived.

The heavy wooden door swung slowly open. An old woman, a black shawl over her head, stared at Clem.

"Good day to you, señora," Clem said, in his fluent but gringo-accented Spanish. "I am Clements. I have come to see Don Enrique."

"Follow me, señor." The ancient led the way through a dark hall into a room lit only with candles. A dozen men and women, all dressed in black, sat quietly. The candles flickered Goyaesque shadows on the walls. In the center of the room, on two carpenter's horses, rested a black coffin.

"You have come only just in time," the old woman whispered. "Don Enrique will be buried within the hour." She crossed herself. "May he go with God."

Clem doffed his hat, lowered his head, and muttered an incantation.

Frank was pleased with his record time. He had picked the three locks on Mack's office door in just under two minutes, a satisfying improvement over the night before, when it had taken almost three minutes, and a *definite* reduction from the clumsy five minutes he had wasted the *first* night. He had the keys to the office in his pocket—Mack had left them, asking Frank to inspect the premises occasionally—but Frank enjoyed the professional challenge, and was rewarded by the knowledge that his fingers retained their touch.

It was black as pitch in the office, but Frank did not turn on the light. Instead, he took a flashlight from his pocket, fitted an almost opaque Celluloid filter over the lens, and switched it on. There was no visible beam of light, but just inside the door a square patch of orange gold radiance glowed on the carpet. Frank stepped over the glow and into the office itself. He turned the flashlight toward the floor under each of the office windows. An undisturbed candescence gleamed in each case as Frank directed the beam on the phosphorescent dust he had sprinkled near the door and under the windows three nights before. There had been no intruders.

Frank closed the office door and, in the elevator, ascended to Mack's apartment. He opened the door and aimed the flashlight at the floor. Luminous footprints led from the entrance to and from the hall which led to Mack's bedroom.

Frank stooped and measured one of the prints with extended fingers, then compared it against his own foot: a man, probably wearing a size eight and a half rubber-soled shoe.

He followed the St. Elmo's path of prints leading to the bedroom. They continued directly to the bathroom. The floor just in front of the toilet was a maze of phosphorescent prints.

Frank turned on the bathroom light and recognized the M–26 grenade even though it was in a plastic bag, as soon as he lifted the lid of the commode. A hard, straight wire led from the lever of the flushing device to the pin in the grenade. Frank squinted through his bifocals to inspect the pineapple-shaped grenade; there were several bright marks scratched on the head of the oval sphere. The customary five-second-delay mechanism had probably been adjusted so that the grenade would explode at the very moment that Mack, next using his bathroom, might flush the toilet.

Frank whistled softly. Normally the prefragmented, spirally wound steel (wrapped around TNT in the M–26) was deadly within a radius of fifty feet. In the small bathroom the expanding force of the water and slivered porcelain would have torn Mack's body to shreds.

Frank carefully removed the wire from the flushing device, leaving it attached to the pin of the grenade. He unwrapped the masking tape which had been used to lash the grenade inside the water closet, and put it into his pocket. When he lifted his arm to look at his watch, Frank saw that his hand was trembling. It would soon be time to meet Mack's plane at Dulles. When he did, Frank decided, he would recommend to Mack that he stay away from his apartment and office for the duration of Operation Carlos.

4.

It was two weeks later when Mack reported to Symser for the third time.

"Mr. Symser?"

"Yes?"

"How long will it take you to go to position Alpha?"

"About twenty minutes."

The Alpha telephone booth number was busy for ten minutes before Symser answered Mack's second call.

"I'm in a bus station," Symser explained. "This Mickey Mouse routine of communications is taking me back twenty years. While waiting for the phone to be free I realized it's been that long since I've ridden a bus."

"I hope I didn't wake you this time."

"No," Symser said, "I was watching the late news. Do you have any info for me?"

"Nothing special to report," Mack said. "Phase One of our endeavor has been relatively successful. We've come up with most of the data we need on the people who might be working with Carlos."

"In less than two weeks?"

"Terrorists are fairly public people," Mack said. "Performers. If they don't make an appearance from time to time they lose their television appeal. Terrorists hope to cause a lot of people to watch and to listen."

"You make it sound like theater."

"Terrorism *is* theater, basically," Mack said. "Three hundred years before Christ was born a man named Herostratos burned down Diana's temple, and later said he did it to make himself famous. Carlos is not much different."

"What about Carlos?"

"It looks as if he's operating on his own. We've yet to find out where he is, or what he plans for the future. But we have a few leads. Has anything happened to your people or your plants overseas?"

"Nothing," Symser said.

Mack thought of the grenade Frank had found in his bathroom.

"Maybe we're keeping him occupied enough so that he will leave you alone while he prepares his next major move. Is there anything planned for your principals which would give him some sort of opportunity? Such as a conference of your senior officers where Carlos could repeat the OPEC scenario?"

"Nothing."

"Let me know if something occurs to you," Mack requested. "Maybe Carlos has just been practicing on you. With a little luck, we should soon know. That's it for now. Not much for your money. I won't charge you for the call. Good night, Mr. Symser."

For the first time since they had been dispatched to Europe, the Middle East, and Mexico, Mack's entire crew was together. They sat around a dining room table in the Washington safehouse Frank and Lucy had maintained in their absence; Skip Wilson was there, again wearing, Mack noted, the Haitian amulet on a chain around her neck.

Mack called the meeting to order.

"Welcome back. You've all done well. In ten days in nine countries and a dozen cities we've managed to accumulate a respectable amount of information about Carlos and his former friends; we know something of his capabilities and intentions; and, thanks to Frank, we have managed to remain alive, despite one attempt by Carlos. Frank found and disarmed an M–twenty-six grenade rigged to blow up my apartment."

"Did Carlos himself plant the grenade?" Emilio asked.

"Probably a henchman. I doubt seriously that Carlos will show up in Washington. But it's a further indication of how careful we will have to be. Watch for surveillance when you are coming and going from this apartment, or to and from your hotels. And this continues to be a 'need-to-know' operation. Only Lucy is to be given complete details, because she'll need everything, including the identity of each source, in order to evaluate the intelligence. Lucy will brief me, and I will pass on to Frank what I think he needs to know. Otherwise, think before you talk. While we should all share the information, nothing is to be said to another of us except in general terms. No specifics about where you've been, whom you contacted, and what your next assignment will be."

"In general terms, Mack, what do we know now?" Skip asked.

"That Carlos is acting alone," Mack said. "He probably has a great deal of money. His share of the OPEC ransom was a minimum share of five million dollars, perhaps as much as twenty-five million. We also know that he has recruited a team of twenty terrorists—the Commando Carlos—and that if one or more becomes inactive, he or she will be replaced. Since there is little question of his connections with the Baader-Meinhof bunch, some are probably women. He is now planning an extravaganza, a spectacular operation which he claims will top his previous exploits. Finally, there is some reason to believe that next time Carlos will strike in the United States."

"In that case," Perry said, "shouldn't we alert the authorities here?"

"No," Mack said. "There's not enough information to be of any use to them. Later, we'll see. Remember that we are going for broke—we want to wrap up Carlos's entire gang if we possibly can."

"Our lady from CIA," Emilio said, "seems like a nice gal. But how do we know she won't run back to Langley and tell them everything she hears here? Then Carlos's source in the Agency will be able to send him daily bulletins."

Skip stared at Emilio coolly.

"Skip has assured me," Mack said, "that she is not going to brief anyone at Langley on what we're doing. I trust her."

"It seems to me," Hyphenated-Jake said, "that we still have a long way to go. What don't we know about Carlos?"

"Where he is," Mack said. "What kind of operation he is

planning and when it will be, and who and where his support chief is. Somehow we have to get into his support apparat if we want to find the answers to the first questions."

"Do we know why Carlos has such a fondness for the M-twenty-six grenade?" Frank asked. "First in Paris, then in your apartment. How does Carlos obtain U.S. grenades?"

Mack turned to Perry, who answered.

"In 1971 Ulrike Meinhof and her friends raided a U.S. military base near Kaiserslautern and scooped up several boxes of M-twenty-sixes. They've been used in terrorist operations all over Europe since, especially in ops by the Turkish People's Liberation Army. About the same time Ulrike led another raid on a town hall in Hessen and carried away blank passports and other identity documents which were used by European terrorists as late as 1975, and probably are still being used from time to time."

"What I wanna know," Clem said, "is when the action begins."

"Just as soon," Mack said, "as we can get a fix on Carlos, and at least a reasonable reading on the twenty people he has selected for his Commando."

"And how do we go about doing that?" Clem asked.

Mack turned. "Lucy."

Lucy Henderson rose, and walked to the end of the room where a bulletin board hung between two windows. A photograph of Carlos—the one which had been used on his Kuwaiti driver's license—was thumbtacked to the top of the board; the space below was empty.

"This board is for what I call Carlos's Gang of Twenty. You folks have to help me fill it up, until we know everyone who's working with him. We can do that by moving three-by-five cards from the other walls." Lucy indicated the cards and photographs which she had taped up and down adjacent walls. She moved to the left wall. "Now you have scratched up so much information—God knows how—that I've come up with almost 300 candidates. This first group I call the 'Probables,' about twenty who seem to me, for one reason or another, just the kind of operators Carlos would seek out. Most of them are terrorists he has worked with in the past."

Lucy moved on, indicating a much larger rogues' gallery. "This bunch I call the 'Possibles.' No direct connection with Carlos that I'm aware of, but all of them fit the mold of the dedicated, audacious international terrorist, so they might have been approached by Carlos." Lucy moved on to another group of cards and photographs. "This group I've dubbed the 'Inactives.' Most of them are in prison. Some of them have simply retired from the terror business. But if they are released from jail, or become bored with a law-abiding life, they might be recruited by Carlos." Lucy moved on and gestured toward almost a score of cards. "The final bunch I call the 'Martyrs.' They're all dead, most of them killed in shootouts with the police. The only reason they're here is to prevent your wasting time if you come across their names."

Mack spoke: "Each of you should study every card and photograph on the walls. That way we can help Lucy decide which candidates should go to Lucy's exclusive Gang of Twenty board."

"So far," Lucy went on, "we're working with the results of your preliminary reports, and there's still a lot of processing to do. I'll want to debrief each of you, in depth."

"Lucy, how can you keep track of all this information?" Hyphenated-Jake asked.

"My little computer, Butterfly, will soak it up. And, besides, I already know a lot of these characters."

"How will you know," Perry asked, "if one of your inactives becomes active? It might be local news if a terrorist in, say, Zurich, escapes from prison there. But it's not the kind of news the *Post* or the *Times* would print here in Washington."

"FBIS," Lucy said. She indicated a stack of pink-covered mimeographed bulletins resting on a sideboard with an imprimatur reading *The Foreign Broadcast Information Service, Central Intelligence Agency* on each of them. "I read the daily FBIS take from Europe, Africa and the Middle East. They reproduce the radio headlines in every area of the world on a daily print-out. We would not only know about a terrorist escaping from prison in Zurich, but about any violent development, anywhere, with political overtones. The most recent FBIS report, in fact, described a kidnapping in Germany where three young women approached the home of the victim carrying a bouquet of red roses. That means the Red Morning organization is responsible, and I would bet the south acre that I have at least one of the abductors hanging in that section." Lucy pointed to her "Probables" and "Possibles" panels.

"Wait a minute, wait a minute!" Emilio turned to Mack. "I thought you told me this was not going to be a CIA operation, except for info Skip brings from Langley. Now you have the CIA listening to radio stations all over the world for us."

"FBIS coverage," Mack explained patiently, "is primarily for government consumption, but it is unclassified and available as a commercial service to anyone who wants to pay for it. Many private firms subscribe to the service and, I would imagine, the Soviet Embassy does the same, through a cut-out. Why shouldn't we?"

"I didn't know that," Emilio said, with an apologetic grin.

"That's it for now," Mack said. "I'll be working on your next assignments today and tomorrow, so stand by. Meanwhile, check with Frank if you had any document trouble on your trip, or if you think it's time for new aliases. Lucy has a duty roster; each of you will be asked to be on call so that this place will be covered twenty-four hours a day. During your free time memorize the facts and faces on the walls of this room. And, again, congratulations on your work so far."

"You'll find beer, liquor, and snacks in the kitchen," Frank said, as the meeting concluded. For a half hour they circulated around the room inspecting the photographs and leaning forward to read the data Lucy had typed on the three-by-five cards. Clem and Hyphenated-Jake, each clutching a cold can of beer, alternated in provoking ribald laughter from the other with whispered asides. Emilio interrogated Lucy as she answered their questions about individual terrorists. Frank held up a blank birth certificate from France to compare it with the one belonging to an active candidate. Perry and Skip talked animatedly as they inspected Lucy's gallery. Indeed, the scene resembled opening night at an art gallery, when the artist's friends, cocktails in hand, circle the work on the walls.

Skip approached Mack. "I'm off, Mack. Back to the salt mine."

"Good to see you," Mack said. "You're looking lovely tonight."

"Perhaps my face is flushed," Skip said. "Perry Allison just asked me to have dinner with him."

"Did you accept?"

"No! He's a child. But I was flattered."

"You owe me a dinner," Mack said. "What about tonight?"

"Oh, Mack . . ."

"Please." Mack reached out and, for a moment, fondled the Haitian amulet. "Please."

"All right. Where?"

"What about your place," Mack said.

"No, Mack."

"Smoked salmon, flank steak, caesar salad. I'll bring the wine?"

Skip turned to look at nothing to her right, then her left. Then she looked at Mack.

"Eight?"

"Thanks," Mack said. "I'll see you at eight."

When Skip went to her bedroom to fetch the sewing basket, Mack, sitting on a sofa cushion on the floor in front of the fire, drained the last of his mulled wine and put the pewter mug on the hearth. He lit a Gauloise and looked about Skip's apartment. A large Haitian painting hung on one wall and a brown and gold batik on another. The room was sparsely furnished, but each piece of furniture was a fine one Skip had bargained for in a foreign bazaar. The copper lamps and table tops were also relics of her overseas tours. The crackling fire and the gleaming reflection of its flames in the room's burnished copper and bronze decorations made it a warm refuge against the cold November night. Mack had not felt so content for a long time. He and Skip had talked through the low stereo music until almost midnight before having their dinner on the floor before the fire. Now he leaned back against a chair and let his entire body relax.

Skip returned, picked up Mack's jacket, and sat on another cushion. "Really, Mack, a grown man mustn't go around with a button missing from his coat." She took needle and thread from the basket and prepared to replace the missing button.

Skip grimaced prettily through her rimless spectacles, then bent over her sewing, her hair absorbing the fire's glow. Mack had never seen Skip wearing glasses.

She sat with legs crossed, Indian style. She wore a pair of ballet-type slippers, raw silk black slacks, and a sheer silk blouse with a full, high collar and a dramatically plunging neckline. Mack's mouth had dropped open when she had greeted him earlier.

"The caesar salad was first-rate," Mack said.

"I expected you to like it," Skip said, "since you taught me how to make it. Coddle the egg precisely thirty seconds."

"I've told you the story, haven't I?" Mack asked. "The two Cardini brothers first made it in Tiajuana. Then they moved to Mexico City and opened what became a popular restaurant, featuring the caesar salad. Everything was fine until a writer for *Life* magazine visited Mexico City to write a story about the salad, which by that time had become a staple in California. He asked the brothers which one actually first dreamed up the salad. 'I,' said one brother. 'No, it was I,' claimed the other Cardini. The dispute became so acrimonious that the brothers split up and, I understand, never spoke to each other again. And that's why today there are *two* Cardini restaurants in Mexico City, each famous for its caesar salad."

"Is that a true story?" Skip asked.

"Absolutely."

"You've never been a trivia buff," Skip said. "What's your point?"

Mack steeled himself and continued: "That it's tragic when two people who should be close, even love each other, are not together, don't love each other."

Mack reached out and touched the Haitian amulet, suspended between Skip's half-exposed breasts.

Skip pushed his hand away, gently. "Things don't always work out for people." She changed the subject abruptly. "You haven't told me how Tom is getting along."

"He was fine," Mack said, "when I visited him at school on parents' day in early October. He'll graduate in June. He has the idea that some day, believe it or not, he will work for the Company."

"So you didn't encourage him?"

"I told him to think about State."

Skip exclaimed in mock horror: "How *could* you?"

It was quiet. Then Skip asked, "Was Elaine there? At the parents' day?"

"Yes."

"Old flame rekindled?" Skip asked seriously.

"You know better than that. We had dinner with Tom. She drove on back to Boston and I flew home to Washington."

"She hasn't remarried?"

"She plans to soon."

Skip pondered a moment.

"Why did you break up?"

"No specific reason," Mack said slowly. "An accumulation of little reasons. The thing that did it, I guess, was that she just got tired of sitting at home alone while the Agency shuttled me around the world on special assignments." Mack suddenly became aware that he was losing the scent. He looked at the wall. "Remember when we bought that painting in Port-au-Prince?"

"Yes, I remember." Skip began to wind the thread. "And I remember Oloffson's and the spooky feeling we had reading *The Comedians* after the manager told us Graham Greene had written it while living at the hotel. There was the empty swimming pool, just like it was in the book, only with a body in it."

"What else do you remember?" Mack asked.

Skip blushed.

"That you made love to me for five days and five nights. That for two of those days we didn't even leave our room. I had to hide in the bathroom when the waiter brought the food and the Barbancourt Rum because you wouldn't let me wear even a pair of panties."

"Do you believe that was almost five years ago?" Mack said.

Skip cut the thread with her teeth and, without lowering her gaze from Mack's, put down the coat and needle and thread. "I haven't been with a man since."

"Tonight," Mack said quietly. "You know it will be tonight."

"I know?" Skip turned away from Mack, then moved backward until she was nestled between his knees, her back pressing against his body, her head on his shoulder.

Mack could feel his heart racing. He had wanted it to come like this.

"Yes, you know," Mack said. "You've worn the amulet from Haiti everytime we've seen each other. And now this blouse. Whenever you wear it . . ." His voice trailed off as he dropped one hand inside Skip's blouse, and caressed her breast. He felt her body grow taut. The blood in his own body ran fast.

"The first time we met," Skip said, "I wondered if I were kinky because I fell in love with the hair on the back of your wrists." She took Mack's hand from her bosom and, in the firelight, inspected the blond hairs which curled on his hands. She put her lips to his hand, then guided it gently back to her breast.

"I suppose I really decided this afternoon," Skip said. "When I dug down to the bottom of my drawer to find this blouse I haven't worn since we were in Haiti."

Mack turned Skip's head toward his and kissed her, gently at first, then passionately when her tongue slipped into his mouth. Then, on the floor, a trembling embrace in the fire's heat.

"Now?" Mack pulled Skip to her feet and they went into the bedroom. They undressed each other slowly. Soon they stood together, naked, bodies pressing one against the other, mouths locked.

Mack lifted Skip onto the bed. He lay beside her and, with his hands and mouth, explored her body. He moved slowly, gently; Skip's hands, too, moved over his body. "The beast with two backs," Mack said softly. "What an ugly image for something so beautiful."

"Yes," she said quietly.

Mack cupped his hands under Skip's buttocks and lifted her body. Then, suddenly, Skip closed her knees and rolled onto her side, away from Mack. She began to whimper.

"Skip? What is it?"

She continued to weep. Then she got off the bed and walked to her dressing table. She kneeled and let her head fall against the dressing table stool. Her body heaved as she sobbed.

Mack went to Skip and stood beside her, caressing her hair with one hand. Mack realized that something was missing from the bedroom. Somewhere, hidden away, there must be a photograph in a silver frame. Skip would have removed it—a picture of a man, taken at least fifteen years ago.

"My darling," Mack said in barely a whisper as he touched her softly. "It's all right, don't worry." Moments passed.

"I'd better go now," Mack said. "I'm sorry."

Skip put her face against Mack's body. For a long time she held him while her body shook with sobs. Then she was quiet. Mack could feel her mouth against him. He reached down, took her head in his hands, and pulled her to a standing position.

"I want you badly, but I want us to have each other. We've got all the time in the world." *Did they?*

Mack began to dress.

Skip sat on the stool and looked at herself in the dressing table mirror. Almost absently, she began to brush her hair.

"I'll let myself out," Mack whispered, bending to kiss her softly on the back of the neck.

When Mack turned, just for a moment, his last view of Janet Wilson was as she sat before the mirror, nude, slowly brushing her hair. Her eyes were bright with tears.

It was three in the morning when Mack left Skip's townhouse. In his lonely preoccupation he did not pick up the pair of headlights behind him until he made the turn onto Route 50 and headed toward Falls Church. Don't be paranoid, he told himself. Moderately heavy traffic on the busy highway was not unusual even at that early hour of the morning. Mack took the loop leading onto the Beltway, the four-lane highway encircling the District of Columbia.

Driving toward the Potomac River, Mack wondered whatever happened to the fifty-five-mile-an-hour speed limit as cars whizzed by and trucks thundered past him. The car which had followed him onto the Beltway hung back. Mack slowed to forty-five; so did the car behind.

Time to be sure, Mack thought, as he swung up the first exit ramp, doubled in a quick U-turn, and gunned the Cougar back over the Beltway overpass. The driver behind followed. After a quarter of a mile Mack turned at a corner where a sign announced "Industrial Park, Three Miles." Mack muttered, "Now we'll find out for damn sure." He stepped on the accelerator until it was flat on the floorboard; the Cougar sped forward registering eighty miles an hour. Now there was no pretense: the twin beams behind grew larger as Mack's pursuer attempted to overtake him. Mack leaned forward over the steering wheel, as if trying to boot his old car into the homestretch. The car behind was now close enough for Mack to discern that it was a dark, low-slung Mercedes with a single occupant.

Time to get out of the boondocks, Mack told himself. Ahead and to his left a glow against the low rainclouds indicated a populated area. He thought quickly. There was no gun in his car, and he never carried one on his person. Was there *anything* inside the Cougar he could use as a weapon, if it came to that? Only an old umbrella with broken spokes.

Mack calculated quickly. Whoever was on his tail—both cars were now hurtling at full speed down the isolated road—intended to kill him. Had his pursuer wanted merely to trail Mack to his new safehouse, he would have turned off and tried another time. I'd better get it in gear, Mack told himself, or my ass is grass.

Mack slammed into second gear to slow the car, hit the brake, and skidded down a side road. The rear end of the

Cougar veered out of control on the stone and gravel shoulder of the road. There was a crunch under the rear of the car; then the wheels spun until they caught long enough for Mack to straighten out. The Mercedes, too, careened around the turn, and Mack could see in its headlights' path the grey mass bouncing down the road behind him.

Mack pumped the accelerator. The Cougar was loosing power; the motor roared but Mack was unable to pick up momentum.

"It's the fucking muffler!" Mack shouted. "Why didn't I fix the fucking muffler?"

Time to dismount. A few hundred yards ahead a billboard announced, "Home of Taystee Treat—Fifty Flavors." The ice cream factory was a low building of concrete blocks surrounded by a fleet of parked delivery trucks, each emblazoned with the Taystee Treat logo and a drawing of a boy leaning over his dog and offering the animal a lick of his cone. Mack drove his coughing Cougar around the perimeter of trucks, and skidded to a halt. Snapping off his headlights, he jumped from the car, and raced the twenty-five feet to concealment behind the nearest ice cream truck.

The Mercedes purred to a stop, its engine idling, just inside the entrance to the parking lot. The headlights flicked off, as the car turned and pulled up along side one of the delivery vehicles.

An outside lighting fixture on each end of the building, and a single globe at a ramp door, illuminated the parking lot. The man in the Mercedes stepped out and crouched in the shadow of the car. At first Mack could make out only the shadowy outline of a head and one shoulder. Then the shadow expanded with an ominous bulge as the assailant carefully raised a stubby machine gun over the car's hood.

The weapon's report was almost polite, more like the *pitchew-pitchew* of a boy's BB gun than the blast of an assassin's weapon.

A floodlight on one end of the ice cream factory roof shattered, went dark; there was a tinkling noise of falling glass shards.

Another genteel burp. The second floodlight burst. Now the vast parking lot was almost dark, its only light shed by the globe at the entrance to the building.

Why? Why the hell, if he is coming after me, Mack wondered, is he extinguishing the lights? How does he expect to hit a moving target in the dark?

Suddenly Mack understood. A tiny, round spot of light appeared on the wall of the building a few feet from the one remaining light fixture. The spot traveled across the wall, like the beam from an electric gun in a carnival shooting gallery, until it was soaked up by the glow of the door-lamp. Burp. The globe shattered. An electric filament fizzed, glowed briefly, then expired. *A laser beam machine gun.*

It was now totally dark in the parking lot except for the small, circular spot of light which remained on the ruins of the lamp, poised, as if waiting to see if the globe would come back to life.

The back of Mack's neck turned icy as he watched the lethal spot of light crawl down the side of the building, flit across the macadam, then probe the delivery truck nearest the loading ramp.

The American 180, only .22 caliber, could fire thirty rounds a second. It could kill at a distance of up to a mile. Marksmanship was not necessary. All one had to do was train the laser on the target and pull the trigger. Several hundred 180's were in use by police departments and law enforcement agencies around the country, but the authorities had taken steps to prevent its falling into the hands of criminals or terrorists.

Until *now*, Mack thought, unless that creep out there is a policeman. *Jesus! Does Carlos have the police working for him, too?*

The spot of light moved from one truck to another, then disappeared.

The assailant would be coming closer now, under cover of the total blackout. Would he have guessed that Mack was unarmed? If so, surely he would have taken advantage of the parking lot's prior illumination to track him down for the kill. Now he would be cautious, on the assumption that Mack also had a gun, but confident that the laser retained the ultimate advantage.

Mack strained to listen for some sound indicating the assassin's movements. Nothing. Probably wearing rubber-soled shoes, size eight and a half, with phosphor dust still on them.

The spot of light reappeared on a truck about thirty yards from Mack. The spot moved to another truck, at the window, beneath the chassis, then moved on, hovering, searching. The circular spot expanded: the assassin was moving closer.

My ass is nearer grass than it's ever been, Mack assured himself. Could he make a break? The parking lot gate was open but a hundred yards away, and the stalker was somewhere between it and Mack. The noise of a desperate dash for the gate would draw the laser immediately. There was, however, a cyclone fence around the lot, Mack remembered, and one section of it would be less than twenty yards behind him. But a break for the fence would unquestionably lead to his untimely crucifixion on it.

The spot methodically explored a nearby truck. Mack stooped and slipped off both his shoes. He stuffed one in his coat pocket and clamped his teeth onto the tongue of the other. With the shoe dangling from his mouth, Mack pulled himself onto the hood of the truck, then slithered over the windshield to the roof of the van. Spread-eagle, the shoe still in his mouth, Mack waited.

The spot appeared, then disappeared. It was larger now, the size of a half dollar. The gunman was close.

Now Mack could hear him. Even with rubber soles, the scratch of an occasional pebble betrayed the assassin's stealthy progress.

Mack waited. He must calculate his move exactly, or the beam and its burst of slugs would find him.

Now. Mack took the shoe from his mouth and, snapping his wrist with a fly-casting flip, threw it into the darkness. The laser blinked in the direction of the sound of the falling shoe. But this time the assassin was so near that Mack detected a telltale glow at the end of the gun barrel.

Mack leapt from the top of the truck. He almost missed,

but one outstretched arm caught the assassin's shoulder and the two men rolled onto the pavement together. Mack could hear the clattering as the machine gun skidded across the ground.

Don't let go! Don't let go, Mack instructed himself, as the two rolled together between the trucks. The assassin pummeled Mack with his fists but Mack was hardly aware of the blows. Don't let go, he told himself.

Mack's head rang with pain as it slammed against the side of a truck. But in the next fraction of a second he was on top of the other man.

Calculating as best he could where the man's genitals would be, Mack slammed his knee into the assailant's groin. There was a sharp gasp; Mack had found his opponent's abdomen. He raised his knee again, and thrust it with all his strength into the man's crotch. This time he found his mark, and a wail of pain pierced the night as Mack's victim shuddered in agony.

Mack grasped the assassin's necktie with one hand, his hair with the other, and counted as he slammed his head against the pavement once, twice, and then three times.

Mack stood over the prostrate figure, then leaned back against the truck, gasping for breath. Then he kicked around in the darkness, feeling with his feet for the machine gun. He couldn't find it. He opened the door on the driver's side of the truck's cab and pulled on the headlights. In the pool of light cast by their beams Mack found the machine gun, lifting it in front of the lights for inspection. He found the button which ignited the laser. He turned the beam on the face of his assailant.

It was not Carlos but Mack recognized the hireling's thin, sallow face and bushy mustache. Most of his white collar was scarlet with blood dripping down from the back and side of his head. Mack turned off the truck headlights, cradled the machine gun in one arm, then reached down and grabbed the terrorist's coat at the collar. With the weapon in one hand, Mack pulled the inert body across the parking lot to the loading ramp of the ice cream factory.

From a distance of four feet Mack put four slugs in the door's lock and pushed the door open. No burglar alarm. Not a lot of thieves stealing ice cream these days.

Mack turned on the lights inside the building, returned to the ramp for his victim, and pulled him inside. Mack kneeled to check the assassin's condition: the back of his head was a bloody pulp, but his breathing was steady and his pulse regular.

Mack inspected the premises. To his left, aluminum vats stretched in rows throughout the production area of the shop. To his right several doors opened into a hall. He found a storeroom, a toolroom, men's and women's bathrooms, a small laboratory (probably where those fifty flavors were concocted), and, farther down the hall, steps leading to a large area where a hundred or so ice cream vendors' carts were parked. Each displayed the drawing of the boy offering a lick of his cone to his pooch and, Mack could now see, a caption: "Which do you like best, Fido, chocolate or vanilla?"

The door to the toolroom was locked, but Mack shot the lock off. He took a pair of pliers and a roll of electrical wire from the shelves and returned to the still-unconscious body of his adversary. He dragged him into the men's room. Then, he clipped a length of wire and wrapped it around one of the man's wrists. He looped the wire around the stanchion supporting the three-quarter-length panel which provided privacy in one of the stalls. Then, lifting the man's body to a slumped standing position, Mack drew the loop together, and lashed the wrists together, using the pliers to make a dozen twists in the wire. He repeated the process at the man's ankles. Now Mack's assailant was securely trussed, and his limp body hung awkwardly against the toilet stall.

Mack searched the man's pockets. He found a Beretta pistol, two clips of .22 ammunition for the laser machine gun, a switchblade, and a ring with three keys. There were also two plastic, tubular pill containers, one holding red and the other yellow capsules. Uppers and downers, Mack surmised. Many terrorists used them during operations. There were no documents.

A washpail and mop had been abandoned in a corner of the bathroom. Mack let two inches of water pour into the bucket from a basin tap, and then emptied it over the assassin's head. The man revived momentarily, then lapsed once more into a stupor.

Mack turned the bucket upside down, sat on it, and lit a Gauloise while he waited for the assassin to regain consciousness. He finished the cigarette and was about to light another when his captive shuddered, blinked, and then revived completely.

"Like some ice cream?" Mack asked. "We have fifty flavors."

The assassin hawked, then spat directly into Mack's face.

Mack reached to his face and removed the phlegm with the tips of his finger. He went to the basin and washed his face. He ripped a paper towel from the container and turned to the urinals. There were three urinals. Mack cleaned them, without haste, with the crumpled paper towel. He turned to the assassin.

"Open your mouth," Mack commanded.

The assassin attempted to spit again but Mack slammed the edge of one hand into his neck, a quick, chopping blow which left the man with protruding eyes and gasping for breath.

Mack stuffed the sopping, urine-soaked towel into the assassin's mouth.

"Now be a good little boy," Mack mocked, "or I'll carry you to my apartment, take you to the bathroom, and make you go potty."

The man spat out the mouthful of shredded paper, then mustered saliva enough to spit again, this time on the floor. Mack sat again on the upturned bucket and lit another Gauloise.

"And now, Giovanni," Mack said. "I expect you to answer some questions."

The terrorist's eyes widened in surprise.

"Giovanni Vasari," Mack continued. "You were with Boudia in 1972 at Trieste. You led the sabotage team which set fire to the oil refinery in the port. A PFLP operation. More recently, you booby-trapped my john. That, and all that dancing in the dark we just went through outside, disturbs me. Consequently, I intend to kill you if you don't answer my questions. If you do, I'll leave you here, unharmed, to explain to the police why you are in this country, illegally. Which will it be, Giovanni?"

Vasari shook his head, but his defiance was little more than bravado.

Mack figured that his chances of persuading the Italian to talk were good. It must have been a shock when Mack identified him. A piece of luck. Some good information and a little luck can topple towers in the intelligence game, Mack reminded himself. Information, from the packet of documents Hyphenated-Jake had brought from Rome; luck because that morning he had run across Vasari's photograph and description in the rogues' gallery Lucy had hung on the safehouse wall.

"Four questions, Giovanni. Answer, and you will be able to call a lawyer after the police come."

Vasari shook his head, negatively.

"Where is Carlos?"

The Italian did not answer.

"What operation is he planning?"

No answer.

"When and where will the operation occur?"

The Italian did not speak.

"Who is your emergency contact when you need money or documents?"

Finally, Vasari spoke. His English was heavily accented.

"I will tell you nothing." The bravado was thin. "I have been schooled to resist torture. Do what you will."

"Torture?" Mack raised an eyebrow. "That would make me uncomfortable, Giovanni. But the prospect of killing you doesn't bother me at all!"

"Then proceed," the assassin said. "I will say nothing."

Mack shrugged. He doused his cigarette in the basin, picked up the bucket, then turned and walked out of the bathroom. He went down the hall, and descended the short flight of steps to the area crammed with parked vendors' carts. He opened the top of a cart and began removing the dry ice, filling half the bucket. He went to another cart, removing enough dry ice to reach the top of his pail. He extracted a popsicle from the cart, and closed the top. He returned to the men's room.

Mack removed the paper from the popsicle and offered it to Vasari. "Which do you like best, Fido, chocolate or vanilla?"

The assassin declined, shaking his head sharply.

Mack entered the stall and dropped several pieces of the dry ice in the toilet. Bubbles formed in the water, and a white vapor rose from the stool. He went to the next stall, and repeated the action, and again at the third.

"What is that?" Vasari asked.

"Dry ice," Mack said. "It keeps the ice cream frozen."

"You are going to kill me with dry ice?" Vasari snorted.

"As a matter of fact," Mack said, "I am."

Mack went to the three wall urinals and deposited dry ice in each, emptying the bucket at the final urinal. The sound of bubbling pervaded the bathroom, and the heavy white mist of smoke produced by the evaporating dry ice spilled from the toilets and urinals until it was hovering thickly on the floor.

Vasari was visibly frightened. "What is it you do?"

"Dry ice," Mack explained, "is carbon monoxide in solidified form. When inhaled, carbon monoxide is a deadly poison; hundreds of people die from it each year in parked cars without proper ventilation. In this enclosed bathroom I suspect it might take a half hour, an hour at the most, before you die. And when they find you in the morning there won't be a clue to the cause of your death. You see, the dry ice will have dissolved by then."

Vasari was shaken. He watched with wide, unbelieving eyes as Mack ripped paper towels from the wall holder, stood on the bucket, and began stuffing them in the ceiling ventilation duct. He gathered up the possessions he had taken from Vasari, ripped more paper towels from the rack, then spoke to the Italian.

"These I will stuff under the door. *Arrivederci*, Giovanni."

Mack closed the door, and stopped to tamp the paper towels in between its bottom edge and the floor. He walked toward the exit, carrying the paraphernalia he had confiscated from Vasari.

"Come back!" The Italian's scream was desperate.

Mack returned to the bathroom, and opened the door. The heavy vapor from the dry ice had reached Vasari's knees; now it spilled out into the hall.

"Where is Carlos?"

"I do not know," Vasari pleaded.

"Where is Carlos?"

"I do not know," Vasari insisted. "I met him only one time, two months ago. I was released from prison in Rome and when I left Carlos was waiting for me outside. He asked me to join him, gave me money and false documents. I have never seen him or talked to him since that day."

"What operation is he planning?"

"I do not know. He said only that I should await instructions, and never to be away from my telephone for more than a few hours."

"Unless you are an idiot," Mack said, "you would have insisted on knowing more about the operation."

"I had no money," Vasari said. "Carlos promised much money, and said we would all be famous. And he said that the operation would strike a spectacular blow against Western imperialism. That is all he told me except that the code name of the plan was to be—he now spoke to me in Spanish —*Operacion Hogar.*"

Hogar? The Spanish word for "home."

"When," Mack asked, "and where is *Operacion Hogar* to take place?"

"I do not know," Vasari groaned. "Undo me. We can talk elsewhere. The police will come here."

"Probably not," Mack said. "Those little poops from your laser gun will not have attracted attention. Where did you get the gun and the grenade?"

"Ten days ago in Rome I found an envelope in my mailbox. It had been put there without postage. Inside were my instructions, money, and a claim ticket. I was to fly to New York, go to the parcel-checking counter at the Grand Central Station, and retrieve a package. I did. The package was marked 'Golf Clubs.' There were golf instruments inside. Also the rifle, the grenade, the pistol. And more instructions for my mission, which included a biography of William McLendon and a map with the location of your office and apartment."

Mack decided that Vasari was telling the truth. He upended the pail, stood on it, and removed the paper towels from the vent in the bathroom ceiling. "And your mission . . . ?"

"To eliminate you," Vasari said, simply. "Then I was to return to Rome and await instructions."

"Who was your contact in the United States?"

"I had no contact plan."

"Now you are lying, Giovanni. Carlos does not practice such poor tradecraft that you would be stranded without money or assistance if something went wrong."

"I had no contact in the United States," Vasari insisted.

Mack stepped onto the pail again, and began stuffing the paper towels back into the ducts.

"Stop it! I will tell you!"

Mack stepped down from the pail.

"I was told that in the event of emergency I was to go to Mexico City. Then I was to do nothing until the Saturday which was the last one of the month. On that Saturday, after eleven in the morning and before midnight, I was to find the mansion called Villa Hermosa located three blocks north of the residence of the president of Mexico in an area known as Los Pinos. I was then to ask for the owner of the house."

"Were you given his name?"

"Yes. Enrique Schwarz."

"Enrique *Schwarz?* Are you positive that was the name?"

"Yes. I was to remember that the man's name was the German word for black."

"You have no documents. Where did you get the Mercedes?"

"It is rented," Vasari said. "The documents and my passport are under the seat."

Mack pondered. His instincts told him that Vasari was telling the truth. He was convinced by intuition derived from years of experience in dealing with pretenders—something he and other intelligence officers tended to value in many situations more than evaluations of lie detector machines.

"Have you told me everything, Giovanni?"

"Everything. I swear. Now please, my wrists pain."

"There is one thing you have not told me," Mack said. "Every emergency contact plan must have an alternative. What if Mr. Black were not at home, ill? What if something had happened to him? What were you to do then?"

"That is true," Vasari said. "Should señor Schwarz not be there, I was to approach the first Japanese person I saw in the house and say that I had come to see the owner on the recommendation of Carlos."

"Japanese?"

"Yes," Vasari said. "Now, will you let me go? I promise that I know nothing more."

"No, Giovanni." Mack gathered together the loot he had taken from the Italian. "I will go now, call the police, and they will release you. You should begin to prepare your explanation —the police will be curious about a man hanging by his wrists in a john."

"Wait! The knife!"

Mack inspected the switchblade.

"What about it?"

"You must use it."

"Use it?" Mack was baffled.

"On my ear," Vasari said. "You must cut my ear. If Carlos finds me with my ears intact he will never believe it when I tell him Mack the Knife overcame me."

"Incredible!" Mack sighed, in exasperation.

"You must," Vasari pleaded. "Cut deep. Otherwise, I am a dead man."

"My surgeon's license has expired," Mack said. "Maybe you'll find a way to mutilate yourself. Be my guest. And now, *arrivederci*, for good, Giovanni."

Leaving the bathroom door ajar, Mack departed from the ice cream factory through the ramp door. He found Vasari's documents under the seat of the Mercedes. Mack went to his own car, started the engine, and drove out of the parking lot. The 1967 Cougar coughed and sputtered without the muffler, but mercifully continued to function.

At an all-night drugstore Mack telephoned Frank at the safehouse.

"Yes?" Frank's acknowledgment was sleepy.

"It's Mack. Are you awake, Francis?"

A yawn. Then: "Yes. Go ahead, Mack."

"Pencil and paper?"

"Yes. But wait until I find my glasses." A pause. "All right."

"Telephone the duty officer at the FBI. Report that the Bureau should check with the Fairfax County police, who will shortly have in custody an illegal alien, probably a parole violator, from Rome. His name is Giovanni Vasari. He entered the country at Kennedy about a week ago with false documents in the name of . . ." Mack consulted the passport he had retrieved from the Mercedes, ". . . Amintore Crispi."

"Anything else?" Frank asked. "What if they ask for more details?"

"Hang up," Mack said. "Then roust Clem out of bed. Have him telephone his friend in Mexico City, Espinosa. Ask him what he knows about a man called Enrique Schwarz—S c h w a r z—who lives in the Villa Hermosa—H e r m o s a —in Mexico City, three blocks north of the presidential residence. Schwarz is probably a financier of some kind, banker, moneylender, investment counselor. If Espinosa doesn't know, have him check and call Clem the minute he has something."

"I've got it. What else?"

"That's all. See you in the morning." Mack hesitated. "Frank, one more thing. What is dry ice made of?"

"Carbon dioxide, I believe. Why?"

"Not carbon monoxide?"

"No. Definitely not."

"Are the fumes from carbon dioxide poisonous?"

"Carbon dioxide isn't toxic; in fact it's used to put the fizz in carbonated beverages." Frank paused. "But I suppose if you were to inhale nothing but carbon dioxide fumes you wouldn't get enough oxygen to survive. What a strange question to ask at four in the morning. Have you been drinking, Mack?"

"No. Just a little mix-up. So long, Frank."

Mack dialed the Fairfax County police. He spoke for a moment with the officer who answered.

"Just a minute, Mister, you'd better talk to the sergeant."

The man at the other end of the telephone line failed to cover the mouthpiece of the instrument: Mack could hear him shout, "Hey, Joe, pick up on thirty-two. This guy must be a nut. He says there's a man hanging himself in the crapper at the ice cream factory!"

"I think we have identified Carlos's support chief," Mack said. "Clem, tell them what Espinosa had to say about Enrique Schwarz."

Clem turned to Frank and Emilio. "My buddy in Mexico City reports that Schwarz is a German-born Argentine citizen who moved to Mexico City in March of 1976. He owns a money exchange and investment business in Buenos Aires. He has made a number of investments in Mexico, even owns controlling interest in one bank. All of this since Vienna, 1975."

"So," Emilio eyed Mack, "you think he has been quietly investing the OPEC ransom in Mexico for Carlos?"

"Not quietly," Clem said. "Schwarz has become a sort of financial celebrity in Mexico City. He operates out of a fancy villa and is famous for his *Ultimo Sabado* or Final Saturday parties. On the last Saturday of each month he is the host of an open house to which he invites just about everybody who is anybody—politicos, movie stars, bullfighters, writers. He's had a problem with the government because he brought a crew of Japanese servants into the country, and they have no work permits. Now he just calls them guests."

"Probably," Mack said, "members of the Japanese Red Army, cooling off until Carlos needs them. Setting up his support shop in Mexico reinforces the hypothesis that Carlos plans his next op in the United States. Maybe we'd better go to Mexico City, perhaps even go to one of Schwarz's parties—the last Saturday of November is only five days from now."

Frank turned to Mack. "Me too, Mack?"

"Hell yes. I want to achieve total coverage of Schwarz's villa. I need to know everything that's said and written, everything that occurs there during the next few days. See any problems there, Frank?"

Frank pondered Mack's query.

"Not with Emilio and Clem to help," Frank said. "Just for one thing: equipment. I'll need cameras, but those I can openly carry into the country. I can buy high frequency radio receivers there. But I'll have to carry in audio gear, my set of picks, and a flaps and seals kit. How will we get *them* past customs?"

Mack turned to Emilio and Clem. "Bribe?"

"Probably would work," Clem said, "but we'd better not depend on it."

"I say no," Emilio said. "Mexican customs people will be cautious with the pressure on them these days because of the government's crackdown on the narcotics trade. We should find another way."

"I don't care how," Mack said. "But don't get caught. It would be hard to explain the audio gear."

"We'll think of something," Emilio said.

"When do we leave?" Frank asked.

"Today," Mack said. "Set up shop, and I'll join you in a few days. I'll be in the bar at the Maria Cristina Hotel every evening between six and eight until one of you contacts me."

The door opened and Lucy entered. She was carrying a stack of pink FBIS reports.

"Lucy," Mack said, "the four of us are going to be traveling. I'll ask you, Perry and Hyphenated-Jake to take turns here as duty officers until we return. It may be a week or so."

"It won't do any good to have a duty officer if we don't know where to contact you."

Mack hesitated. "I'll be at the Maria Cristina Hotel in Mexico City."

"The snow birds," Lucy said, "always fly south at this time of year. Anything else?"

"One thing," Mack said. "Giovanni Vasari, there in your list of 'Probables.' You were right, but now you can move him to the 'Inactives.' "

Lucy removed a three-by-five card and a file photograph of Vasari from one wall, and taped it to the other. "Don't tell me what happened to him," Lucy said. "But the idea *is* to move them to the bulletin board."

"Let's hit the trail," Clem said, standing and donning his Western hat, "and head south."

5.

"I can report some progress," Mack spoke into the receiver. "Phase One of our operation has been reasonably successful."

"Phase One?" Symser was at a public telephone in Los Angeles.

"Gathering enough information about Carlos and his bunch to make some plans," Mack explained. "We still need more, but can go into Phase Two because we've identified Carlos's support chief, and we're preparing to zero in on him. Three of my people have already gone to the field, and I'll be joining them in a couple of days. I'll call you again when I return."

"Where will you be?" Symser asked.

Mack hesitated. "Abroad."

"Sorry I asked," Symser said. "You're not exactly loquacious when you call to make these little reports on how our money is being spent. Incidentally, I made the deposit you asked for."

"Mr. Smyser, it won't do you any good to know more than you need to know. And we must continue to be careful. Carlos very much wants me dead. One of his thugs tried to kill me last night."

"I see." Symser cleared his throat. "What happened?"

"In a nutshell, he botched it, and he's now in jail in Virginia."

"Crassweiler really finds it strange when I give him such, uh, terse reports. Can I tell him what follows your Phase Two?"

"Phase Three," Mack said, "will be to discover where Carlos himself is these days, and monitor his activities and contacts. Tricky business, and the reason I'm charging you a thousand dollars a day."

124

"I didn't mean to complain," Symser said. "But your expense claims have been rather steep."

"Mr. Symser, I'm asking friends to perform some tough chores for me. All of them know they might not survive. The least I can do is to see to it that they go first class, and that if anything does happen to them it won't be because we've saved a few dollars for Scott-Wagner Petroleum."

"You're right," Symser conceded. "I won't mention the expenses again."

"There won't be any more when we finish Phase Four," Mack said.

"Phase Four?"

"The wrap-up, Mr. Symser. If I don't put Carlos out of business soon my own chances of survival will be quite slim. I'll check in again next week."

In Mexico City Emilio Gonzalez introduced himself as Alfonso Arenales to the owner of the large house not far from the president's residence.

"Special unit of the tax department?" Sr. Bustamante glanced at Emilio suspiciously. "I have never heard of such an office."

"We conduct our business as quietly as we can," Emilio said, "and report directly to the president, your neighbor. I will only take a few minutes of your time."

When the two men had ascended to Sr. Bustamante's upstairs studio, Emilio spoke assuringly. "Yes, we try to go about our task in as discreet a fashion as possible. It is an onerous task we are charged with. Without money our government obviously cannot function, but there are so many scoundrels like your neighbor, Sr. Schwarz, attempting to avoid payment of taxes. I am sure you agree, Sr. Bustamante, that it is the patriotic duty of each citizen to see that taxes are paid promptly."

"But yes, of course," Bustamante said.

Emilio walked to the window and gazed out on the gardens of the mansion next door. The house was a three-story fortress of Moorish architecture.

"Yes," Emilio said, "your neighbor Enrique Schwarz is cheating us. A foreigner, too. I'm sure you will assist us in obtaining proof which can be used to prosecute him and serve as a warning to others. Have you ever met Schwarz?"

"Never. I have only seen him on a few occasions, when he was entering or leaving the house, but I hear the noise from his parties too frequently." Bustamante was uneasy. He was a successful manufacturer of concrete pipe and, thus far, an evader of taxes himself. When Emilio had introduced himself as a tax inspector, a chill had run through his body. It had been a relief to find that his visitor was only concerned with the next-door neighbor.

"Certainly I will do what I can to assist you," Bustamante said. "But I cannot leave my home. There is my wife, five children, a son-in-law . . . and the servants. Where will they go?"

"I will need your home for only a few days," Emilio said. "And of course the government will reimburse you for the inconvenience. Perhaps your family would enjoy a vacation in Acapulco?"

"I cannot abandon my house," Bustamante said. "And I don't understand how it would help the case against my neighbor Schwarz."

"We must observe the comings and goings at his house," Emilio explained. "Yours is the only home in the neighborhood which offers a good view."

"In that case," Bustamante said, "I will invite you to be my guest here. But I cannot and will not leave my home in your care."

Emilio was becoming impatient; there was a great deal of work to be done before Mack arrived.

Emilio said, "I must insist, Sr. Bustamante. It is best that you vacate your house. You see, before approaching you, I checked your tax file. It is very curious indeed. You sold such vast quantities of concrete pipe and yet paid so little income tax last year. I am confident, of course, that an investigation would reveal nothing irregular, and besides, it would be tedious. I was planning to return your file to the archives where, undoubtedly, it would lay forgotten and undisturbed for some time."

Bustamante sighed, then shrugged stoically. "My house," he told Emilio in the traditional gesture of Spanish courtesy, "is your house."

Frank Coughlin sat behind the wheel of the rented Ford and served as a lookout while Clem negotiated on a nearby street corner with the trash collector. After ten minutes Clem handed the man a roll of pesos and returned to the automobile, settling in the front seat beside Frank.

"That garbage man displayed a total lack of curiosity," Clem said. "You would think he was approached every day by people wanting to buy his trash. And he was greedy, too— insisted on a hundred pesos when I offered him fifty for each sack. We settled on seventy-five when he finally agreed to remove the food and deliver only papers."

"How often does he pick it up?" Frank asked.

"Three times a week. That means two deliveries before the Saturday night fiesta, one today and another on Friday. He'll drop the Schwarz bags in Bustamante's receptacles. Think two deliveries will be worthwhile?"

"Who knows?" Frank said. "Now let's check out the telephone lines."

They drove slowly down the street, past Bustamante's home and the mansion where Enrique Schwarz lived.

"No lines in the front," Frank said. "Let's try the back street."

A narrow, dirt road ran behind the two residences, the only dwellings on the block. Both homes were isolated from the road by high stone walls with jagged shards of glass fixed in the cement along the top of the wall to discourage intruders.

"Stop the car for just a minute," Frank instructed. He leaned out of the window and looked at the top of a telephone pole. "That's a common junction box. The lines from both the Bustamante and Schwarz houses meet there. Should be easy. No more than five minutes at the most."

"Are you going to shinny up that pole, Frank?"

"Yes. They won't be able to see me from the Schwarz place.

Too many trees. But we'd better not take any chances. You'll have to rent a lineman's truck for me, and if you can, lineman's equipment. If that's not possible, we'll just have to manage with a ladder."

"Need any special tools?" Clem asked.

"No. Bustamante left plenty." Frank accelerated and they drove back to their temporary residence. Emilio was standing at the front gate, talking with the postman.

Frank got out of the car and Clem slipped under the wheel.

"Is it okay if I have my friend Espinosa help me buy these things?" Clem asked. He glanced at the shopping list Frank had drawn up for him.

"Sure, as long as you don't let Espinosa know where we are."

"It's quite a shopping list." Clem looked at the paper and read aloud: "Hamburger meat and phenobarbital, camera tripod and a complete developing kit, a five-channel high-frequency radio receiver, a walkie-talkie set, etc, etc, etc."

"And one more thing, Clem. Do you think your friend Espinosa could obtain builder's plans of the Schwarz place for us?"

"Maybe," Clem said. "Might find them in municipal files or the architect's office, if he's still around."

"Have him try," Frank said. "You'd better get going. We need to set up shop before Mack arrives."

Clem drove off and Frank met Emilio at the gate.

"The postman has agreed," Emilio said, "to make a mistake every day between now and Saturday. Here's the first mistake." He handed Frank a dozen letters, each addressed to Enrique Schwarz.

"Good," Frank said. "We'll photograph them and they'll be ready for tomorrow's delivery next door. How much did he want?"

"Nothing," Emilio said. "He refused when I offered him a bribe. Said he was a church-going, family man. So I told him I was a private investigator working for Bustamante. That Bustamante had taken his family away when he found out that Schwarz had tried to seduce his fifteen-year-old daughter. The postman was shocked, and agreed that he would help in seeing to it that Schwarz is the one who gets screwed this time."

"Why is Emilio in the tree?" Mack asked.

"One of the branches is in the line of sight between here and the front entrance of Schwarz's place," Frank explained. "Can't get a clear shot at people going in and out." As Frank spoke Emilio, wearing the clothes and straw sombrero Bustamante's gardener had left in the tool shed, sawed through the branch and it fell. Emilio looked toward the window. Frank squinted down the telescopic sight on the tripod-mounted camera aimed at the entrance of Villa Hermosa. He lifted a slat of the venetian blinds sufficiently to signal Emilio, forming an okay ring with forefinger and thumb. Emilio began a cautious descent, his two hundred forty pounds bending the branches precariously.

"Sure would be good," Clem said, turning from the chair where he sat before a recording machine, "to get a snapshot of one of Carlos's gang showing up tomorrow for this month's final Saturday party."

"I have a dozen good pictures of Schwarz, about fifteen visitors, and, so far, nine Japanese, all of them living with Schwarz at the villa."

"Is night photography a problem?" Mack asked.

"I have an infrared attachment." Frank flipped through a stack of photographic prints, selected two, and gave them to Mack. "There's the dog, and the other is one of the Japanese on a two A.M. walk in the garden."

The prints were dark but the figures and features of a large Doberman pinscher and a short, stocky Japanese wearing a bathrobe and carrying a machine pistol were clearly distinguishable.

Mack turned from the window and went to a table where a faded blueprint lay face up, its curled edges weighted with books. Frank had sketched several comments and question marks on the plans of Villa Hermosa. Mack looked up at Frank.

"Frank, are you going to be able to make an entry, rummage

around for documents or records, photograph them and then get out and back here without being seen?"

"I think so," Frank replied, peering over his bifocals at the blueprint, "but it's going to be hairy. These floor plans that Emilio's friend Espinosa purchased from a clerk at the construction company which erected the place are almost twenty years old. There have been a couple of rooms added, but what alterations might have been made inside we don't yet know. Getting over the wall into the garden won't be difficult; it's not that high and Emilio has already filed the glass shards from a space large enough for me to slip over. The dog, I trust, will be sleeping while I'm working. We tossed him a dozen meat balls laced with one-tenth of a phenobarbital and he appeared to snooze twenty to thirty minutes after eating them. A full dose before I go in should keep him sleeping."

"What about the Japanese guards?" Clem asked.

"Fortunately they are methodical, and have established a pattern. One of them patrols the gardens every half hour, on the hour and half hour. They've never been more than a few minutes off schedule." Frank paused. "Of course, we can't be that sure of their schedule during the fiesta tomorrow, or about their movements inside the house."

Emilio entered, pulling behind him a large plastic sack which he dumped on the floor in the middle of the room.

"Hi, Mack, welcome to the Annex, Villa Hermosa."

Mack acknowledged the greeting, then chuckled at Emilio's appearance, especially the gardener's pants which were several sizes too small.

"It's not funny," Emilio said, pretending irritation. He removed the dirty, frayed straw sombrero, sniffed the almost black headband, shuddered, then skipped the hat into a corner of the room. Then, gesturing at the plastic sack, Emilio spoke to Clem. "Clem, it's your turn to check the garbage."

"Sorry, pardner. Too busy here. Real interestin' conversation goin' on right now." Clem turned away, covered his ears with earphones, and bent over the row of four tape recorders.

"Scummy jobs I keep getting around here. Climbing trees, working on walls, picking through the damned garbage."

Emilio started to squat on the floor, couldn't make it, opened and unbuttoned the gardener's pants, then sank to the floor and opened the bag.

"Could be worse," Frank said. "One of my first assignments for the Company was to obtain a urine specimen from a foreign minister."

"Any luck in the trash, Emilio?"

"Not so far, Mack. A few interesting things—some handwriting in Japanese, a page from last month's calendar with some notes and telephone numbers, odds and ends—but they must be burning anything important or sensitive. I tried to check out the telephone numbers without much luck. They don't have a crisscross directory in Mexico City, and the numbers I called myself turned out to be a dry cleaner's, a pharmacy, and the local weather service. The weather," Emilio added, continuing to assay his pile of trash, "will be good for the op tomorrow."

Mack turned to Frank. "What about the mail?"

"Seems to be legitimate business correspondence, and some personal notes and bills. You can be sure they have a mail drop somewhere in the post office for sensitive mail. There's been nothing, for instance, in Japanese, although there was a letter in Spanish from the Sony people in Japan to Schwarz, saying one of their executives would visit him soon to discuss the possibility of his handling a franchise for them."

"SW?" Mack asked.

"No secret writing that I can detect," Frank said. "I've scorched a few letters in the oven, but nothing appears. Have to wait until we're back in Washington to test them with chemicals."

"The phones?"

"Two lines, and we're on both of them. Clem is listening to one now." Frank removed the earphones from Clem's head, and offered them to Mack.

The conversation was in Spanish, but Mack could detect an occasional guttural accent. Enrique Schwarz was discussing fluctuations of foreign currency exchange with someone who, Mack recognized instantly, spoke with an Argentine accent.

"So our friend is in residence," Mack said, returning the earphones to Clem.

"Yes," Frank said. "He nearly always is. He has two offices downtown, but he seldom visits one and spends only an hour each morning at his bank. Then he's back here, where he operates out of his hip pocket, conducting his affairs by phone. No secretary, no Mexican servants. The second telephone line is used by the Japanese, and only to call shops to order food in atrocious Spanish. The line Clem is monitoring is in Schwarz's home office, with an extension to his bedroom. If there are any records about Carlos's operations, they have to be in that office. In any event, that will be my target for the entry tomorrow night. Sundown will be at seven-twelve. I'll go in soon after that, presuming Schwarz will be occupied with his guests."

"Frank, I'm not sure about this one." Mack paused, and tugged at his ear thoughtfully. "The risk factor is sky-high. Even if you get into the office you probably will have to open a safe. Schwarz certainly wouldn't leave documents concerning Carlos in file cabinets or desk drawers. How long has it been since you cracked a safe?"

"Almost eight years." Frank turned both hands inward, and rubbed the tips of his fingers with his thumbs. "But unless it's something entirely new I can open it."

" 'Unless' is not good enough. I've been thinking about it, Frank. The whole idea of your being surprised in that office by Schwarz or his terrorist-trained Japanese is just too risky."

"Don't worry now," Frank said. "Clem and Emilio will be mixing with the guests. I'm going to wire them for sound. If I'm in trouble you can instruct them to come to my rescue."

"But how will I know what's happening to you in the office?"

"Oh, that's simple," Frank said, touching the edge of his spectacles with the gesture, Mack had learned over the years, which indicated that he was pleased with himself. "I have placed an audio device in Schwarz's office. Come listen."

Frank turned to a radio receiving unit, to which a recorder, tapes rolling, was attached. He turned up the volume knob.

Enrique Schwarz's voice was clear. Clem was listening to the conversation at the adjacent recording machine.

"How the hell . . . ?"

"I hoped you would be pleased, Mack, with the efforts of your aging, feeble-minded colleague whom you did not trust to operate efficiently overseas." Frank touched his glasses again, this time with both hands, a sign of immense self-satisfaction. "The letter from the Sony people turned out to be quite useful. I had Emilio buy the very latest portable Sony he could find in Mexico City. It's only a small television set, but cute as a bug—in fact, it *is* a bug, since I've fixed it—and will cost your business sponsors dearly. Emilio had a little boy deliver the small but expensive TV to Villa Hermosa, with a note describing the rich gift as a token from the Sony Corporation. It was sent in the name of the Japanese gentleman whom Schwarz expects to visit him soon. It was my hope, obviously, that Schwarz would take it to his office. As you can hear, he did." Frank turned down the volume knob.

Mack smiled, and placed a hand on his friend's shoulder. "Not only am I pleased, I am—"

"Eureka!" The shout from Emilio interrupted Mack. "I've found it, I've found it!" Triumphant, the grinning Emilio held aloft a plastic cartridge, black and square.

"A typewriter ribbon! An *electric* typewriter ribbon!"

Mack inspected the find. "Great work, Emilio. Schwarz might be careful enough to burn his confidential papers, but Carlos should have warned him about typewriter ribbons, especially this kind, which receives only a single row of strikes from the keys and can be read easily."

Frank congratulated Emilio and Clem rose from the bank of recorders, putting aside the earphones. "Time to celebrate. How many beers?"

Emilio and Frank nodded, but Mack declined.

"Not even in Mexico?" Clem queried. "I have Carta Blanca and Dos Ecces."

"All right," Mack said. "A Dos Ecces for me." Clem went downstairs to fetch the beer and Mack spoke to Frank, as

Emilio began the tedious task of making notes from the type-writer ribbon.

"Frank, the ribbon might give us what we need, if Schwarz used it to type up his notes on Carlos. Maybe we can scratch your mission next door."

"I'm beginning to lose my patience with you, Mack." Frank was exasperated. "I'm not too old for this job, and I don't want to call it off now."

"It looks hairy and I see no reason for your indulging in arcane art just for art's sake," Mack insisted. "You've told me about the outside of the villa, and you know something of what's going on in Schwarz's office. But you don't even know where the office is. Nor do you know where alarms might be located. How can you be sure one of the Japanese Red Army types isn't always sitting behind a one-way mirror or in front of a monitor with a television view of the office? How will you get in and out?"

"My original plan was go in as an uninvited guest," Frank said, "along with Emilio and Clem. But that's no good—the *guests* are just the ones the Japanese guards will be watching."

Clem returned from the downstairs kitchen with a tray of beer bottles.

"Leave the ribbon for now, Emilio," Frank said. "Let's brief Mack on the op."

The four men sat around the table on which the blueprints of Villa Hermosa were spread. Frank opened the venetian blind so they could see the mansion.

"Lookee there," Clem said. "There go two of the little fellers now." Two Japanese, dressed in dark suits, white shirts, and black bow ties, strolled in the yard. The Doberman pinscher trotted behind them, stopping occasionally to sniff along the ground near the wall which separated the two homes. "And there's the doggie, scratching around for some more of that gussied-up hamburger I've been throwing to him. That dog looks fierce, all right, but those little Japanese fellers don't look very mean. Ain't they little, though? Reminds me of my poor Uncle Ebner, who just could never seem to make any money at business. Once he opened a tall man's store in Tokyo—"

"Shut up, Clem," Emilio said. "Go on, Frank."

Frank pointed to a metal grill on the nearest side of the Villa Hermosa, then located it on the blueprint. "I'll carry a few tools, and make my first entry attempt by removing that grill, which leads to a crawl space running under most of the house. There might be some sort of trap door leading up to the main floor, or into the basement. If I can't find one, I'll have to go outside again and get through this side door because all the windows have grills, and the *other* doors will be crowded with Japanese or Final Saturday guests."

"Okay," Mack said. "Once inside, how will you know how to reach the office?"

"I suspect it's right here," Frank said, touching a blueprint area which read *Biblioteca*. "If the other rooms and halls haven't been changed around I should know how to get to the office. The trick will be to do it without being seen."

"What if you're wrong about the location of the office, or if the interior of the house is not the same as shown in the blueprint?"

"In that case, Emilio or Clem will have told me about it before I make the entry."

"How?"

"Each of them will have one of these Kel-Cams in their shirt pockets," Frank said. He held an aluminum transmitter, the size of a box of kitchen matches; from it hung a plastic-coated wire. "And this antenna will go through a hole in their shirts, and around their necks at the collars. They will be walking radio stations. You and I here in the listening post will hear any conversation they have, and they will be able to communicate with us by muttering in their beer."

"I plan to mutter into a glass of Walker Black Label," Clem said. "Espinosa says this guy serves nothing but the best."

"What if Schwarz doesn't welcome two strangers to his fiesta, and asks them to leave?"

Emilio answered. "Espinosa says it's an open house attended

sometimes by two or three hundred people. Guests often bring along another, uninvited one. But, just in case, Espinosa has checked out newspaper photographs of previous parties, and has given each of us the name of a Mexican who has been there before but who Espinosa knows is now out of town. We'll use the name if Schwarz is curious."

"Emilio and Clem," Frank said, "will go to the party about noon. It starts at eleven each final Saturday. I trust that we can expect them to stay out of trouble and not offend their host until I'm ready to make my entry. Their job in the meantime will be to check out the entire house, and to confirm to us here, using the Kel-Cams, the location of the office, or to tell us about any changes which have been made in the layout of the interior."

"But I thought Emilio and Clem were also to help you out of any scrapes?" Mack questioned. "Once you're in the office they can't hang around the door."

"I told you there would be two way communication. Each of them will carry one of these." Frank displayed a dark, rectangular box about the size of a deck of cards. "Commercial beeper, rented from a local call service. I've wired the beepers so that I can activate them with this." He showed Mack a standard walkie-talkie.

"What if one of the beepers buzzes while Emilio or Clem is talking with someone else? Do they plan to pretend to be doctors?"

"No buzzing. Just a thump."

"What will the thump mean?" Mack said.

"You'll be here," Frank explained, "and able to hear over the TV audio device. I can speak to you directly through it if I'm alone, or you will hear what's happening if Schwarz or his goons surprise me in the office. Then you can signal Emilio and Clem. One thump: I'm in the house, no problems. Two thumps: I've entered, finished the job, and they can leave the fiesta. Three thumps, however, indicate that I'm in some sort of trouble, and they must create a diversion to cover my exit. Four thumps: Frank's in real trouble, try to rescue him.

Finally, five thumps means that I'm in so much trouble that Clem and Emilio should clear out without me."

It was quiet for a moment.

"I just can't remember all that," Clem said. "Better forget that number five thump." He glanced at Emilio.

"That's right," Emilio said. "Too complicated. Four thumps will do."

Mack rose from his chair and gazed out at the Villa Hermosa. It was easy enough to envisage sending his friend Frank into the inhospitable mansion; imagining him escaping was a different matter. Mack turned.

"Clem and Emilio should be armed for this one," he said.

"The thought occurred," Clem said. "I have a nifty little thirty-eight Police Special for each of us."

"Traceable to Espinosa?" Mack asked.

"Nope. Bought 'em downtown myself with one of Frank's phony papers for identification. Used to be able to buy a gun in Mexico in five minutes. Now they've tightened up the gun laws and it takes almost ten minutes."

"What if the Japanese Red Army guards frisk you, or spot the bulge on your belts?"

"There would be no fiesta, if that was a problem," Emilio said. "At some Mexican social affairs only about half of the male guests carry guns; at the others everyone does."

"Schwarz himself always carries one at the party," Clem added. "Right on his hip in a holster. Fancies himself pretty good at pistol shooting, Espinosa tells me, and he dresses up for the *Ultimo Sabado* in tight pants and a great big sombrero."

Mack turned to stare out the window. The Doberman was barking at a passer-by outside the high iron fence in front of the Villa Hermosa. Hairy.

"I'm going back to my hotel," Mack said. "You can reach me in room 627 at the Maria Cristina. Better check your car, and I'll do the same. We might have to get away from this place in a hurry tomorrow night. We'll have a final run-through in the morning."

Frank followed Mack from the room and to the head of the

stairs leading down to the front door. He stopped Mack before the latter began his descent.

"You're worried that I won't be able to pull it off, aren't you, Mack?"

"If anyone can, you're the rascal," Mack said kindly. "And the way you've covered the Villa Hermosa should be used as a case history for the kids at The Farm. But I am worried about your safety, Francis. Whether you like to admit it or not you're almost seventy years old. You haven't done an entry of this nature for years—so you're damned right I'm worried about your climbing a wall, getting into a locked office, staying there long enough to photograph documents, and then getting out past that dog and an army of Japanese. That's going to require a lot of luck, not to mention stamina."

"It will work, Mack. Schwarz might be fast with finances, but there's no indication he's ten feet tall in security. I don't think he's clever enough to catch me."

"It's not Schwarz I'm concerned about," Mack said. "It's Carlos."

"Carlos?"

"Schwarz's elaborate Saturday entertainments provide good cover for members of Carlos's band when they need to contact Schwarz. But they also could be a cover for meetings between Schwarz and Carlos himself. Sleep tight, Frank."

When Mack opened the door of his hotel room at the Maria Cristina he found a visitor waiting for him. Someone was stretched out on his bed reading *Excelsior*. Mack could see only parts of the man's partially propped up body—the soles of his shoes, his long legs, fingers holding the edges of the daily newspaper, and the top of a bald head just visible over the headline which proclaimed a new petroleum discovery in Chiapas. The intruder neither moved nor lowered his newspaper when Mack spoke.

"Keep both hands in view," Mack instructed, "while you introduce yourself."

There was no acknowledgment of the instruction from the reclining figure.

Mack repeated the injunction, in a louder voice, in Spanish.

This time there was a reaction: the man on Mack's bed let the newspaper fall, smiled faintly and greeted Mack.

"Hi, McLendon." The CIA Chief of Station, Mexico City, turned up the volume knob of the hearing aid he wore on his left ear. "I always turn this damned thing down in the noise of traffic, then forget to turn it up again. How you doing?" Fred Bond laid aside the newspaper, punched the pillow behind his shoulders to make himself more comfortable, and regarded Mack through narrowed eyes.

"I'm all right, Fred. Why don't you make yourself comfortable?"

"Appreciate that." Bond gestured toward a chair. "Have a seat, McLendon."

Mack sat in the chair and waited for his former colleague to speak.

"At first I was afraid I had the wrong room," Bond said. "No booze anywhere. I even went through your luggage. Are you on the wagon or something?"

"What are you doing here, Fred?"

"No, no, no," Bond said, waving a finger at Mack. "The question is, what are *you* doing here? I have a perfectly valid explanation of why I'm in Mexico City. I'm here in my official capacity as the ambassador's principal advisor on intelligence matters. What I want to know is why Mack McLendon is here?"

"They say," Mack said, "that there are more than five thousand tourists here on any given day. I'm one of them."

"The other tourists," Bond said dryly, "do not enter the country and register at a hotel under an assumed name."

"How did you know I was here, Fred?"

"I'm tempted to boast that it was efficiency," Bond said. He folded the newspaper into a neat square and placed it on the bedside table. "But the truth is that one of my junior officers was on the flight with you from Washington. He walked through the first-class section and recognized you. He came into the office this morning all excited, telling us at the staff meeting that he had seen the famous Mack the Knife. I'm surprised he didn't ask for your autograph. He recognized you from the halls at Langley, and apparently believes the horseshit legends about your career as—" Bond paused, chuckled, "—the James Bond of the Company."

Mack began to laugh as he extracted a Gauloise from his pack. "Coming from you, that's a compliment." Mack laughed heartily.

"Up yours, McLendon." Bond's face flushed, but then he too began to laugh with Mack, for Fred Bond really was the James Bond of CIA. When Ian Fleming's hero became the personification of the audacious intelligence operator, the real James Bond had found it necessary to drop the James and use his middle name of Frederick.

Bond sat up and swung his feet to the floor. "All right, McLendon. That's enough ho ho ho. What *are* you doing in Mexico?"

"I'll tell you," Mack said. He lit the cigarette with his cheap lighter. "But tell me first how you knew where I was staying and how you got into this room."

"I wanted to know why you were here. We checked the passenger list but your name wasn't on it. There were only three unaccompanied males in first class; one of them had to be you using an alias. So I dug a photo out of the files. It was on a phony document you used several years ago when you tried to recruit the KGB agent, Seymonov, here in Mexico City. One of my fellows showed the picture to hotel clerks around town until the one downstairs allowed, in return for a hundred-peso bill, that you were registered. As for getting into your room, one of my officers collects master keys to the important hotels as a sort of hobby. Now it's time for you to answer some questions."

"Fred, I'm here because I believe that Carlos now has his support base in Mexico City. I'm trying to track him down before he kills more of my friends—station chiefs like Fred Bond."

Bond regarded Mack. "I'm going to blast somebody about this—the first time headquarters has ever sent someone into my territory to operate without my consent or knowledge."

"No, Fred. Langley doesn't know I'm here. I'm working on my own."

"Horseshit," Bond snorted. "The cable that advised us in the field about Carlos was 'eyes only' for the COS. We're supposed to watch our own asses without alerting the people working for us. They don't want the word to get out. How the hell would you know that Carlos is gunning for us unless you're aboard again with the Agency?"

"The outfit did tell me about Carlos," Mack said, "and knows generally what I'm doing. But I'm not on the payroll and they don't know I'm in Mexico. And I'm going to ask you not to tell Langley. Somewhere, somehow, Carlos has my operation penetrated, and it might be at headquarters."

"What's that? What's that?" Bond fiddled with the volume control of his hearing aid.

"Carlos has a line into my operation, maybe through Langley."

"Jesus!" Bond used the Spanish pronunciation of His name. "Remember when the spy business used to be an orderly profession? Now we can't even keep secrets from international bums like Carlos. And I have to find out from you that he may be in my own territory. The headquarters cable didn't alert me to that possibility."

"What do you know," Mack asked, "about Enrique Schwarz and the Villa Hermosa?"

"He's notorious here," Bond said, "as a financial wheeler and dealer. His *Ultima Sabado* fiestas are famous, but I don't know of anything which connects him with Carlos."

"You'd better check. He has a crew of Japanese with him, probably from the Red Army. And his Final Saturday parties are probably just a cover so that members of Carlos's band can get in and out of his place when they need money and documents. Ask Buenos Aires for traces. I would imagine Carlos picked Schwarz to manage the money because he was doing the same thing in Argentina."

"All right, McLendon," Bond said. "What can I do to help *you?*"

"Nothing," Mack said. "I have a contract on Carlos, but part of the understanding with Langley is that I'm not to expect help from the Agency. For your information, I'll be running an entry during the party tomorrow night at the Villa Hermosa. It'll be best for me, and probably for you, if you stay on the sidelines. The new Director will blow his top if he finds you're mixed up in this operation."

"Screw the new Director," Bond said. "I've had to learn a lot of new rules, but I'm goddamned if I'll sit around on my duff while Carlos knocks off my friends. Isn't there anything I can do to help you? What about surveillance? I have a top-notch team."

"No thanks, Fred. Better that you and the Agency not be involved. But you might watch your rearview mirror with a little extra attention."

"Why?"

"If Carlos ever travels to Mexico City," Mack said, "it's probably around the last Saturday of the month. If I were the CIA station chief in Mexico I believe I would take a little extra care."

"Yeah," Bond said. "I guess you're right. I'll take care. I have a piece of real estate close to one of the new courses at Pinehurst and only need two years for retirement pay. I'd hate to be snuffed out by that bum at this late stage."

Bond stood, and began putting on his coat.

"I'll tell you what, Mack. I'll skip a social evening my wife and I had planned for tomorrow night. Instead I'll come back and wait here in your room while you are trying to sneak in the Villa Hermosa. That way I'll be here if you need something—maybe a 'get out of jail free' card."

"You fellows are missing quite a party. Don't believe I've ever seen so much to eat and drink and so many pretty girls. Never had so much fun with my clothes on."

The voice was Clem's, and he was addressing Mack and Frank, both of whom were stationed by one of Bustamante's windows, through the microphone in his pocket.

Frank Coughlin listened to the report originating from inside the Villa Hermosa as he continued to take photographs of the guests as they arrived at the entrance. Mack looked at his watch: it was almost six P.M. Emilio and Clem had been mixing with the guests at Enrique Schwarz's *Ultima Sabado* fiesta since shortly after noon.

"Yes, siree," Clem continued, the sound of his voice metallic as it came through the receiver. "Must be two hundred folks here now, and they're sopping up Scotch whiskey and tequila like it's about to go out of style. Everytime you turn around one of those little Japanese fellers is at your elbow with a tray of goodies. The girls sittin' around the swimming pool are just about naked. Can you hear that mariachis band singing 'Guadalajara'? When they take a break the marimba band comes on. Hope this little ole CB's working all right so you guys can hear what you're missing. Signing off now. Must look kind of stupid standing here talking to myself."

A few minutes later Mack and Frank could hear Emilio's voice. Each time he spoke there was a hollow echo.

"I'm in the downstairs bathroom," Emilio reported, "and it might be a problem for you, Frank. People going in and out all the time and the more the guests drink the more traffic there'll be. Trouble is that the john is in a hall with a clear view of the door to Schwarz's office. Not much question that you figured out the location right. A few minutes ago I checked the door. It's locked. There's no other room on the first floor Schwarz would use as an office. When Mack signals that you're inside, Frank, we'll hang around that area the best we can to cover you. If necessary, I can knock out the electricity. I wandered into the kitchen asking for an aspirin and located the switch box, so if—"

There was the sound of gunfire from the gardens of the Villa Hermosa. Mack moved quickly to the window and Frank turned from his camera.

"Don't worry about that," Emilio reported. "There'll be a lot more. Schwarz has challenged his guests to a pistol-shooting competition. He's offered a case of Dom Perignon fifty-five to anyone who can turn in a better score than he can. See you later; I'm going out to join the party again."

Frank went to the table and began kneading raw hamburger into a patty.

"Time for the Doberman's last supper?" Mack asked.

"Not his last one," Frank said. "Just enough to be sure he sleeps through the rest of the evening. One full phenobarbital should do it." He began mixing the white powder into the meat.

"Frank, use three or four capsules, just to be sure."

"Can't do that, Mack. Might kill him. He's really a handsome animal."

"Frank . . ."

"Oh, all right. I'll use two, then."

Frank left the observation post, went downstairs, and, outside, tossed the hamburger over the wall. He returned to the room just as Emilio spoke urgently into his microphone.

"Better tune in Clem's frequency," Emilio whispered. "Schwarz has braced him—"

Mack turned up the volume control of the receiver which carried sound from Clem.

". . . and I'm pleased as can be to meet you, Mr. Schwarz. I've heard about your parties for a long time, and it's a pleasure to be here."

"My house," Schwarz said, "is your house. To whom do I owe the honor of your presence, Mr . . ."

"Puller," Clem said. "Jethro Puller. My old friend Humberto Medrano from Jalisco suggested I look you up. Said you were the most hospitable man in Mexico City, and just the fellow to help me with some business I have."

"Medrano? From Jalisco. I'm not sure I remember . . ."

"Humberto said you were a financial wizard and the man to talk facts and figures to when it comes to investing money."

"I don't remember Medrano," Schwarz said. "But then I have a poor memory. What sort of business are you in, Mr. Puller?"

"I'm here in Mexico representing a Texas friend who wants to invest money down here. Thought you might help me do it for him."

"This sponsor of yours from Texas," Schwarz asked, "he is a wealthy man?"

"Right well fixed," Clem said. "I first worked for him in the thirties, when I was about eighteen. He hired me to go around all the small towns in Texas, knocking on doors. I was selling a religious lithograph for fifty-five cents. Really were fine drawings, printed in Philadelphia, and they cost my boss almost a dollar each."

"I do not understand. How is it possible to profit from selling pictures which cost one dollar for fifty-five centavos?"

"They was eight-sided," Clem explained. "Octagonal in shape. Everybody out in the boondocks snapped 'em up, especially the Baptists. Should have, too; they were a real bargain. Once I had made a sale, my boss would come along behind, maybe one or two days later. He sold picture frames. Specialized in eight-sided frames, which just happened to be a perfect fit for my lithographs. Octagonal picture frames are hard to come by. So he paid thirty-seven cents apiece to have them made, and sold them to all those folks for a buck and six bits. Now, I ask you, Mr. Schwarz, if you were sitting in the middle of Texas with an eight-sided picture, would you be able to say no?"

"Ingenious," Schwarz admitted. "What does your friend from Texas do now?"

"He's in the land business. Owns a couple of acres."

"Two acres? In Texas? That is nothing."

"His little parcel," Clem said, "is in an area commonly known as downtown Dallas."

Schwarz guffawed. "We will do business, I can see that. Meantime you must enjoy the party. I see by your attire that you are a man of the West. Do you shoot? A case of champagne if you beat me—but it will take four tens and a nine for your five shots."

"I'm a little rusty," Clem said.

"But you are a man of the American West. Your hat? It is a Stetson?"

"Yup," Clem said.

145

"Would you forgive me if I ask the price of such a hat?"

"One hundred twenty hard ones," Clem said, "at the factory. But my hat's not nearly so pretty as yours, Mr. Schwarz."

"Do you know what a *charro* sombrero like mine costs?"

"With all that fancy filigree I would guess more than mine," Clem said.

"Almost three hundred American dollars," Schwarz confirmed. "Come, let's watch the competition."

Back at the listening post Frank asked Mack: "That story about the eight-sided picture frames? Is it true?"

"Clem swears it is," Mack said. He watched Frank with interest; he was standing in his undershorts, busily smearing his chest and legs with cooking grease. Once finished, he stepped into his pants and donned his shirt.

"Is that really going to do any good," Mack asked.

"Has once before," Frank said. "In some Asian countries housebreakers make their entries entirely in the nude, with their bodies covered with pig grease. If they're surprised it's not easy to hold on to them. If I have to make a fast break from the Villa Hermosa I just might shed some clothes first."

"When do you go, Frank?"

"It should be dark in another half hour. I'll go as soon as the Japanese on duty makes his turn around this side of the house." Frank cocked his head. "Listen. Schwarz is giving Clem a hard time."

They could hear Schwarz and Clem talking, and the sound of other guests in the background.

"Quiet! Quiet!" Schwarz was shouting to his guests. "Another challenger. Mr. Puller is an American cowboy. We will see if he can shoot better than I!"

"Come on, Mr. Schwarz. I really don't believe I'm up to you."

"I insist. Here, take the gun. Five shots at the target. Quiet everybody, while our cowboy shoots."

"Well, all right then."

It was quiet, then through Clem's microphone and through the open window Mack and Frank could hear five shots.

"Applause, applause for him," Schwarz shouted. "Not bad at

all! Three tens, a nine and a seven. Not bad at all. But not good enough to win the champagne. But wait. I'll give you one more chance. Give me the pistol." A pause. "And now, Mr. Puller, will you give me your hat?" Another pause. "Regard the hat! A fine Stetson, with a price at wholesale of more than a hundred American dollars."

"That's right," Clem said. "Now may I have my hat back?"

"No," Schwarz said. "This is your chance. I will throw your Stetson as far as I can, and will not shoot at it until it is within one meter of the ground. If I hit, you lose. If I miss, the Dom Perignon fifty-five is yours."

"Thanks, Mr. Schwarz," Clem said, "but I'd just as soon not. My hat, please . . ."

"Too late! Attention!"

It was quiet. The sound of a single shot. Then the receiver from Clem's microphone emitted a chorus of laughter. Finally it was quiet again.

"Mr. Schwarz, you shot a hole in my hat."

The laughter resumed; it was derisive.

"I don't call that a very neighborly thing to do," Clem complained, his voice strained.

"Only a wager between friends," Schwarz laughed. "Only one little hole between friends. Now, come friend Puller, and I'll introduce you to a film star."

I must remember, Mack said to himself, to compliment Clem for keeping his cool. He was peering through the infra-red attachment of the camera, watching Frank work on the iron grill on the side of the Villa Hermosa. He had slipped over the wall a moment before and crossed the swath of lawn without incident.

Frank removed the grill, and slithered into the opening which led to the crawl space under the mansion. Mack watched the grill for five minutes; he was about to activate the walkie-talkie which would thump Clem and Emilio with the signal that Frank was inside the house, when Frank reappeared. He replaced the grate and walked the thirty steps to the heavy, wooden side door. For two minutes he leaned over the lock. Then the door opened, and Frank went into the house.

Mack alerted Clem and Emilio. One thump, on the beepers they carried.

Several minutes passed. Then Mack, standing near the receiver which carried the transmission from the Sony television, heard from Frank.

"Hi, Mack," Frank reported, his breathing heavy. "No problem so far. One of the Japanese was in a position to see me cross the room for this hall, but I sneaked past." There was a pause. "This is Schwarz's office, all right. Bookshelves all up and down the walls, but there's only one book in the room. The shelves are filled with papers, and there's a stack of them on the desk. I'll go through them as quickly as I can. I've had to lock the door with an inside bolt, because there's no place to hide in here."

Five minutes of quiet, although Mack could hear muted sounds as Frank thumbed through Schwarz's papers.

"There's nothing worth photographing that I can find," Frank informed Mack. "Anyway there's so much paper I wouldn't know where to begin, even if I did understand the Spanish and German most of them are written in. Can't see a safe, either, but I'll look first behind a painting . . ."

Mack could hear Frank exhale gratefully.

"Just like the movies, Mack. Here is it, a wall safe, behind the painting."

Then: "Oh, no."

Frank continued after a pause. "Can't open it, Mack. I know about the model. It's a modern one. A French firm manufactures it. There's no way I can deceive the damned tumblers the way I've done with older ones. Sorry, Mack, but I'll have to come back empty-handed, I'm afraid."

Mack heard nothing for several moments but the sound of Frank moving about the office. Why the hell wasn't Frank getting out of there?

"Think I'll just take a couple of minutes to look around," Frank advised Mack through the Sony. "You know lots of people invite thievery in their homes by thinking they've cleverly concealed the front door key under the mat. Same thing with safes. Remember Schwarz told Clem he had a poor memory. Maybe he's hidden the combination somewhere around the safe in case he can't remember it."

Mack waited tensely in the listening post.

"Looked everywhere, and can't find it. Guess I'll have to—wait a minute! I've found some penciled numbers on the back flyleaf of the book. Looks like a date, and the price. I'll try just in case."

It was quiet.

"Mack, the safe is open."

Mack could imagine Frank touching the side of his spectacles with the gesture which indicated that he was pleased with himself.

Then: "Oh, no. Oh, no!"

Frank explained: "Mack, you wanted me to photograph the documents, then replace them and get out so Schwarz wouldn't know they were compromised. But that's going to be impossible. There are no loose papers in the safe—only a bundle of money and a manila envelope that's almost completely covered by Scotch tape. Schwarz has written his signature across the tape a hundred times. There's simply no way I can open the envelope and then close it without his realizing he's been burgled. Sorry, Mack, I'll have to bring the envelope with me, but as soon as someone opens the safe they'll know I've been here."

Mack was standing at the wall when Frank climbed over it and dropped into Bustamante's yard. They returned to their observation post.

"There it is, Mack." Frank handed Mack the pack of money, but kept the envelope. It was an eight-by-eleven rectangle swathed with Scotch tape which had been wrapped around it dozens of times. Every half inch of the tape contained the signature of Enrique Schwarz. "You can see that opening it, even if we slit it on one edge, will leave evidence that it's been tampered with."

"Doesn't matter, Frank," Mack said. "The important thing is that we have it, and I would guess that it contains what we want to know about Schwarz's bookkeeping on the Carlos account. I'll signal Emilio and Clem that you're out, and they can leave the party. Then we can all get out of here."

Mack picked up the walkie-talkie.

"Hold it, Mack." Frank turned the bulky envelope in his hands, scrutinizing it carefully. "Just how important is it that Schwarz doesn't know we have his papers?"

"Important, but not vital," Mack said. "The best intelligence about Carlos that we could have would be whatever we know that he and Carlos don't *know* we know. When Carlos realizes that we have this haul, he'll be able to change his plans."

Frank continued to examine the envelope. "I have an idea that might work. Just a minute." Frank went to Bustamante's desk and began to rummage through it. He looked in the pigeonholes and drawers. Finally he removed a manila envelope, which was the same size as the one he had taken from Schwarz's safe, and carried it to the table. He compared the two envelopes: the empty one from Bustamante's desk and the stuffed one wrapped in bands of Scotch tape.

"Not precisely the same," Frank said, peering over his bifocals, "but close enough that it will probably pass inspection. Anyway, what can we lose?" Frank picked up a pair of scissors, cut a slit in the package he had taken from the Villa Hermosa, and then, with his hands, ripped the envelope apart. Inside there was a two-inch-high stack of papers.

"Start photographing these, Mack." Frank handed the documents to Mack. "I'm going to be busy for a while."

"But what's the idea, Frank? Let's just take our find and get out with it."

"Give me twenty minutes. Then I may make a proposal."

Mack placed the stack of documents under a table lamp and, one at a time, photographed them.

Frank sat at the table, putting a blank piece of paper before him. Alongside he laid a strip of Scotch tape which bore Enrique Schwarz's signature. Without haste Frank began to write, across the paper in front of him, 'Enrique Schwarz, Enrique Schwarz, Enrique Schwarz.' He stopped, compared his duplication of the signature with the original, then wrote it again and again.

As he moved the documents rapidly under the camera lens Mack whistled softly. "This is it, Frank. All written by hand. It's a ledger of expenses, with date and names. And there's one page of nothing but code, all of it in numbers, but it has the word *Hogar* as a title. That's Carlos's big operation. If we can unscramble the code, we'll be five steps ahead of Carlos when he tries to pull it off."

"Okay," Frank said, "I'm ready. Let's see how it looks."

Frank stacked Schwarz's documents together in the order in which they had been arranged in the original envelope and inserted them in the envelope from Bustamante's desk. Then he wrapped the new envelope thoroughly, laterally and diagonally, with Scotch tape. Then, without haste, he began to scribble his version of Enrique Schwarz's signature across each band of tape, over and over again.

With one hand Frank passed the reconstructed package to Mack; with the other he touched the edge of his spectacles. "Not a bad job, if I say so myself."

Mack turned the spurious envelope from one side to the other. "It's an incredibly good job, Frank. I don't believe Schwarz himself would recognize that it's not the original. But I can't let you do it. It's just too dangerous."

"It'll be simple," Frank said. "Much simpler than before. I know exactly where I have to go and what I have to do. I'll slip in, return this to the safe, close it, and Schwarz will never know he's been had. And we'll know something about Carlos and his operation that he won't know we know."

"Two entries? That's really stretching your luck, Frank."

"I feel lucky, Mack." Frank stood, and stuffed the envelope into his waistband. "Why don't you gather up anything in here you wouldn't want found later, especially those old scraps of Scotch tape, and put them in the car. It shouldn't take me more than five or six minutes. As soon as I come back we'll decamp, and Emilio and Clem can do the same."

"We can quit while we're ahead, Frank. Are you sure?"

"I'm sure, Mack." He extended his hand. "And I'll have to take the money back, as well."

Mack rifled through the stack of bills, held together by rubber bands, and whistled softly. "There must be several hundred thousand dollars here, mostly in U.S. bills."

Frank took the currency. "If we keep it they'll know they've been had." He smiled. "Besides, that would be stealing . . . I'll see you shortly."

Frank went out of the room, descended the stairs, went to the wall and vaulted into the darkness of the Villa Hermosa garden.

After opening the side door Frank stood for a moment in the foyer. He could see only part of the lower level of the house, but there was no one in his field of vision. He strode briskly through a large room and into a hall. At the door of Schwarz's office he inserted his pick in the lock; the door opened almost immediately.

Frank stepped inside and turned quickly to be sure his entrance had not been observed, only to find himself gazing into the eyes of a fat Japanese guard, his round face registering surprise at finding the intruder in the hall.

Frank slammed the door and threw the inside bolt. If he was to be apprehended, it might as well be under circumstances which would convince Schwarz that his secrets remained undiscovered. He went to the safe and began to spin the combination lock.

Enrique Schwarz was the center of attention as he stood before a large portable grill near the side of his pool. He joked with his guests as he served them ample portions of lobster tails, sweetbreads and strips of beef and pork, sizzling hot, from a bed of glowing coals. Occasionally Schwarz would pause to drink from the glass of champagne extended to him by a striking young actress in a skimpy bikini. The group of mariachis, resplendent in their *charro* costumes, sang with a gusto derived from hours of drinking.

Clem and Emilio regarded their host from a distance.

"I don't think you like Schwarz," Emilio said.

"The son of a bitch," Clem muttered. He removed his Stetson and thrust a wiggling finger through the hole Schwarz had shot through his hat. "If he's circumcised, I hope he was cut on the bias so he pees on his foot."

Emilio was worried. He looked at his watch. "Frank has been in that office almost an hour. Either he's found a hell of a lot of stuff to photograph, or he's in trouble."

"I certainly thought we would have the signal by now," Clem said. "What do you figure is going on?"

"Damned if I know," Emilio said. "Have you felt anything?"

"Nope," Clem said. "I hope these beepers are still working."

"*Huevos de Oro,*" Schwarz shouted, holding a portion of meat aloft on a fork. "Who will have the golden eggs?" An enthusiastic guest accepted the bull's testicles.

Frank reported to Mack as he opened the safe.

"I've been spotted, Mack. One of the Japanese saw me come in. He knows I'm inside the office, and he and his friends will be breaking down the door. I'll only need a minute now to replace the envelope, but after that I'll need help to get out of here."

Mack, at the listening post in the Bustamante house, activated the walkie-talkie three times.

"Did you feel that?" Clem asked.

"Yes," Emilio said. "Three times?"

"Yup," Clem said.

"Get started then. Create a diversion!"

"What kind of diversion, for Christ's sake?" Clem asked.

"Why don't you go kick Schwarz in the balls? I'm going to try and find Frank."

Emilio moved hurriedly into the house. Clem scratched his head, shrugged, pulled up his pants, and marched along the side of the swimming pool through the crowd of guests. Clem confronted Enrique Schwarz.

"Just a minute! Just a minute! I want to make a bet with you, Schwarz."

Schwarz laid aside his serving fork

"Why it's our gringo friend Puller. What is it you want to wager, friend Puller?"

"You shot my hat," Clem said. "I'll bet you I can shoot your hat better."

"But my sombrero is three times larger than your hat," Schwarz said, reaching up and touching it. "Of course you could put a bullet through it."

"But I'll do it with your gun," Clem said. "That looks like a thirty-eight-caliber revolver that holds six rounds. Harder to handle than that fancy little target pistol you used to drill my Stetson. I'll bet you I can put all six shots through your fancy sombrero."

Schwarz chortled. He spoke to his guests.

"I'm afraid our friend Puller has been drinking too much. Even *I* could not hit this hat six times out of six." Schwarz put his hand on Clem's shoulder. "Friend Puller, I cannot take advantage of you. Have another drink."

"A man," Clem said, "would give me the opportunity."

Schwarz narrowed his eyes and glared at Clem. He pulled his revolver from the holster. "Stop the music!"

The sound of *Cielito Lindo* faded into silence. The guests gathered around Schwarz and Clem.

"Take the gun." Schwarz handed the revolver to Clem. He removed his sombrero.

"Ready, Puller?"

"Let 'er fly," Clem commanded.

It was quiet as Schwarz sailed his hat across the swimming pool. The floodlight around the bathing area illuminated the graceful arch of its flight.

It was still quiet as the hat hit the ground on the far side of the pool.

Clem did not hurry as he shuffled to the corner of the swimming pool, turned, then turned again and approached the fallen hat. Standing directly over it, he fired six times. The sombrero danced with the impact of the bullets.

Clem turned and smiled at Schwarz. "I won."

Schwarz swore and began running around the pool toward Clem.

As the commotion around the pool continued, Emilio stepped into the kitchen. Two Japanese were leaning out of the kitchen door staring into the garden, seeking the origin of the shots that had just interrupted their chores. Emilio fired three times into the electrical switch box.

The Villa Hermosa and its gardens were plunged into darkness. A woman's scream could be heard.

Clem scampered around the pool, Schwarz behind him. Clem lifted one end of the long brazier of glowing coals and cooking meat and pushed it into the pool. There was a whishing sound and clouds of smoke billowed from the bubbling water. Clem turned, and, in the darkness, ran into a guitar held by one of the troubadours. "Play the national anthem," Clem hissed.

Emilio stood in the darkened house near the entrance to Schwarz's office. Three Japanese were there, a thin one holding a flashlight while a bald one worked in the light of its beam with a crowbar to open the office door. The fat guard who had discovered Frank held a machine pistol at the ready. Emilio drew his gun and tightened his wrist as he aimed the sight at the man's head.

The door opened into the office with a wrench of broken wood and bending metal. Frank Coughlin crouched on the floor, naked except for his spectacles and pair of knee-length undershorts. As the flashlight beam shone on him, Frank lowered his head and shoulders and, like an elderly fullback going through the middle of the line, catapulted his wiry body forward. Two of the Japanese grabbed him, and the three men crashed to the floor in a melee of twisting arms and legs. The fat Japanese with the machine pistol danced erratically as he sought the opportunity to fire at Frank without hitting one of his companions. His body fell with a thump when Emilio smashed the butt of his pistol into the back of the Oriental's head; the machine pistol slid along the floor into the darkness.

Emilio turned to help Frank but it was not necessary. The

older agent slithered out of the grasp of the two Japanese who had momentarily pinned him to the floor. They could not hold on to Frank's grease-covered body. Frank eluded both men and pranced down the hall, knees high, in the direction of the door leading to the garden. The thin Japanese retrieved the flashlight and used its beam to probe the darkness for the machine pistol. He found it and with his free hand reached for the weapon.

Emilio's ears rang at the blast of a pistol shot from just behind his head. The thin Japanese screamed in pain, then stared at the back of his hand: there was a small round hole in it. He turned his hand over and found the palm was blown away. "Banzai," Clem said, raising the pistol above his head in a gesture of triumph.

Emilio turned as the bald Japanese who had been wrestling with Frank lunged for him. Emilio met his rush head-on, lifted the small assailant, and slammed the man's body into the wall.

Emilio and Clem ran to the door. Another flashlight beam, from near the back of the house, swept up and down the swath of grass between the Villa Hermosa and Bustamante's house. It caught Frank halfway across the yard. He was running in a low crouch, one hand holding his spectacles in place and the other keeping his shredded underpants from falling around his knees. There was a staccato burst from behind the flashlight, and the ground near Frank's feet jumped as the bullets ripped into the dirt.

Now the din increased with the barking of the Doberman who was streaking across the yard in pursuit of Frank, now dashing toward the wall.

Clem and Emilio, firing together, shot half a dozen rounds into the darkness behind the flashlight. There was a moan and the flashlight fell to the ground.

Frank beat the Doberman to the wall by a close margin, dove to the top of the wall, rolled over it, and dropped into Bustamante's garden.

Emilio turned to Clem. "Whenever you're ready?"

"Now," Clem said. "Let's haul ass."

Pandemonium continued inside the Villa Hermosa as Clem and Emilio walked through the darkness toward the gate and the car they had parked just beyond it before entering the party. Schwarz was bellowing instructions. There were imprecations in Japanese, and women were sobbing in the darkness. A single guitar was strumming the refrain of the Mexican national anthem.

Clem and Emilio waited in their rented car until they observed Mack and Frank drive out of Bustamante's gate and speed away toward the center of Mexico City. Frank, putting on a shirt, waved a good-bye.

Emilio backed the car into a side road, turned, then drove rapidly in the opposite direction.

Clem looked to the rear. "Emilio, we forgot something."

"What, Clem?"

"We shoulda done somethin' to Schwarz's cars. Because two of 'em just came out of his gate."

Emilio adjusted his rearview mirror and could see the headlights behind. "Fasten your seat belt, buddy." He put the accelerator on the floorboard.

The road curved into a long straight stretch. Emilio leaned over the wheel as if using his weight to increase the vehicle's speed. Now the car was trembling under the strain of its own force.

"Those are big ole cars," Clem said. "I'm afraid they're gaining on us." He checked his gun.

Emilio could see a fork in the road ahead.

"Do you know where we are, Clem?"

"Don't have the foggiest. But better we bear to the left and head toward city traffic. This heap won't outrun those big ones behind us."

At the fork Schwarz's two cars split; one taking the right turn, the other continuing in pursuit of Emilio and Clem.

"I hope," Clem said, "they don't know something we don't know, and that other car won't be able to head us off at the pass."

Now they were in a suburb where high walls lined the narrow street. Emilio twisted the wheel and hit the curb to avoid colliding with a slow-moving truck. He fought to keep control, and then sped on.

"Watch it!" Emilio slammed on the brakes and the car skidded to a halt.

One of Schwarz's cars had come from a side street, stopped, and was completely blocking the way. Two Japanese Emilio and Clem had not seen before jumped from the black limousine and stood at its front and rear. Both lifted machine guns to the alert.

Emilio looked back over his shoulder and could see the lights of the car behind growing larger. There were no alleys, no spaces between houses.

"Hold tight, Clem! I'm going through!"

"In this little-bitty car? You'll kill us!"

Emilio stepped down hard on the gas. The car lurched forward, gained momentum, and sped directly toward Schwarz's car. Forty. Fifty. Sixty miles an hour.

Schwarz was sitting in the back seat of his car. His astonished face was clearly visible in the headlights' beam as he realized that Emilio was about to crash deliberately into him. The two Japanese began shooting, the mouths of their gun barrels flickering red.

At the very last moment Emilio turned the steering wheel slightly. His car smashed into Schwarz's automobile at the rear wheel. The large vehicle spun, its rear lifting into the air. Metal crunched, as tires screamed, and a man shrieked. The limousine was on its side.

Emilio's car had been slowed by the impact but it did not stop. One fender was torn loose and hanging; sparks flew from the macadam as it bounced on the street.

"Well if that ain't the Goddamnedest thing I ever saw!" Clem exclaimed. "And look there!"

A ball of flame rose into the air as the gas tank of Schwarz's car exploded. One of the Japanese guards rolled on the ground, his clothes afire.

Emilio turned at the next corner. One tire was flat and the car limped badly. The windshield blurred as water drops formed on it.

"Radiator's busted," Emilio said. "But we can go up to five miles before the engine seizes."

"Lordy." Clem made a strange noise of relief. "Where did you ever learn how to knock around big cars with such a little one?"

"It's called defensive driving," Emilio explained. "If you hit the other car at just the right place, either front or back, you can knock aside a Cadillac with a Volks. But it has to be just right, and you have to keep your foot on the gas all the way."

"I think I'll learn that little trick," Clem said.

"Why not? They teach the course at a place in Detroit. Five hundred bucks. Anyone behind us?"

"Nope. Looks like we're home free."

"Let's find a place to dump this thing," Emilio said, "and then get out of town."

"One thing?" Clem asked.

"What's that?"

"Tell me, Emilio. When you rented this car, did you take out the extra insurance?"

"I'll check out," Mack said, as he stepped from the car, "and then we'll head for the airport."

Frank, who by now had dressed himself from the suitcase in the back of the car, nodded. "I'll wait here."

Mack ascended the elevator to his floor and went to his room. He opened the door. Bond was again stretched out on the bed, seemingly asleep, a magazine across his lap.

But James Bond was dead.

Mack walked to the side of the bed. He lifted an inert eyebrow, and felt Bond's pulse. A small caliber bullet had gone into the side of his skull and erupted from the other side. The smaller hole in Bond's head was ringed with a powder burn. Whoever had shot Bond had been standing almost at his side. The hearing aid was intact.

Mack walked to the hotel room desk and consulted the telephone directory. He called the American Embassy.

"American Embassy. Marine guard speaking," a voice responded.

"Would you make a note of what I'm going to say, please? It's important."

"Who is this?"

"A friend," Mack said, "and this is an emergency. Call Mr. Bond's duty officer and tell him that Bond has been killed. His body is in room 627 at the Maria Cristina. The duty officer had better hurry if he wants to get there before the police. If you can't find the duty officer, deliver the same message to anyone who works in Bond's office—his deputy, his secretary . . ."

The young Marine was hesitant. "Look, Mister. You're going to have to identify yourself. Who are you?"

"A friend of the Marine Corps commandant," Mack said, "and I'll be checking with him to see how promptly you delivered this message."

Mack hung up and consulted the directory again.

"Policía del Distrito Féderal."

"There has been a shooting at the Villa Hermosa near the presidential residence," Mack said in Spanish. "Several Japanese with illegal documents are involved and the owner of the place, Señor Enrique Schwarz. With so much commotion so near the home of the President of the Republic, I would suggest you investigate immediately."

Mack dropped the telephone into its cradle. He scooped his belongings from the dresser drawer and put them into his valise. He went into the bathoom for his toilet case.

The message on the bathroom mirror was in block letters, scrawled in soap: *"Saludos,* McLendon. *Y hasta la vista."* It was signed, "Carlos."

Mack checked out of the hotel and got into the car.

"You think we'll make the flight?" Frank asked. "It's the last one before morning."

"We should make it," Mack said. "You've just run a good operation, Frank. You put that package back together so cleverly that I don't believe Schwarz will realize we were inside it. Certainly the Villa Hermosa has to be abandoned now as a support base for Carlos. And if we can decipher the coded paper about Operation *Hogar,* we'll be one up on Carlos when he launches it. But I'm going to ask you not to mention it to Emilio or Clem."

"I don't understand, Mack. They know I made the entry."

"But they don't know you opened the safe, or what you collected about Carlos's finances and plans for Operation *Hogar*. I'd rather no one else knew that, at least for now."

"To be honest," Frank said, irritation obvious in his tone, "it bothers me to think that you don't trust Emilio and Clem, and that I will have to lie to them, especially after what they did for me tonight."

Mack decided to wait until they were airborne to tell Frank about Fred Bond; Frank and Fred had been friends.

"We've spent our lives in a shitty business," Mack said. "A young officer named Philip Agee once worked for me, and I trusted him. And I have British friends who trusted their chief of Soviet operations, Kim Philby; Prime Minister MacMillan defended him on the floor of Parliament."

"I still feel creepy," Frank said.

Mack made the turn at the John F. Kennedy housing development and headed toward the airport lights. He was thinking about Fred Bond. He had served quietly and competently as a minor proconsul in a dozen countries abroad. His job had offered scant recognition but Bond believed it had to be done. Had he stayed in his native Utah, he probably would have been a successful businessman, important in country club circles. Now his only recognition would be an anonymous star carved in the marble plaque at Langley. He would not enjoy his retirement home on the links at Pinehurst.

That was not all. Mack realized with a shudder that Bond had died because he was in the line of fire between Mack and Carlos. Carlos would not care, but Mack did.

6.

The next morning Mack placed a call from Washington.

"Mr. Symser, please."

"This is Mrs. Symser. I'm sorry, Allen's not here. Is this a long-distance call?"

"Yes," Mack said.

"Allen's in Dallas today. He'll be back tomorrow."

"How can I reach him in Dallas?"

"He's staying at the Adolphus Hotel. He said that a man with a voice like peanut butter might be calling. You sound like the man. He's in room 312."

"Thanks." Mack paused. "Mrs. Symser, do you like peanut butter?"

"Crazy about it. Have been since I was a kid."

Mack chuckled. "Thanks. I hope to meet you some day, Mrs. Symser. Good-bye."

Mack rang the Texas hotel.

"Allen Symser."

"Good afternoon, Mr. Symser."

"Hi there. I'm afraid I don't have any all-night drugstores cased out around here."

"It's all right," Mack said. "I just wanted to tell you that Phase Two of our operation is over."

"The support thing?"

"That's right. We located Carlos's support chief in Mexico City, and now he's out of business, at least temporarily."

"What happened?"

"The fellow had a party and we sort of broke it up."

"Very illuminating. Does that mean that Carlos is out of business as well?"

"Not at all," Mack said. "But it will be more difficult for him to operate, and he might take some short cuts which could lead to mistakes. It will take time for him to set up another support base."

"So now you're ready for Phase Three?"

"Yes," Mack said. "Locating Carlos himself, and monitoring his activities as well as those of all his cohorts, so that we will be ready for his next operation."

"How long do you think that will take?" Symser asked.

"Let's see." Mack paused. "There are only twenty-four more shopping days till Christmas. I suspect Carlos will act within a few weeks, less than a hundred days from the day we signed the contract."

"You sound optimistic."

"Not really, Mr. Symser. The truth is that I'm frightened. My friends are being killed off at an alarming rate. Have a good holiday, Mr. Symser."

Mack hung up.

Later in the morning, Lucy looked up from a stack of documents as Mack entered the safehouse apartment. Mack presented her with a gift of large paper flowers, purchased the night before in the Mexico City airport.

"Thank you, Mack. That's sweet. Especially as busy as you fellows must have been in Mexico. There's enough here to keep me occupied for a week, what with all the notes Emilio and Clem dictated, the financial records, and the typewriter ribbon. And Frank says he has almost two hundred photographs."

"We had a busy time," Mack confirmed. "You might ask Frank sometime to tell you the story of how he almost lost his ass—literally—because he was too kind-hearted to give a proper dose of sleeping pills to a very large dog. Any calls while we were gone?"

"Skip. She telephoned about ten times, wanting to know if there had been any word from you, and when you would be back."

"Anything else?"

"A man with a British accent telephoned and left a message," Lucy said. "It was a short one: Barton Wheeler departed

London for New York on BEA on two December, using the assumed name of Justin Smith.' "

"Who is Barton Wheeler?"

"Notorious British terrorist. Was a chum of Carlos's when Carlos was in London."

"Then he's probably one of the Gang of Twenty, coming over for the operation."

"That's my guess," Lucy said. She pointed toward the bulletin board at the end of the room. "At least I'm sure enough about it that I've put him in my rogues' gallery."

Mack went to the board and studied the photograph Lucy had pinned there. Of course, Carlos would be calling on associates who spoke English for an operation taking place in the United States, just as he had, according to Seymonov, recruited two Puerto Ricans in New York who knew the area.

"No long-distance calls from Rio de Janeiro?"

"No."

"What about Perry and Hyphenated-Jake? Will they be here at five?"

"Yes, they've checked in or called every morning since you've been gone. I told them you wanted to get together this afternoon. Clem and Emilio came here straight from the airport to deliver their loot; they're getting some sleep, but they'll be here too."

"And Skip?"

"Oh, yes." Lucy's eyes twinkled. "I couldn't keep her away if I wanted to."

"What about the haul we brought back from Mexico? Have you found anything worthwhile?"

"The photographs will be ready early this afternoon," Lucy said. "Maybe I can match some of them with my friends here." She motioned toward her photographic display of terrorist suspects.

"But the financial ledgers are a gold mine full of nuggets," Lucy continued. "Amounts, places, dates, code names—all bits and pieces now, but they just might fit together later. I've found two items that you should know about now. Remember that you once told me a good intelligence officer shouldn't track gnats when there are elephants tromping by? I found two elephants in the ledgers. Carlos is paying two people very large sums of money on a regular basis. The first is named Black, or at least that's his funny name."

"Black is Schwarz, Carlos's support chief," Mack said. "I knew he would be well-paid."

"Oh." Lucy was disappointed. "Well, there's one more. An entry made in the journals each month, going back at least five years. See, here it is: 'Monthly Humboldt Payment— US$10,000.' Now all of this is written in German or Spanish, so I've been working with German-English and Spanish-English dictionaries. And I can't find Humboldt anywhere. But somebody, somewhere, has been paid ten thousand dollars a month by Carlos for a long time."

"You won't find that word in the dictionary. It's a man's name. But thanks, Lucy, that is an elephant."

There was a ring at the door. Mack opened it, and Frank entered.

"He can't do it," Frank said. He handed *Operacion Hogar*, the paper he had pilfered from Schwarz's safe, to Lucy. "I left him a Xerox, but he's not optimistic. Says it's too short to work with."

"What's this?" Lucy asked.

"An important piece of paper," Mack said. "We brought it back from Mexico. It's in code, so this morning Frank took it to Hal Benson, an old National Security Agency hand who retired recently. He's just about the best cipher man in Washington. If he can't break it, no one can." Mack turned to Frank. "What's Hal's problem?"

"Hal is convinced this code which uses numbers instead of words is a simple one requiring the use of duplicate texts available to sender and receiver. If both have, say, identical copies of a travel guide, the digits 23-7 mean something like the twenty-third word on page seven. But what texts are being used by Carlos and Schwarz? Identical editions of a magazine? The Bible?"

It was quiet for a moment. Mack pulled at his earlobe.

"Frank, do you remember telling me that you found only

one book in Schwarz's library, a book with some lucky numbers written in it?"

"Yes."

"Do you remember the title of the book?"

"No," Frank said. "It was in Spanish. But I do remember that the author was Cervantes."

"Not *Don Quixote*?"

"Of course not. I would have remembered that."

"Was it a collection of plays?"

"No."

"Was it called *Novelas Ejemplares*?"

Frank shook his head, negatively.

"Was it *Galatea*?"

"That's it! I recall that somehow it made me think of *My Fair Lady!*"

"Find a copy. It was the key to the safe for you, and it just might be the key that Hal's looking for so he can break out the message from numbers to words."

"How do I find a book in Spanish?" Frank asked.

"Foreign section at the Library of Congress," Mack said. "Or the libraries at the Pan American Union or the OAS. State Department. Call a buddy at the Agency library. The Spanish Embassy. Keep trying until you find it, and hustle it out to Hal."

"What's all this about?" Lucy asked.

"Lucy, we might be able to learn the details of Carlos's operation if we break the code on that paper. If we do, don't say anything to the others. Just put it into your files and talk about the information, but not the source."

"I still feel guilty about not telling the others," Frank said. "Can't we trust each other?"

"Somehow," Mack said, "Carlos knows everything we're doing." Mack placed his hand on Frank's shoulder. "Sorry, but we'd better keep everything on a 'need-to-know' basis. I was going to tell you on the plane last night, Frank, but you fell asleep so quickly I decided to wait until today. When I went to my hotel room to check out, Fred Bond was there. He was dead. Carlos left a message, saying he had done it."

Lucy gasped.

"Fred?" Frank was stunned. "He was in my OSS unit."

"He was a friend of mine, too." Mack went to the door. "I'll be back for the meeting at five. First, though, I'm going to play some golf."

Philip Layton tugged at the glove on his left hand, then smoothed the leather wrinkles from each finger, as he looked down the first fairway at the Kenwood Country Club. He took one slow practice swing. Then Layton turned to Mack.

"A wager, Mack? Ten, ten, ten?"

"Five, five, five," Mack said. "Don't be greedy, Phil. Your handicap is four, I believe."

"Three," Layton corrected Mack.

"And mine is twelve," Mack said. "I'll need the strokes. Haven't played in a long time. If I lose, I'll challenge you next to a game of tennis to get my money back."

"Fair enough," Layton said. He rested the end of his driver against his abdomen for a moment while he warmed himself by running his hands briskly up and down his arms. Layton was a small man, but his shoulders were broad and his body tapered to narrow waist. Despite the heavy sweater he wore, it was easy to see that he was in good physical shape. He had dark skin and his face was handsome with a rough Mediterranean cast.

Layton addressed the ball, squinted again into the bright December sun, and, with what appeared to be an almost leisurely swing, drove the ball two hundred forty yards down the middle of the fairway.

"Fine shot," Mack said. His own drive was poor, half the distance of his opponent's. The ball landed in the rough.

The men boarded the golf cart and rolled quietly down the hill toward Mack's ball. The grass was sere, the green had disappeared from the fairways in the low temperatures of late November and early December. The sun shone in a cloudless sky.

"What a great day," Layton said, breathing deeply, "and a great idea, Mack. Much better than wasting our time in a restaurant."

"I wanted to see you, Phil," Mack said, "and I recalled your saying one time that you tried to play golf at least once a week unless there was snow on the ground. When I looked out the window this morning and saw what a fine day it was I decided to tempt you."

"You did, and it cost me a good column," Layton said. "I cancelled a lunch with a senator who had promised to give me the inside story on the administration's position on the peace talks next week in Geneva."

Mack stopped the cart and waited for Layton to make his shot.

Mack knew that Philip Layton had worked his way through journalism school, often as a dishwasher in all-night cafeterias. For two decades he had been a relatively obscure working journalist but in recent years had become a well-known political commentator. After the *Washington Post* had made his column a regular Op-Ed page feature, Layton was syndicated to fifty newspapers and his swarthy countenance was familiar to television talk-show viewers.

Layton swung a crisp seven iron, lofting his second shot to the green. A moment later Mack put his third in the bunker and the hole was Layton's.

At the ninth hole Mack was three down, despite the advantage strokes his higher handicap gave him. He managed to stay even with Layton through the twelfth, and the two men sat in the cart at the tee of the par three thirteenth waiting while two women played out the hole in front of them.

Layton declined the cigarette Mack offered him.

"What's on your mind, Mack? You said it was important that we see each other today."

"I need some help," Mack said, lighting a Gauloise in cupped hands.

"You know I'll do what I can," Layton said. "God knows we've been able to help each other in the past. All those lunches over the years, beginning in Buenos Aires back in—When *did* we first meet, Mack?"

"That was in fifty-nine, Phil, when you were covering the southern cone of Latin America for Associated Press."

"That's right." Layton nodded. "That was when it was politic for CIA station chiefs and correspondents to take turns buying each other lunch and exchanging information. Not now, though. Do you realize, Mack, that if you were still with the Agency I would have to be crazy to be in touch with you—too much of a chance someone would claim I was on your payroll. Bradlee and Graham would scream bloody murder."

The ladies putted out and went on. Both Mack and Layton drove the green. In the cart again, Mack explained to his golfing partner. "I need some information about Carlos— the kind of information that I'll probably find nowhere except down deep inside the Mossad."

"Carlos, the Venezuelan terrorist?" Layton pursed his lips. "Of course I know about him. Just sort of disappeared in recent years, hasn't he?"

"From public view," Mack said. "But he's around and planning something big. I'm trying to stop him."

On the green Layton shot first, a long breaking putt which stopped when the ball was only three feet from the hole. Mack stroked his ball to within six inches and Layton knocked it away, conceding Mack's par.

"And how can I help you with the Mossad?" Layton asked. He surveyed the degree of break in the short, easy putt which would give him his par three. "I suppose some of the people I know at the Israeli Embassy here must be intelligence, in touch with Langley. But not with me. The truth is, Mack, I don't even know what Mossad means."

"An acronym," Mack said. "Hebrew, for 'Central Institute for Intelligence and Security.' Also known as Shin Beth. And I suspect you're lying when you say you don't know it."

Layton, about to putt, stood erect and glared at Mack. "I don't like to be called a liar."

Mack shrugged. "It goes with the profession. Cover is worth protecting."

"Cover?" Layton's face was grim.

"You are a successful journalist," Mack said. "I also believe you to be a successful Mossad agent. Except for perhaps one of your colleagues under official cover in the embassy, I expect you are the most senior Mossad agent in the United States."

Layton laughed. "That's a romantic notion, Mack, but the fact is you're full of shit."

Mack said nothing.

Layton chuckled again, leaned over his ball, and putted. He missed the cup by several inches.

On the fourteenth tee Mack and Layton again had to wait before driving. They both had bogie fives and continued, with Mack two down.

On the fifteenth hole the women golfers, searching for a ball gone astray in the rough, beckoned the men to pass through. As they approached the green in the golf cart Layton spoke.

"Curious," Layton said. "Why do you believe me to be with Mossad?"

Mack paused, then related the background of his suspicion. He reminded Layton that he had been a guest in Layton's home in Argentina in 1959 when another visitor was the AP chief from New York. The AP chief commented to Mack that Layton and his wife must have really coveted the Buenos Aires job, because Layton had turned down an assignment to work in Rome. Then, over a period of two years, Mack learned of Layton's diligence in covering stories about Nazi war criminals in Paraguay, Bolivia, and Argentina—stories which were of interest to AP readers, but of even higher priority for an Israeli intelligence officer. Then Mack learned from his own sources that Layton had been personally involved in the kidnapping and spiriting out of Argentina of one of the most notorious of those war criminals.

On the sixteenth tee Mack explained further. "But the thing that gave you away, Phil, was that you made a mistake an intelligence officer should always avoid: you established a pattern. Each time we met, at each of those lunches we had in Buenos Aires, and later during the years in Washington, you always introduced some single question, a query about something which would generally be of more interest to an intelligence service than to a press service. You would just slip it into the conversation, casually, but it was always there."

Mack stopped the cart at the edge of the green. His ball was several feet off the green, but he selected a putter for the approach.

"You should be ashamed," Layton said, "using a Texas wedge."

Mack stroked the ball and it came to rest four inches short of the hole. "The ends," Mack said, "sometimes justify the means."

Layton made a routine two-putt and they tied the hole, going into the seventeenth with Mack still two down.

Mack went on with his explanation. "Once I began to believe that you might be Mossad, I became more interested in your life style. Sure, you're making plenty of money now with your column. But in those early years you lived very high on the hog for a man who had to subsist on a journalist's salary. Twice-yearly vacations, always first-class. At your home the gin was always Beefeaters and the whiskey Black Label—enough to make the AP auditor blow his stack. And remember introducing me to your parents in Washington when they were visiting your rather grand house on Foxhall Road? Your father told me how generous you had been, sending monthly checks."

Layton's ball was in the trap. He stepped down from the golf cart and pulled his sand-wedge from the bag. He walked into the bunker, twisted his body until his feet were firm in the sand, and prepared for his shot. But then he stopped.

"Mack," Layton said, "you're fishing. You're throwing out bait waiting for me to bite. It's all conjecture. I happen to be a Jew who decided a long time ago that I was going to make it, and I have. I'm not proud of everything I've done—you will remember that my father's name is Myron Latviski—but I promised myself, when I was almost falling asleep over a tub of dirty dishes in the greasy spoons where I worked to get through college, that I was going to make it. And I have, as a newsman, not a spy."

"I knew I was right," Mack said, "when you invited me to the White House correspondents' dinner just before I retired from the Company in early 1975. Big deal for you guys. Each journalist on the presidential beat in Washington invites two people, and you all play the game of who can bring along the most VIP guest. Bill Colby was there, and another ex-Director of CIA, Red Raborn. I was the only other spook. Mack McLendon, under State Department cover, nonentity. Why did you invite me, Phil?"

Layton looked up at Mack, from the depth of the sand trap.

"You were a friend," Layton said. "I thought you would enjoy it."

"I hope that was part of it," Mack said. "But your other guest was one of the country's most famous novelists, with a book at the top of the best-seller list at the time. Then why the spook nobody had ever heard of? Because, I told myself when I was putting on the tux I hadn't worn in five years, you had a question. A *big* question. I drove down to the dinner wondering just how you would slip it to me, at just what point you would think I was heady enough, consorting with all the famous people, to be caught off-guard."

Layton shook his head and closed his eyes, as if the scenario Mack described was ludicrous.

"Your wedge just touched the sand," Mack said, "but I won't call you on the penalty stroke. It came just after the president made his speech. We were chatting about nothing special when you asked, almost idly, 'Mack, I hear they've changed the date for the underground tests in Nevada next month. Will it be the fifth or the eleventh of the month?' Hell, I didn't even know there were any underground tests scheduled, but I checked the next day. Sure enough. You knew, but you didn't know when, and you were trying to get the date from me so you could send a report back to Tel Aviv."

It was quiet for a moment. Layton lowered his head, drew back his club, and swung down fast and hard into the sand. The ball moved a few inches. Layton looked up at Mack.

"That," Layton said, "is the first time I've failed to get out of a trap in five years."

At the eighteenth tee Mack was one down. He had no advantage stroke on the par four final hole. Both were in the fairway, and both men reached the green with their second shots. Mack was away, and he putted the ball to within a foot of the hole. He tapped it in for his par four.

Layton was twenty feet from the hole. He putted, hit the edge of the cup, and his ball went two feet beyond. Layton walked to the hole and, placing the head of his putter in the hole, measured the distance.

"That's in the leather, Mack."

"No concession for the match, Phil," Mack said. "Putt it out."

Layton stood erect, leaving his putter on the ground.

"Mack, you are a hard-nosed bastard. What the hell is it you want?"

"Get off a fast cable to your headquarters. Tell them I need help and I need it fast. Don't let them check with Langley; it may be that Langley's leaking. Tell them I know Carlos is planning a major op in the United States sometime soon. I need to know exactly what, when, where and how. If there's a service in the world that has a penetration of Carlos's group it's the Mossad. Even if you don't, Mossad can help me with information on the people who work with him."

"Mack, you're being unreasonable. You've put together a hypothesis based on guesswork and suspicion. You know, it's just possible that you're wrong, that I'm not a Mossad agent."

"It's possible," Mack admitted. "But if you're not with Mossad you work for someone else. Maybe the Soviets. I've been in the business a long time, Phil, and I can spot a spook from a hundred paces. Now I'm standing five feet from you, and I *know* you're an agent."

"And if I am, and if Tel Aviv says no?"

"In that case," Mack said, speaking evenly, "I'll blow you out of the water. I'll expose you."

"Blackmail?"

"Blackmail," Mack confirmed.

Layton leaned over his ball. His hands were trembling. He looked up at Mack.

"You really should give me this little one," Layton said.

"Not a chance," Mack said. "Putt it."

Layton missed the putt. The match had ended, even.

"You are a tough bastard," Layton said. Despite the crisp December air his forehead was dotted with perspiration. "I'll be in touch."

When Mack returned to the safehouse his team, with the exception of Frank, was gathered around Lucy at the dining room table. Emilio and Clem were joking with Hyphenated-Jake, trying to mollify him after the two had refused to tell him their whereabouts during the past week. Perry was complaining of a hangover, and intimating his previous night had been a memorable, romantic evening. Skip was lovely in a leather pantsuit. The Haitian amulet, Mack noted, again hung round her neck on its gold chain.

When the door opened Mack said, "We were waiting for you, Frank. Let's begin."

Frank touched the edge of his spectacles. "May I see you for a moment, Mack?"

Mack excused himself and accompanied Frank into an adjoining bedroom. Frank was smiling broadly.

"The book was the key," he said, removing a single, folded piece of paper from his pocket and handing it to Mack. "Didn't take Hal more than a half hour to break the message. Look."

Mack unfolded the paper and read:

OPERATION HOGAR

Carlos to Black:
1 November

Load all drops. Each comrade will need sufficient funds to obtain new false documents, round trip air passage to U.S., and per diem for ninety days.

Rogelio and Fermin need money to purchase weapons, which must be sterile. Suggest six thousand dollars.

Pepe and Bart require funds and credentials to rent ten-passenger jet with fuel capacity for international flight. Pepe to pose as wealthy playboy; arrange to cover him in Mexico or Argentina.

Once under our control, our guest will be in custody of Pepe, Bart, Rogelio, Maria, and Fermin (and me). Reload all other drops with promised bonus and living funds for six months. Explain that no further contact to be expected for at least that long as Washington will be investigating through all friendly services.

"Well, Mack?"

Mack looked up at Frank. "A giant leap forward."

"I thought you would be pleased," Frank said, touching the frames of his glasses with both hands.

"Let's join the others," Mack said.

The two men went into the safehouse dining room and sat at the table. Mack addressed his group.

"Sorry, but I'm going to ask you to travel again," Mack said. "For about ten days, but you'll be home before Christmas. Maybe you can see your families during the holidays. Tell them what we need, Lucy."

Lucy Stevenson rose and went to her bulletin board.

"You can see that so far we have identified only one person as almost certainly a member of Carlos's Gang of Twenty. He's an Englishman named Wheeler."

Lucy moved to the wall where several score photographs and typed three-by-five index cards were taped in her gallery of suspects.

"But a number of our 'Probables' are much closer to becoming candidates for the Gang of Twenty board." She pointed to eight photographs of Oriental men. "Any one of these, for instance, might be joining Carlos for Operation *Hogar*."

"What does 'might' mean?" Hyphenated-Jake asked.

"You'll have to ask Mack about that," Lucy said.

"They are all members of the Japanese Red Army," Mack explained. "I'm not sure at the moment what their status is. Some of them were . . . injured . . . recently."

"That turkey on the end won't be doing much of anything for a while," Clem said, as he exchanged glances with Emilio. The photograph to which he referred was of the Japanese man he and Emilio had last seen rolling, his clothes afire, on the street in Mexico City.

"What happened to him?" Perry asked.

"He was fricasseed," Clem said, grinning.

"That's enough, Clem," Mack snapped.

"The point," Lucy continued, "is that we now have a great deal of information about the suspects, most of it collated and fed into my computer. I can push a button and Butterfly will give it back to me with any related data. But most of what we have is history, what all these people did in the past. Mack wants you to travel again for the *now* information. Where are they? Are they coming here to the States for Carlos's operation? In short, we need new, fresh information."

"How much more do we really know, now, about the specific operation Carlos is planning?" Skip asked.

"I do have some new information," Mack said. "The operation will take place before the end of January, probably sooner. Carlos plans to kidnap a U.S. government official—who and where I don't know—and fly him out of the country."

Lucy glanced at Frank; now she knew why he had taken Mack into the other room.

"But who?" Perry asked. "Which government official? Carlos will have to go pretty high in the pecking order to top the OPEC kidnapping. The president?"

"Could be," Mack said, "but I doubt that Carlos would challenge the phalanx of Secret Service men who always surround the president. But it could be the vice-president, the secretary of state, the chief of the joint chiefs of staff, the Director of Central Intelligence. Certainly someone of that rank."

Hyphenated-Jake expressed himself by whistling softly.

"Lucy will give you your assignment sheets for Phase Three," Mack said. Then he spoke emphatically: "Don't compare notes. Just get your job done, and be back with any new information for Lucy within ten days. And, before you travel, study Lucy's rogues' gallery again. Remember, Carlos may be using anyone from any of the terrorist groups, including German and Arab women."

For a moment no one moved and it was quiet. They are

beginning to understand, Mack told himself, just how hairy this operation has become. He wondered if the others were as frightened as he was.

The quiet was broken by Clem, who blurted out one of his old one-liners. As the others gathered around Lucy and inspected the stack of photographs Frank had taken at the Villa Hermosa, Mack drew Skip aside.

"Dinner?"

"Yes," Skip said. "If you promise not to visit an ice cream factory afterwards. I read in the *Post* about the Italian terrorist arrested near my place."

"That's a promise," Mack said. "I need to speak to Perry for just a minute, and then I'll try to wrangle a table at The Company Inkwell."

Mack spoke to Perry, alone.

"There's one base we haven't touched yet," Mack said. "Caracas. You said that the former Venezuelan security chief who set up your meeting with Carlos knew a lot about him, was even a friend of Carlos's father. Is he still in Caracas?"

"As far as I know," Perry said.

"Then let's visit him. Both of us will be traveling during the next few days, but let's meet in Venezuela. Call and see if he's there. If I don't hear from Frank or Lucy that he isn't, I'll meet you in the Tamanaco Hotel bar a week from Friday between noon and one. Okay?"

"Fine," Perry said. "I was beginning to feel left out of the action you promised. I'll see you at the Tamanaco."

The big, heavy man with the red face stood, heaving himself from his chair with obvious effort. Sir Michael was, Mack judged, six feet three and weighed close to two hundred fifty pounds. He wore a speckled coat, probably a Harris tweed. He took the briar pipe from his mouth and extended a huge paw to Mack.

"Good to see you again, McLendon." The chief of the British Secret Service shook Mack's hand enthusiastically. "I must say you look younger than when I saw you last—five years ago, I believe."

Mack, who was not feeling well at all, bone-weary from the night flight across the Atlantic which had arrived at Heathrow only two hours before, made an effort to respond in kind. He was, after all, in the presence of "C."

"It is very kind of you to see me on such short notice, Sir Michael."

"Not at all," was the bluff response. "Rollins here tells me you flew to London for the sole purpose of speaking with me for five minutes. A tedious journey for such a brief encounter. Do sit down." Sir Michael turned to Mitch. "You, too, Rollins."

The three men sat in their chairs in the paneled office, adorned with ancient volumes in bookshelves, and a carpet which must have been brought back to England from Arabia by some vice consul fifty years before. Sir Michael tamped his pipe, and spoke to Mack.

"I do have to run along shortly to see our foreign minister," Sir Michael said. "But I am *intensely* curious about what I can do for you in just five minutes."

"First," Mack said, "I want to thank you and Mitch for the word you sent to me in Washington about Wheeler, and his trip to New York."

"Not at all," Sir Michael said. "Nasty chap. Glad to have him out of the U.K. I won't be at all dismayed, in fact, if he never returns."

"Secondly," Mack said, "I want to borrow Mr. Rubbers."

"Mr. Rubbers?" Sir Michael turned to Mitch Rollins, who formed with his lips a name Mack could not discern.

"Oh. How curious! Why in the world would you want to . . . borrow . . . Mr. Rubbers?"

"Every service has its resident expert on terrorism and terrorists," Mack said. "I understand from Mitch that Mr. Rubbers is your man. I would like him, on loan, for a few days."

Mitch interjected: "I told him, Sir, that it was im—"

"A moment, Rollins." Sir Michael peered at Mack. "How could Mr. Rubbers be of use to you?"

"I'm sure Mitch has explained that I'm attempting to thwart

an operation by Carlos which will occur soon in the United States. I need Mr. Rubbers to come along and help us spot Carlos and his cohorts."

Sir Michael turned to Mitch Rollins. "Has . . . uh . . . Mr. Rubbers ever had an overseas assignment?"

"I believe, sir," Mitch said, "that he has never been farther from London than Brighton, where he vacations summers."

The MI–6 chief turned back to Mack. "In that case I really don't believe I should trust the innocent overseas, most especially when he would be engaged with a terrorist such as Carlos."

"He will not be involved in an operation," Mack said. "I need him to assist a woman now working with me. She, like myself, was once with the CIA, and was, more or less, the counterpart of your Mr. Rubbers."

"There's no physical danger involved?"

"No, Sir Michael. Mr. Rubbers would be removed from any action aspects of the operation. But, with his knowledge of terrorists and terrorism, his presence would be invaluable."

"His presence where?" Sir Michael asked.

"I'm not quite sure," Mack replied. "Somewhere on the eastern coast of the United States, sometime in the next few weeks." Mack saw Sir Michael and Mitch Rollins exchange glances. "I would, of course, be responsible for any expense involved."

Sir Michael looked at his watch. "I really must run along." He rose, and walked to the window. After a moment he turned to Mack. "I recently had lunch with your new CIA chief. Staunch enough fellow. He assured me that your efforts against Carlos were only indirectly connected with your government. I would like to help. You may have Mr. Rubbers, on two conditions."

"They are, sir?" Mack asked.

"One: if your operation is successful I will expect you to pass to our service all the intelligence you have acquired during your endeavor. Tit for tat type thing. Two: if your operation succeeds, you will send me a letter stating that your

British cousins were instrumental in achieving success. I would expect such a note even if it were hyperbole. I don't know how your fiscal year works out in America, McLendon, but we are approaching budget time here. I need money to keep Her Majesty's Secret Intelligence Service on track. The morale of my officers is low; our capabilities have been reduced drastically—to no small degree, I might add, because of the debris washed up on this side of the Atlantic following the tidal wave of criticism of your service in Washington. I warn you that I might even exaggerate somewhat our role in the demise of Carlos, should it occur, in order to justify my new budget. Are those conditions acceptable to you?"

"Absolutely, sir," Mack said.

"Prepare Mr. . . . uh . . . Rubbers for his assignment," Sir Michael instructed Mitch Rollins. "He probably hasn't had a physical for twenty years."

Sir Michael offered Mack his large hand.

"Good-bye, McLendon, and good luck. Any man who would try to neutralize Carlos and nurse our Mr. Rubbers at the same time deserves my condolences."

Mack sipped a cup of coffee while he waited for Boris Seymonov to appear for his morning swim. The beach crew which cleaned up Copacabana each morning, wearing bright orange shortsleeved shirts and shorts, moved southward filling their bags with rubbish and smoothing out the sand with long-handled rakes. No sooner would they pass, however, than the surface of the beach would be dappled with the footprints of soccer players and featherball buffs. The December sun was blazing, even at that early hour of the morning.

Boris Seymonov, wearing only his bathing suit and black swim cap, came out of his apartment building and jogged through the warm sand toward the Atlantic. Halfway to the water's edge he saw Mack, and approached him.

"You are here, William, without invitation," Seymonov said, his countenance grim. "Nor, as far as I am aware, did you even telephone to verify that I was in Rio."

"I haven't heard from you, Boris."

"Because I have been instructed not to see you again, or to talk to you. I am going to take my swim. Please do not be here when I return."

Seymonov ran to the surf and plunged into a breaking wave. He swam out to sea until his black rubber cap was a speck bobbing in the water.

Mack waited. Ten minutes. Fifteen. Twenty.

Finally Seymonov swam slowly back to shore and, shaking his body as a dog will to rid himself of dripping water, approached Mack again.

"I told you, William. I cannot see you."

"Why, Boris?"

"Orders from headquarters. The center did not react to your threat of blackmail. The reply to my cable was negative. My service will not support your charade against Carlos, and I, personally, am to avoid contact with you."

"Carlos has murdered another of our station chiefs," Mack said.

"In Mexico?"

Mack nodded.

"Yes, I read of Bond's death. I knew him slightly when we were in Tokyo. I'm sorry, William."

"Then help me, Boris, if you hear of anything. I now know what Carlos is planning, and approximately when. It will be in the United States, as you told me before. I need to know where. Is there no chance you can find out from the two Puerto Ricans you told me about?"

"That contact," Seymonov said, "is . . . indirect."

"Through the Cubans?" Mack asked.

Seymonov did not reply.

"You still have my telephone number in Washington. Let me know if you can."

"How strange," Seymonov said. "The world's most notorious terrorist is now stalking his victims in the United States, yet it is a retired intelligence officer who attempts to thwart him. Are your government services in such low repute, is their morale so bad, are their capabilities so diminished that protecting your nation's safety must be the task of a—pardon me, William—burnt-out case?"

Seymonov paused long enough to admire a lithe, bikini-clad girl.

"In the Soviet Union, William, it is different. Our intelligence officers are highly thought of, and given the highest honors when they are successful. Colonel Abel is a hero of the students in our schools. Philby, they tell me, has one of the three Rolls-Royces to be found in Moscow. We have even had an opera about a spy—*Richard Sorge,* the story of our agent in Japan who provided us with the precise date of the Nazi invasion in 1941."

"But," Mack said, "Stalin refused to believe the information. So Sorge, who was hanged by the Japanese, worked for nothing."

"True." Seymonov sighed. "As I told you before, our work is not that of the Boy Scouts. Good-bye, William. Do not contact me again. It will be dangerous for me."

Seymonov turned away, ran quickly with long steps across the hot beach, and disappeared into his apartment building.

"Fifty bucks," Mack said. "I had to pay the room clerk fifty bucks before he was able to find, to his astonishment, that he did have a room available after all."

"Hotel rooms are tight in Caracas," Perry said. "I had the same problem, but because of my Venezuelan accent paid only twenty. The clerks always keep a few rooms on standby these days."

Perry and Mack had met in the bar at the Hotel Tamanaco, as they had planned to do before leaving Washington. Now Perry was chatting in his fluent Spanish with the driver as their taxi ground up a winding street in the hills above the Venezuelan capital. Below them the lights in the center of Caracas were a bright blaze until they stretched out toward the suburbs into a maze of soft twinkles. The illumination stopped sharply at the mountain which stood between Caracas and the airport at the port of La Guaira. Here the darkness was broken only by the distant strand of lights on the funicular ascending to the circular hotel on the top of the mountain.

"Tell me about Lorca's background," Mack said.

"Roberto Lorca," Perry said. "He will be pleased if you address him as *Doctor* Lorca; he has a law degree. He will expect me to refer to him as Don Roberto. He immigrated to Venezuela in the thirties, while he was still a young man, when his father was imprisoned in Spain. His father later died in one of Franco's jails. Roberto Lorca became a Venezuelan citizen. He went to work with the civilian security service and became something of a national hero because of his success in countering Castro's efforts to sabotage the elections in 1958. He had some help from the Agency in doing it, and has been a friend of Uncle Sam since. He became chief of the service around 1970. I've met him only once, when he improvised the 1973 meeting during which I tried to recruit Carlos. He lost his job when a new party came into power later that year. I don't know what he's been doing since, but when I talked to him on the telephone he said life was treating him well, and he looked forward to seeing us tonight."

"Was he curious about me?" Mack asked.

"No. I only said you were a former colleague named Williams and that we wanted to consult him on a matter of some urgency. He's not the kind of person you might expect. He's a cultured man, fond of the best in everything—music, books, fine food." Perry waved his hand at the expensive houses along the road they were traveling. "He must have money now. Houses in this section of Caracas go for the same price as the ones in Beverly Hills. I wonder if he went on the take when he knew he would be losing his job?"

The taxi stopped at an entrance gate in a high wall which blocked off the view of the city. Perry paid the driver while Mack rang the bell.

"¿Quien?" The query came through an intercom.

"It's Perry Allison, Don Roberto. And his friend."

"One moment. It will take time for me to reach the gate."

It was several minutes before Lorca opened the door to welcome his guests. He was breathing heavily.

"*Perricito!*" Lorca exclaimed, as the two men embraced.

"Don Roberto." Perry turned to Mack. "Please meet my friend, Sr. Williams."

"You are welcome, Sr. Williams. Come in, come in."

When they passed through the gate Mack could understand why Lorca was short of breath. To meet them he had ascended a long flight of steps through a garden, leading up from one section of his home. To their right was an illumined pool, the pale blue water flecked with red and gold tropical fish. The garden dropped precipitously to another brightly lit pool, its slightly larger surface strewn with water lilies, its depths alive with colorful fish.

"Follow me," Lorca said. "You must see my home. We are alone. I sent away the servant for the night so that we could talk freely. But first we will drink and dine. Come."

Lorca, stepping carefully, led them down the stairs. He was a very tall man, even taller than Perry, with a slender body and a sallow, Spanish face. He wore extremely thick glasses. Exhibiting the customary caution of a man with poor vision, he looked at his feet as he went down the stairs.

When they reached the first landing Lorca led them through his dining room and, with evident pleasure, a large modern kitchen. He indicated a parlor on the side of the landing, then led them through another door.

"Regard," Lorca said.

"Incredible," Perry said. "Don Roberto, this is the sexiest house I've ever seen."

"It is," Lorca acknowledged, "exotic."

A second flight of stairs, like an ornate ship's gangplank, went to the upper story of what was, in fact, a completely separate house. And a third stairway went down to the lower floor of that building. Dozens of tropical plants hung at different levels and orchids were in bloom. A third pool separated the two sections of the home, gleaming like the others from submerged lights.

Lorca led the way into his living room. The furnishings were elaborate but in good taste; one end of the enormous room was covered with paintings, the other with bookshelves from floor to ceiling. The remaining two walls were glass. The lights of Caracas spread like a blanket of jewels two thousand feet below.

"One final exhibition," Lorca said, "and the tour will be finished."

Lorca walked to the entrance and flipped a switch. He turned and looked at the pool which ran the entire length of the room outside the plate glass and under the stairs leading to the upper house. In a moment the waterfall began, slowly at first, then until it was a cascade spilling a thick shaft of silver water into the pool.

"Fantastic!" Perry exclaimed.

"I am impressed," Mack added.

"I designed the system myself," Lorca said. "A pump takes the water from the lower pool and raises it eighty feet to the first pool, the one near the gate you entered. From there it goes by pipe to the second pool and then here to the lower house in the form of an instant waterfall, which stops or flows at my command. Is it not ingenious?"

Without waiting for a reply Lorca went to a cabinet filled with liquor bottles. He picked up a bottle of Chivas Regal and turned to his visitors. "You will have scotch?"

"Thanks," Perry said, "straight, please."

"If you don't mind, Dr. Lorca, I would prefer gin on ice, with a few drops of cognac."

"Of course, Mr. Williams. Forgive me. You see here in Venezuela one presumes that a guest will drink scotch. There is an interesting statistic: more Scotch whiskey is consumed per capita in Venezuela than in any other country in the world—including Scotland!"

Lorca made the drinks and handed them to Mack and Perry. He poured his own scotch on ice in a crystal tumbler.

"Before we sit, gentlemen, see this lovely thing." Lorca motioned to a plant which hung in long tendrils beside the artificial waterfall. A single bloom, just opening, adorned the plant. "In English it is known as the night-blooming cereus. In Spanish we call it *Belle de Baile*—Beauty of the Ball—as it blooms just once during the year, and then always at night, opening to its fullest at midnight. Then the bloom closes, not to reappear until another year passes. Now we will drink, then have the dinner prepared before I send my cook away to insure our privacy. Then we will talk."

"You said that life was treating you well," Perry said. "I can see that it is."

"I have been fortunate," Lorca said, looking directly at Perry. "Since last we met I have . . . uh . . . come into some money. It is a pleasure, I find, to spend money for beautiful things."

Lorca turned to Mack. "You must think me a sybarite, Mr. Williams. For many years I was poor, living on a bureaucrat's salary. My wife died when she was very young, leaving me with only one child, and I have never remarried. Now my son has his degree and has made me a grandfather twice over. This house will be his, and all the fine things in it." Lorca motioned toward the bookshelves. "My collection of Garcia-Lorca—he was a distant relative—most of them first editions and signed by the author. My records. The paintings, some of them quite valuable. Even the stamp collection, which my son and I began together when he was fourteen."

The three men talked over a second drink. Then Mack spoke.

"Perry told you why we have come to Venezuela to see you, Dr. Lorca?"

"Yes," Lorca said. "You want to ask me about Carlos. His father is a millionaire, you know, and lives not two miles from this house. I see him occasionally at my club; we even play a game of dominoes from time to time. But as for his son, I have not seen Carlos—Ilyich—since 1973 when I introduced him to Perry. An unsuccessful attempt at recruitment, alas."

"But if you will tell us everything you can it might help. Any detail, however trivial, which might assist our investigation."

"With pleasure, Mr. Williams. But first we must dine.

Then I will reach back as far as—"

A buzz interrupted.

"Excuse me," Lorca requested. He went to the intercom. "Yes, who is it?" Lorca listened. "All right. It will be a minute."

Lorca turned to his guests. "Someone is at the gate, to deliver flowers, they say. I know of no occasion . . ."

Mack stood. "Allow me, Dr. Lorca."

"No, no, please sit down, Mr. Williams. The voice was female. Of course I must satisfy my own curiosity as to what lady brings me flowers."

Lorca started climbing the stairs.

Perry went to the bar and made himself another drink. When he finished he turned to Mack. "One more?"

"No thanks," Mack said. "I imagine Lorca will serve wine, and that'll do for me."

Mack and Perry talked for a few minutes about the house, Lorca's devotion to it, and the fine things it contained.

Finally Mack said, "Lorca's taking a long time. Do you suppose—"

Mack broke off in mid-sentence. Perry was staring past him, his eyes wide.

"Mack, look! The waterfall—it's changing color!"

Mack turned. Where there had been a silver white cascade, there was now a torrent streaked with pink.

"Blood!" Mack exclaimed. "Let's go!"

Mack and Perry ran up the stairs, taking three steps at a time, until they reached the landing at the front gate.

Roberto Lorca was floating, face down, in the upper pool. In the water, like flowers at a funeral bier, dozens of red roses surrounded his body.

Perry jumped into the water and propelled Lorca's body to the edge of the pool, then lifted himself out to help Mack pull the former security chief onto the grass. Mack turned over the inert figure. Lorca's breast was wet with water and blood: he had been stabbled repeatedly, and his throat was cut so deeply that his severed windpipe was visible.

"He's dead," Mack said.

"No way?" Perry asked.

"No way," Mack said. "He just can't be put back together again." Mack stood, and went to the pool. He plucked one red rose from the surface of the water.

"The Red Morning group," Mack said, twisting the flower in his fingers. "How stupid I was not to suspect something when Lorca told us a woman was delivering flowers. Carlos is really moving his troops around the world. There must have been at least two of them to have overpowered Lorca, even after they got a knife in him the first time. Carlos's imported *frauleins*."

"What are we going to do, Mack?"

"Get the hell out of here. But two things first: you go down and wipe clean anything that might have our prints; I'll call the police and tell them to start looking for German girls who have entered Venezuela recently."

Mack and Perry walked a dozen blocks before taking a bus, then a taxi to their hotel. They checked out and rode in another cab the twenty miles down the mountain to the Caracas airport. The first flight out was the same Mack had flown into Venezuela, the Pan Am plane from Rio de Janeiro which stopped in Caracas en route to Miami.

Two seats were available in the tourist section. There was a long wait. Mack stopped a passing stewardess.

"What's the delay?"

"Some sort of fuss at the ticket counter," the stewardess replied. "The police took away two young German girls who were about to board. I don't know why. But we're cleared now for takeoff."

"Two young girls." Perry shuddered. "I'm scared shitless, Mack. Carlos knows everything we're doing, everywhere we go."

"Yes." Mack was pulling at his earlobe. "Perry, is your Spanish accent authentically Venezuelan?"

"Sure. I was born here, and didn't leave until I was in my teens."

"I was listening carefully, without knowing why, when you were talking with the taxi driver on the way to Lorca's." Mack paused; he was clearly troubled. "Now I know why. It made me think back to the night I had that telephone call from a

man claiming to be Carlos. Perry, it wasn't Carlos. It was someone impersonating Carlos."

"How do you know?"

"Because two nights before I had dinner with Skip at The
Angler's Inn. I chatted with the waiter. He was an Uruguayan
and spoke with the same accent as the man who telephoned
me at the apartment."

"Jesus, Mack. What does that mean?"

"I'm not sure," Mack replied. But he did know. It meant
grandmother was on the roof.

The jet roared down the runway, soared over the Caribbean,
and banked toward Florida.

7.

Mack made his fifth call to Symser the next day.

"Yes," Symser said, "I'm at telephone Alpha. And I appreciate the fact that it's not the middle of the night. I'll be able to go right on from here to my office."

"A routine report," Mack said. "We've been traveling, and now we're preparing to collate our information. It's going relatively well."

"Not with Scott-Wagner," Symser said. "One of our local managers was kidnapped yesterday in Ecuador. We had hoped you were keeping Carlos sufficiently occupied so that he wouldn't be molesting our people. The abductors are demanding $500,000 for his release."

"That won't be a Carlos operation," Mack said. "He's beyond such picayune activities. And, anyway, we have been keeping him jumping." He paused a moment and then continued. "Really, you mustn't believe that putting Carlos out of business will solve all your problems overseas. International terrorism is going to be with us for a while. The most recent statistics I've seen were for 1976, but they showed that more incidents of terrorism had occurred that year than ever before, and that the percentage of actions directed against Americans and American firms had increased. Removing Carlos from the scene will help you, but won't, by any means, make the problem go away."

"I'm sure you're right," Symser said. "Is there anything I can report to Crassweiler? I believe you are in . . . was it Phase Three of the operation?"

"That's right."

"Have you located Carlos and his bunch? Do you know yet what they plan to do next?"

"We've had some luck," Mack said. "We know enough now that we might go into Phase Four any day. Perhaps before Christmas."

"Let me know if there is anything I can do," Symser said. "How's the money holding out?" The question was cautiously put.

"I doubt there'll be more extraordinary expenses—unless that insurance company which is covering me and my friends finds that it's made a bad investment. Carlos is still trying to kill me and the people who are in a position to help me. I'll be glad to see the end of this operation."

"It's amazing," Symser said, "what you've done on your own thus far."

"With help from others," Mack said. "Even some international assistance. I'm on my way now, as a matter of fact, to meet with someone who might really be in a position to participate in the final act of this show. I'll keep in touch, Mr. Symser."

Philip Layton was standing in front of the bas-relief world map in The National Geographic Building when Mack entered the lobby. He approached the journalist and stood beside him.

"Good morning, Mack."

"Good morning, Phil."

"As you can see," Layton said, pointing to the huge map, "it's bedtime in Tel Aviv."

"Before the office closed," Mack asked, "did anyone respond to your message?"

"Yes," Layton said. "Have you ever been in this building, Mack?"

"No."

"Convenient to my office. And one of the few places in town where you will never see a Washingtonian—sort of like the Statue of Liberty in New York, frequented only by tourists. Let's see the exhibition."

Mack and Layton strolled through the small but expertly designed museum.

"What was the response?" Mack asked.

"Somewhat to my surprise," Layton said, "Tel Aviv has given in to your threat. They have asked me to pass on certain information. First, Carlos is using a trusted lieutenant named Khalil in his upcoming operation."

"Yes, I had presumed that. But what is the operation?"

"An abduction," Layton replied. "Carlos is planning to kidnap one of your government officials."

"Who?"

"We don't know."

"Where?"

"Somewhere near Washington. How near we don't know."

"Why? Simply for ransom? To make some demands related to the Middle East?"

"We don't know the motives behind the abduction," Layton said. "Only that it has been meticulously planned over a long period and Carlos has invested a great deal of time and money in the operation. It must be something transcendental, if it is to compare with the OPEC kidnappings. But, according to our source, Carlos has run into a problem of some kind with his support apparat; nevertheless he has instructed his people to proceed with the operation."

The two men were quiet as a tourist leaned between them to read the inscription describing an exhibit. Then the intruder moved on.

"I want to thank you and your people in Tel Aviv," Mack said, "but your information is more frustrating than anything else. You've been telling me things I already know."

Layton smiled. "We've come up with negatives on who, where, and why. The what is the abduction. But if you were a newsman, Mack, you would ask one more question."

"When?"

"That's it," Layton said. "The kidnapping is to occur three days from now. Now you have at least two of the elements needed for a good lead paragraph."

"How good is your information?"

"Reliable," Layton said.

"You do have Carlos's group penetrated, then?"

Layton shrugged.

"You must have an agent working for Carlos," Mack said. "That kind of information doesn't come from analysts. What role will your agent play?"

"When we last heard from him, which was some time ago, he knew only that he would be one of a five-member squad under Khalil's command, and that they would pretend to be airport employees while carrying out the abduction."

"Five in the squad?" Mack was perplexed. "I've had information that Carlos would utilize twenty of his people. Would he attempt to kidnap an important U.S. official with only five?"

"In Vienna," Layton reminded Mack, "Carlos, Khalil, and four others killed three people, held seventy hostages in the OPEC offices, some of them among the then most powerful men in the world, and eventually flew out of Austria with forty-two hostages, including eleven oil ministers."

"Has your agent said where he will be going when the victim, whoever he might be, is flown from the country?"

"On the contrary," Layton said. "He has told us that he will remain in this country, a member of a team which will guard the hostage wherever he is hidden."

"Anything else you can tell me?" Mack asked.

"Nothing. At least for now." Layton paused. "I told you I was surprised that Tel Aviv agreed to pass information to you from our man. In fact, I'm astonished. Our agent has been working for five years to insinuate himself into Carlos's group, and was only recently successful. I had thought he would be saved to thwart an operation against Israel, not against this country."

"Maybe," Mack said, "your chiefs realized what a flap there would be if it was revealed that you, a prominent American journalist, are a spook. When do you expect the agent's next report?"

"That's the pity of it," Layton said. "Now that Carlos's operation is in the final stages, he may not have the opportunity to report to us again. You've been in the counterterrorist trade a long time, Mack. You know how these things work. No chance to use a telephone. No time to write a note and no opportunity to mail one."

"Yes," Mack said. "Once a terrorist cell is briefed on the final details of its mission, no one is allowed to be alone."

"Precisely," Layton said.

"Once in Latin America," Mack recalled, "the American ambassador was kidnapped and held for two weeks. I was the station chief, and had an agent in the cell assigned the task of keeping the ambassador hidden. He was no help, though; they wouldn't even let him, or any of the other terrorists, go to the john alone."

Layton looked at his watch. "I must go, Mack. There's really nothing else I can tell you, unless the agent manages to convey additional information. But I doubt that will occur."

"I need one more thing," Mack said. "Your service must have one person who is an expert on individual terrorists. I may need him, or her, very shortly. A temporary duty assignment."

"Not a chance!" Layton scoffed. "Not a chance Tel Aviv would agree to that."

"Advise them to mull it," Mack said. "I'll need such a person to help me trap Carlos and Khalil and the rest. Think of the haul. Your WOG teams have been after most of this bunch for years."

"Exaggeration," Layton protested. "All those stories about WOG teams assassinating people are greatly exaggerated."

"I recall reading," Mack said, "that Golda Meir made a speech on the floor of your Parliament, a few days after Munich, saying that Israel intended to track down terrorists wherever they could be found. Carlos has assembled a group of anti-Zionist killers. Tell your headquarters they will be able to claim credit when I finally net all of them."

"All right, Mack. I'll alert them, but I doubt they'll agree."

"And send thanks for their information."

"I will." Layton reached out to shake Mack's hand. "Merry Christmas."

Mack's team was gathered, once again, around the dining room table in the safehouse headquarters. Mack spoke to them.

"If everything goes all right," Mack said, "you'll all be home by Christmas. We know more now than when we last met. Then we knew only that Carlos's Operation *Hogar* called for the abduction of a senior U.S. official. That's been confirmed, several times over. But we still don't know who that official is, or what Carlos plans to gain from the kidnapping, or precisely where it will take place. All we do know is that it will be somewhere near Washington. We have about seventy-two hours to find the answers to those other questions, because the operation will take place three days from now."

"There's another photograph on Lucy's board," Hyphenated-Jake said. "Who else do we think will be involved?"

"That's Khalil," Lucy said. "He was at the top of the list from the beginning, because he's worked with Carlos before."

"And," Mack added, "he's the one man we know of with the balls to carry on with the rest of the group if anything ever happens to Carlos. We want him."

"I'm nervous about this," Emilio said. "Isn't it time we notified the proper people around government, here in Washington? I don't want to be a part of some snafu where one of our top officials is kidnapped or harmed because we've been so cozy."

"Yes," Mack said. "We're closer to that time. But I don't want word to get back to Carlos that his target has been alerted. He'll cancel the operation and then we'll be back at square one."

"We still have those questions without answers," Clem observed. "What can we do to find them?"

"Lucy and Frank have drawn up a list of assignments for each of you," Mack said. "We have seventy-two hours."

"The first assignment is for you, Clem," Lucy said. "The customs service here has about 2,000 names and 5,000 passport numbers in their computer—all of them political crackpots, criminals or suspected terrorists. I have a list of names and passport numbers I need checked through their system. Do you have friends at Customs?"

"Sure," Clem said. "The number-three man is an old pal from our days together on the Texas border. I can manage it."

"I agree with Emilio," Perry said. "We should be talking with the FBI and the Secret Service."

"If necessary," Mack said, "but not yet. We're too close to wrapping up Carlos and his entire gang to trust the operation to the bureaucrats. But, in addition to trying to put more candidates on Lucy's board, we need to do all the scratching we can to find out who Carlos's intended victim is. We need to obtain the personal agenda for the next few days, and especially for three days from now, of all the wheels in Washington, beginning with the president. Each of you will have places to visit and people to see, with the single objective of getting those schedules. The vice-president, the secretary of state, congressional leaders, the VIP bunch." Mack turned toward Skip. "You need to find out what the Director's plans are."

"I'll call Cook," Skip said.

"We'll meet here again tomorrow at eleven in the morning," Mack said. "Meanwhile go about your work. But from this time on it's strictly the buddy system. Work in pairs. None of us is to be alone. No telephone calls unless someone else hears what you are saying. No letters. No notes dropped out of windows. Sack out here in the apartment if you like. If you need clothes, or want to buy something, take someone with you. Let Lucy or Frank know where you can be reached at all times."

"I'm not so sure I'll buy that," Emilio said, his face flushed. "What you're saying is that you don't trust us. Maybe I'll just tell you to take your goddamned op and stick it."

"Just for three days, Emilio. We have a problem. There's a strong possibility that one of us is leaking information, intentionally or unintentionally, to Carlos. Maybe not. But whatever the case, the safest thing for all of us is to see to it there's no way anyone can communicate outside our circle until this operation is over." Mack stood. "I'll see you all tomorrow at eleven."

When the meeting was finished Mack spoke to Skip. "Shall we go in your car, or mine?"

"Where?" Skip asked.

"To your place," Mack said. "I'm going to spend the night with you. My muffler's been fixed, and the car's parked down the street."

"Don't you trust anyone, Mack?"

"It's not just a question of trust, Skip. Carlos is still trying to kill me and my friends. I don't want you to be alone tonight. And there's another reason." Mack reached out to touch the Haitian amulet. "If I stay with you enough, things are bound to go my way, sooner or later."

Skip smiled. "I like that reason better. I'll call Cook, then we'll go in my car. It's more reliable."

Skip and Mack were drinking Kahlua on the rocks in front of the fire when the doorbell rang.

"That will be Willard Cook," Skip said, rising gracefully from the floor where she had been sitting at Mack's feet. She went to the door and opened it.

"My God, but it's freezing out there," Cook said. "There'll be ice on the road tonight for sure." He took off his coat and handed it to Skip, who hung it in a closet near the door.

"What about something to warm you up?" Skip asked.

"A quick one," Cook said. "Shot of brandy, if you have it. Have to pick up my wife at the PTA meeting. Seems some of the kids have been breaking windows at the school and our boy is the ringleader. Hi, Mack." Cook warmed his hands at the fire.

"Hello, Will. What's new at the Pickle Factory?"

"Everything is about the same," Cook said. "Because of the energy shortage the lights are so low you can't recognize your friends in the halls. Wouldn't want to, anyway; morale's so low the conversation is depressing. They just announced another personnel cut in the DDO. This town is soon going to be filled with unemployable ex-spooks."

"Here, Willard." Skip offered a brandy snifter.

"Cheers," Cook said lamely. He drank half the cognac in one swallow. "Remember when the spy business used to be fun?"

"Do you have the Director's schedule?" Mack asked.

"That's why I'm here," Cook said. "He asked me to deliver it to you personally—but not before you answer some questions."

"What questions?"

"First, what makes you think that Carlos, or the Sovs or Cubans, have a penetration of the Agency? The Director has the counterintelligence crew working nights looking for an American Philby."

"I've never said I believed that," Mack said. "Although it's always a possibility."

"Then why won't Skip tell us what the hell you're up to? I've never seen anything like it in my twenty-two years with the Company. One of our own officers refuses to tell us how she's spending her time. It was part of our agreement—we pass on FOI information on Carlos, and Skip stays out of operations. Do you remember, Skip?"

"Of course, Willard." Skip blinked her eyes innocently. "I'm just a fly on the wall when I'm with Mack."

"I've asked Skip not to brief you on our operation," Mack explained, "simply because we are being careful. If the Agency doesn't know what we're doing, it won't be responsible if things go wrong, and there won't be a leak if Langley is penetrated."

"What the hell are you doing? That's what the Director wants to know. The cables have been coming in from all over, from Europe, the Mediterranean, the Caribbean. That wild-eyed crew of yours is breaking regs all over the world. What are they doing?"

"Have you forgotten, Will, that it was you who persuaded me to take on this assignment for Symser? How do you think we're going to catch Carlos—by sneaking up behind him and putting salt on his tail?"

Cook finished the brandy with a second gulp. "But Jesus Christ, Mack, what are your cowboys doing? The damage assessments from the stations they've visited are scaring the hell out of the Director. If this keeps up he could be called down to the Senate committee to explain why your wild bunch has been breaking laws in two dozen countries."

"We're engaged in espionage and covert action," Mack said. "Specifically, we're in the serious business of counterterrorism, which involves some of both. I don't know how to conduct such an operation using the rules and moral standards which prevail at Sunnybrook Farm. I realize the Director is new, but you might remind him that espionage and covert action are illegal in every country in the world. What is it that bothers him so much?"

"You've been contacting our liaison services," Cook said.

"That's true," Mack said. "They seem to be more comfortable working with me than with the Agency these days."

"Your crew has been contacting their old agents, some of whom are still working for us."

Mack shrugged.

"At least two of them have been blackmailing our agents, forcing them to cooperate."

"I know," Mack said, sipping his drink. "It's a dirty business, all right."

"Your people have been in touch with criminal elements."

Mack nodded.

"They've also been soliciting information from, even recruiting, people on the no-no list. Newsmen, for instance. You know that contact with journalists is against the rules now."

"Your rules," Mack said, "not mine. I'm trying to be very careful about whatever we do domestically, because I don't want to go to prison, nor cause my friends to go. Otherwise there are no rules in a knife fight with someone like Carlos. If it will soothe the Director, tell him I solemnly promise not to approach anyone in the Peace Corps."

"It's no joke, Mack." Cook's face flushed. "We might find ourselves in a shitpot full of trouble because of what you're doing. Fred Bond dead in your hotel room in Mexico City. Lorca found with his throat cut in Caracas, while two men fitting descriptions of Perry Allison and you are seen leaving on the next flight out. Nothing very funny about those developments."

"No, nothing amusing about them at all." Mack lit a cigarette, his hand shaking. Skip reached out to put her hand on Mack's, then she turned to Willard Cook.

"I've known Mack for a long time," Skip said, looking straight at Cook, "and I've never seen him as furious as he is at this moment. I suggest that you knock it off—now."

"Do you have the list of the Director's appointments?" Mack asked.

Cook did not reply, but reached inside his coat pocket and removed an envelope, which he handed to Mack.

"Does this include everything he plans to do three days from now, on the nineteenth of December?"

Cook nodded.

"Then our business is finished," Mack said. "Toddle along to the PTA meeting."

Cook rose and went to the door. Skip followed to give him his coat. As Cook opened the door, Mack called after him.

"Will, I want you to deliver a message to the Director."

"What message?"

"This." Mack held one little finger in the air.

"What's that supposed to mean?" Cook asked.

"The little finger," Mack explained, "is when you don't want to send the best."

Cook turned and stalked out. Skip shut the door behind him, leaned against it, and exhaled slowly. Then she walked to Mack and stood beside his chair. Mack was staring glumly at the fire.

Skip put her hand under Mack's chin, tilted his head toward her, leaned down, and kissed him on the lips. Then she stood again.

"What about a stiff one now? You deserve it."

"Thanks, Skip. I'm fine. Just sit with me."

Skip sat on the floor, her body between Mack's knees, and leaned back so that their bodies were touching. For several minutes they did not speak. There was an occasional pop from a dying ember. The music from Skip's stereo was low and tranquilizing. Finally Mack spoke.

"Where do I sleep tonight, Skip? On the sofa?"

"No," Skip said. "With me."

"I'm not sure I can handle another night as frustrating as the last one we had here."

"Nor can I." Skip turned her head so that her lips were brushing the hairs on the back of Mack's wrist. "God knows I don't want to do that again—to either of us."

"I understand about Webb," Mack said. "But I'm a big boy and you're a big girl. Big boys and big girls shouldn't spend the night together without loving each other."

"There's something Puritan in me that's been fighting to escape," Skip said. "I think it will tonight. I'm tired of loving you in a dream, remembering the time we were together in Haiti. Tired of fantasies, my hand between my legs. And it's always you, Mack. I imagine all sorts of things. Kinky things, sometimes. And it's always you."

The telephone rang.

"Shall I take it off the hook?" Skip asked.

"Better not," Mack said.

Skip rose and went to the telephone. She listened, then turned to Mack.

"It's Lucy. She says it's urgent."

Mack went to the telephone.

"Yes, Lucy?"

"I just had a call from a man who identified himself as Boris. He said you would know him. He wanted the number where you could be reached. I wouldn't give it to him."

"I know him," Mack said. "Was it an overseas call?"

"No. He gave me the number of a local pay phone. He said he would be waiting to answer it. That you should call at once, because it was important."

"Give me the number," Mack said. He poised the pencil attached to a notepad near Skip's telephone and jotted the number on the pad.

"Thanks, Lucy. It may be an elephant." Mack hung up.

"What was all that?" Skip asked. "What's an elephant?"

"A man from Rio de Janeiro," Mack said. "I saw him there only a few days ago. Now he wants to talk to me here."

"Go ahead," Skip said. "Call him."

"He's a Russian. A KGB officer. I believe he's a friend, but it could be a provocation. Why don't you pick up the extension in your bedroom? Make notes, because it could turn out to be important—one way or the other."

"All right." Skip turned and went into her bedroom.

Mack dialed the number and, when he heard the first ring, called to Skip. "Okay!" He could hear the click as Skip picked up the extension.

"Yes?"

"Boris?"

"This is William?"

"Yes, Boris. Where are you?"

"In the lobby of a shabby hotel in your nation's capital."

"Why are you here?"

"I have been called back to Moscow for temporary duty. They told me it was to serve on a promotion panel. Perhaps that is true, although there is the possibility I will be questioned about our meetings in Rio, especially if we were detected together during your most recent visit. Foolishly, I did not report that encounter. The matter has taken a serious turn. At this moment a security man from my embassy here is seated in an all-night restaurant across the street from this hotel—a clumsy surveillance I easily detected."

"Why are you in Washington, Boris?"

"I came to keep an option open, William. You. My flight from Rio terminated in New York, where I was to wait for the Aeroflot plane which departs tomorrow afternoon. The regular courier in our office at the United Nations mission was ill. I volunteered to carry the pouch to Washington for him. Generally couriers stay at the embassy overnight, but I wanted to talk to you so I used a device which is venerated in my service: I told the chief of center that I would be spending the night with a lady friend."

"What is the option you want to keep open, Boris?"

"The possibility that I might need a friend in the West," the Russian said. "I have no intention of becoming a traitor, but neither am I fool enough to remain passive if threatened with Siberia, or worse. You were interested in the activities of the Puerto Ricans working with Carlos. In New York I found that one is a pilot who recently rented an aircraft to perform a mission for Carlos. My colleagues in New York have been following the affair with detached amusement, monitoring developments in an . . . indirect manner."

"The Puerto Rican," Mack said, "talks to the Cubans and someone in the Cuban service gossips with your friends?"

"Something like that, William," Seymonov said. "In New York I found myself alone in an office. On the desk was a report concerning the Puerto Rican who works for Carlos. Attached to the report was a map of the State of Virginia, and to the map, a chart of some kind. It appeared to be a magnification of an aerial chart with the location of a landing strip. I could make no sense at all from the chart, but I made a copy for you. A gift, intended to keep my option open."

"I need the gift, Boris, and somehow I must get it from you tonight."

"That will not be necessary, William. For all my good intentions it will be useless. As I was leaving the office in New York, the chart in my pocket, I was informed that the Puerto Rican's mission for Carlos has been cancelled. He will not be flying the plane; it has already been returned to the company from which he rented it. So the chart is history; of no value."

"It might be of great value," Mack said. "Do you still have it?"

"Yes."

"Boris, I must see you. Tonight, or tomorrow morning at the latest."

"No, William, it is impossible. I must return to New York in the morning. The man across the street might be relieved by another. Certainly there will be someone watching when I leave the hotel tomorrow to go to the airport. It could be a routine surveillance; it is not unusual for our security staff to spot-check our movements. But I cannot take a chance. I will go now to the desk clerk and ask for a whore who will spend the night with me. That will not be difficult to arrange at this hotel. If you like, I will mail the chart to you from

New York. In the meantime, you must not come to the hotel or send anyone else."

"It's essential that I obtain the chart," Mack said. "I can't wait for it to arrive in the mail from New York."

"I tell you it is impossible." The Russian was adamant.

"There has to be a way," Mack insisted.

"No, there is no way." Seymonov hesitated, then chuckled. "Unless you know a whore you can trust completely, and have her present herself in my room within the hour, ready to stay the night. Then I will give her the chart and she can bring it to you in the morning."

The line was quiet.

"William? Are you still there?"

"What hotel, Boris?"

"The Smith House. On Sixteenth Street."

"Your room number?"

"611," the Russian replied.

"Boris, don't hang up. Give me a minute to think." Mack placed his hand over the mouthpiece of the telephone. He raised his eyes when Skip appeared in the doorway.

Skip shook her head from side to side.

"I haven't asked you to do anything," Mack said.

"But I know what you're thinking," Skip said. "No way."

"We need the chart," Mack said. "What can we do?"

"You can take any of my dresses you want, you son of a bitch, and visit your KGB buddy in drag. That's what you can do!"

Mack removed his hand from the mouthpiece, started to speak to Seymonov, changed his mind, and covered the telephone again. I suppose I am one, he said to himself, before speaking again to Skip.

"For Chuck Leonard?" Mack asked. "For Cartwell? Robertson? Bond?"

Skip glared at Mack, closed her eyes, then opened them to stare at him again. "I'll get dressed," she said, and turned into her room.

"Boris?"

"I'm here, William."

"A colleague of mine will be coming to see you." Mack paused. "You can trust her. She is an intelligence officer, and she deserves your respect. She'll be there in about an hour, and will stay about an hour."

There was the sound of laughter at the other end of the line.

"You are a true professional, William." Seymonov laughed again. "Nothing deters you. Of course I will respect your friend. But tell me about her. After all, I have my reputation to think of. The word will spread quickly tomorrow at the embassy if she is seen. Is she fat? Is she ugly?"

"She's beautiful," Mack said.

"And how will I know she has been sent by you?"

"On a chain, around her neck," Mack said, "she will be wearing an ebony amulet."

"You promise me she is beautiful? How delightful." Seymonov chuckled again. "What a pity that Soviet intelligence officers do not write their memoirs when they retire, as your people do, Mack. You have provided me with so many amusing anecdotes."

"Let me know if you need help, Boris. I hope you are not in trouble."

Skip did not speak during the thirty-minute drive to the center of Washington. Christmas lights decorated store windows, and on the car radio Bing Crosby sang "White Christmas." Mack drove carefully on the ice-covered streets.

Mack parked Skip's car in an all-night garage on 14th Street. On the sidewalk he handed Skip the parking ticket.

Skip looked up and down the street and its gaudy façades of porn shops and topless bars. In spite of the cold, two prostitutes were wearing only hip-length coats as they solicited passing pedestrians.

"You'd better walk the rest of the way," Mack said.

Skip glared at Mack. "And you'd better be careful. I read in the paper today that the police are cracking down on the pimps in this area."

Skip turned and walked down the street.

As he watched her walk away toward 16th Street Mack considered calling her back, telling her to forget it. But he decided not to, and hailed a cab.

When Skip entered the safehouse a few minutes after eleven, Mack and his friends were seated around the dining room table, which was littered with papers and photographs. Mack rose and went to Skip.

"Here's your chart," Skip said, challenging Mack with her eyes as she handed it over.

Mack unfolded the chart, glanced at it briefly, then started to speak.

"Don't say anything!" Skip commanded. "Don't say anything at all."

"Not even thanks?" Mack asked.

"Especially that," Skip said. "Let's not mention that little episode ever again. The one thing I will say is that your friend Boris is a very attractive man. Think about that for the rest of your life, but don't say anything—ever!"

Mack hesitated, then motioned at the group at the table. "We're about to begin. I hope you will understand if you find that I'm not being completely candid with them."

"You mean I'm not to contradict you if you lie to your friends," Skip said. "Don't worry, I'm used to it."

They went to the table and sat with the others.

"Here's just about everything we know," Lucy was saying. "Carlos's operation is to take place the day after tomorrow, the nineteenth of December. He plans to abduct a U.S. government official, somewhere near Washington. We also know that he plans to fly his hostage out of the United States, but again we don't know where they are going, or what demands Carlos will make."

Skip glanced at Mack. He said nothing.

"So what we need to know most now," Hyphenated-Jake said, "is where and who?"

"That's right," Lucy said. "You've all done a good job of coming up with the appointment schedules of the top people in government. We even have the president's schedule for the nineteenth. We can find out *who* if we find out *where*."

"Skip's brought along something that might be the key," Mack said. He threw Seymonov's chart on to the table. "As far as I can figure out, that's a blow-up of an FAA aviation chart. There's good information that the plane which will fly the kidnap victim out of the country will take off from the strip on the chart. I can't make out where it is. But I know it's somewhere in Virginia."

"Let me see it," Perry said. "I'm a pilot, and I had to learn to read these things." He studied the chart. "The symbols mean than it's an unused landing strip, for emergencies, but there's no tower, no beacon, no runway lights, no terminal. We'll have to obtain the entire chart from FAA to find where this piece fits. There are no towns named on the chart but its edge cuts through the name of one. Whatever the town's full name is, this indicates there's a railway line running through it."

"What are the letters you can make out?" Frank asked.

"The final letters of two words," Perry said. "——fton, and ——orge. That doesn't mean anything to me."

"Let me see that," Lucy asked. "Why, I know what town that is. It's Clifton Forge, Virginia. Junior used to travel to the train station there summers, when he was working. He waited on tables at a fancy resort in the mountains not far away."

"What was the name of the resort where Junior worked?" Mack asked.

"At that ritzy place, the one with all the golf courses and tennis courts and skiing in the winter."

"The Homestead," Frank said. "I've been there many times."

"That's right," Lucy confirmed. "That's where Junior worked summers, maybe four or five times."

"Mack?" It was Emilio who spoke.

"Yes, Emilio?"

"*Operacion Hogar.* In Spanish *hogar* means home. It also has a secondary meaning—homestead."

"Just a minute! Just a minute!" Lucy flipped quickly through the papers on the table before her. "Here it is! The secretary of state will deliver the principal address at an international conference on the night of the nineteenth—at The Homestead in Warm Springs, Virginia!"

"What's the conference, Lucy?" Mack asked.

"It's an annual thing." Lucy consulted the paper. "Third World Symposium. The secretary is going to speak on 'Human Rights In a Changing World.' More than two hundred delegates from about thirty countries."

"Just the cover Carlos would need," Hyphenated-Jake said, "in order to bring into this country a gang of so many different nationalities. I was stumped, wondering how he was going to manage that."

"Can you imagine the international furor Carlos can create," Perry said, "if he can hold the secretary of state hostage?"

Frank spoke. "There's something that's not clear to me. I flew to The Homestead once. You have to fly into Hot Springs. The Homestead is a twenty-five-minute drive from the airport, at Warm Springs. Why, then, will Carlos's plane be at an emergency landing strip which is considerably more distant than the airport at Hot Springs?"

"I would guess," Mack said, "because he won't have to worry about tower clearances and the checks which the Secret Service would make on a private plane at any airport where the secretary's plane would be landing. With his Gang of Twenty at the hotel to carry off the kidnapping, it will be easier and safer to spirit the secretary away to the abandoned strip, then fly him out of the country."

Perry nodded in agreement.

Skip was staring at Mack. He avoided her gaze.

"I declare," Clem said, "it looks like day after tomorrow is going to be—"

Emilio interrupted: "Do we advise the Bureau and the Secret Service now, Mack?"

"Not quite yet," Mack replied.

"What the hell do you mean?" Emilio turned to Frank. "Are you going to tell him, or shall I?"

Frank turned to Mack. "You should know that you're about to have a mutiny on your hands. We've all been talking about the latest developments. Our consensus is that you are being too cozy in this operation. We're only forty-eight hours away from the convening of the world's most dangerous terrorists. That, in itself, is certainly a grave matter. We now believe that these international thugs intend to kidnap the secretary of state. The time has come to warn the Bureau and the Secret Service of the danger."

"Goddamned right!" Emilio slammed a massive fist on the table. "You're spaced out, Mack, around the bend. We can't screw around any longer with your crazy scheme. We have to tell the FBI now!"

Mack lit a cigarette. He pondered for a moment.

"It's true," he said, "that Virginia will be host to some of the worst murderers in history, all congregated in one building. That also gives us a unique opportunity to wrap them all up at once. It's true we must protect the American secretary of state. But if we tell the FBI and the Secret Service now, they will have no choice but to cancel the secretary's speaking engagement. When word of that leaks, Carlos will call off his operation. And we will have lost the opportunity to snare them all—Carlos, his gang, and the one man who might take over from Carlos in the future, Khalil."

"You know we're with you," Hyphenated-Jake said, "but we're wondering if you're not obsessed by this thing. The flap potential seems to spiral higher and higher."

"That's right," Lucy said. "It makes us nervous to allow the authorities to climb out on the same, long limb we're all perching on now."

"I understand how you must all feel," Mack said, "and I'm sorry this has turned into such a hairy situation. But we have to do it my way. I'll make one concession. I'll advise the Bureau, today, about Carlos's plan to use the airstrip outside Clifton Forge, but without telling them why. If I tell them that field may be used by terrorists, they will be waiting when Carlos's plane arrives. Then if something goes awry with our operation at The Homestead, we can at least be sure that no one will be flying the secretary of state out of the country."

209

Mack snuffed out his cigarette in an ash tray, and continued, "Do I hear any nays? If so anyone who wishes to withdraw can do so now without hard feelings. What about it?"

Mack's crew exchanged glances, but there were no dissenting voices.

"Good," Mack said. "We have a lot to do before we go to The Homestead day after tomorrow. I'm going to ask you all to stay here in the safehouse tonight and tomorrow night. Frank's brought in some cots, and there's plenty to eat and drink. You may leave if you have to, but only if someone else is with you. And, in that case, I'll depend on each of you to be sure the person you're with doesn't make any phone calls, mail any letters, drop any notes."

Clem stood. "All this makes me so nervous I want to drink away the shakes. Come on, folks. I'll serve the drinks."

Lucy approached Mack. "I have a chore I just have to do. Christmas isn't Christmas at my house if I don't serve suckling pig to Junior and his friends. There are two waiting for me, and I'd better pick them up before they're sold. Is it all right if I go for them?"

"I'll be your escort," Frank said. He turned to Mack. "May I use your car?"

"Sure," Mack handed Frank the keys to the Cougar. "It's just around the corner."

Frank and Lucy went out in search of suckling pig.

Skip approached Mack and handed him a glass of gin on the rocks, with a few drops of cognac.

"Thanks, Skip."

"Mack, I'm frightened."

"It is getting sort of scarey, isn't it?"

"That was quite a performance you just put on for the benefit of your friends. Remember, I was on the extension when Boris told you the plan to use a plane had been abandoned. Mack?"

"Yes?"

"You really believe one of us is reporting to Carlos, don't you?"

"I know that Carlos knows everything we do."

"Do you suspect me?"

"No."

"Then you suspect one of the others?"

Mack was quiet and looked out the window.

Skip shuddered.

The apartment rocked from the blast of an explosion.

"What's that?" Emilio shouted.

"Jesus!" Mack exclaimed. "My car! Carlos must have booby-trapped my car! Let's go!"

Mack, Frank, and Albert Stevenson waited outside the operating room. Albert paced back and forth.

"I told you not to worry, Albert," Frank said. "She's all right. Your mother was never even unconscious."

Albert looked at Frank, then at Mack. "I knew, that day I met the two of you in my mother's office, you were up to something that would get her into trouble. What's been going on?"

"Lucy has been working with us," Mack said, "in an effort to apprehend a dangerous terrorist called Carlos. He's been trying to kill me. You mother's been hurt because I was stupid and allowed her to use my car after someone had planted a bomb in it."

"It wasn't a bomb," Frank said. "It was an M-twenty-six grenade, the kind Carlos used in *Le Drug Store*. If Lucy hadn't forgotten her keys, both of us would be dead now. She opened the door of the car, started to get in, but then remembered that she had left her house keys in the apartment. She closed the car door and both of us walked away to return to the apartment. Apparently the grenade was not connected to the ignition, but was wired to the door so that when it opened the pin was pulled. Thanks to the five-second delay fuse, Lucy and I were far enough away from the car to escape the force of the blast. Good thing. The inside of the car was torn to shreds."

The surgeon came out of the operating room and approached Albert.

"Your mother's all right," the doctor said. "We had to remove a piece of metal from her leg, but it's not serious. She'll just have to stay off her feet for a few days. Your mother's quite a woman, young man. We used a local anesthetic, and all the time I was digging that piece of metal out of her leg she was trying to convince me that this hospital should use her computer service." The surgeon smiled and walked away.

The doors of the operating chamber opened and a nurse pushed a hospital bed into the hall. Lucy greeted them cheerily.

"I'm going to be gimpy for a while," Lucy said, "but the doctor says I can leave in the morning. I'll have to use a wheelchair for a few days, but I'm all right. What about you, Frank?"

"I'm fine, Lucy. Wasn't even touched."

"It was Carlos, wasn't it?" Lucy asked Mack.

"Yes. I'm sorry I was dumb enough to let you borrow the car. I should have anticipated something like this."

"That man is beginning to irritate me," Lucy said. "I'll rest tomorrow, but don't get any ideas about leaving town the day after tomorrow without me."

"We'll see," Mack said. "We'll see what the doctor says."

The nurse interrupted. "If you give me five minutes to make the patient comfortable, you can go to her room." The nurse pushed the medical cot down the hall.

"What's this about day after tomorrow?" Albert asked.

"If all goes well," Mack said, "we'll be confronting Carlos and his accomplices then."

"Can I help?" Albert asked.

"No, Albert, I—"

"Just a minute." Frank spoke to Albert Stevenson. "Lucy said you once worked at The Homestead in Warm Springs?"

"That's right. I was a bus boy for two summers, and waited tables for two more."

Frank surveyed Albert's rugged six-foot-four frame, then spoke to Mack.

"I'll be putting together an operational plan tomorrow," Frank said. "Albert's knowledge of The Homestead might be very useful. Albert, could you persuade a half dozen of your football friends to come along with you?"

"If I ask them, they'll come."

"Good. We'll put them to work. Okay, Mack?"

Mack hesitated. How many friends had he already placed in jeopardy? How many lives, other peoples' lives, had he already laid on the line?

"Sure," Mack said. "Okay."

8.

"Mr. Symser, please."

"I'm afraid he's not here. Is that you, Mr. Peanut Butter Voice?"

Mack chuckled. "Yes. What time do you expect him, Mrs. Symser?"

"Not until late. This is poker night. I can give you the number."

"Never mind. I just wanted to leave a message. Would you tell him that I called, and that Phase Four has begun."

"Phase Four? Will he know what that means?"

"I think so."

"This is the most frustrating time I've ever gone through," Mrs. Symser said. "All these mysterious calls at strange hours. And Allen refuses to tell me anything about it. We were childhood sweethearts, and he's always told me everything."

"When you and Mr. Symser were sweethearts," Mack asked, "did you ever go to the Roller Derby?"

Silence. Then, "Once or twice, I think."

"Then just tell him that I called . . . and that the jam is on. Good-bye, Mrs. Symser."

The Piedmont Airlines prop jet left National Airport a few minutes after ten in the morning, stopped briefly in Staunton, then flew on to Hot Springs, Virginia, arriving just before noon. Mack, Perry, and Albert Stevenson rented a car at Ingalls Field airport, and drove toward The Homestead, seventeen miles away. As they approached the vast estate of the famous resort, Mack pointed out the first of three golf courses. It was laid out in 1892, qualifying as the oldest course in continuous use in the United States. Behind the dozen buildings comprising

214

the hotel, the ski slope was a swath of artificial snow laid down between leafless laurels and oaks.

At the reception desk Mack flipped open his wallet, told the clerk he and his friends were from the Secret Service, and asked to speak to the manager.

"Taylor, Roy Taylor," the manager introduced himself. "And this is my security chief, Paul Nelson. Have a seat gentlemen. Coffee?"

"Please. Black for me," Mack said.

Albert accepted a coffee, and Perry declined.

"Well, what can I do for you gentlemen?" Taylor was cheerful-looking but his ready smile was tempered by the serious mien of a man who is called on in the middle of the night to cope with unexpected problems, be they messy suicide attempts or brawls between husbands and wives.

"Mr. Taylor, my name is Frank Johnson. My colleagues are Mr. Richards and Mr. Little."

Taylor acknowledged the introductions, but chided Mack.

"We may not be far from Washington," Taylor said, "but you are in the South. Please, I'm Roy."

"All right, Roy," Mack said.

"You know we really are pleased to have this conference," Taylor said. "We've been in business for a long time and like to think we have just about the finest resort and convention center in the country. George Washington never slept here, but a number of presidents have. Not in my time, though, so I'm gratified to know that we will have the secretary of state as our guest tonight. We have a truly colorful collection of people here for the conference. They've come from all over the world. It's quite an event."

"Roy, we're here to provide the secretary of state with extra protection tonight. I'm the chief of what is called the Special Duty Squad of the service."

"And you're welcome. You're probably on per diem, too, which might not meet our rates. Don't worry. I'll give you a special rate so you won't be out of pocket."

"We appreciate that, Roy. We'll just be staying the night."

"But why the sudden attention, from . . . uh . . . the Special

Duty Squad? Your Mr. Beckwith spent the entire afternoon with Paul here yesterday. He checked everything: the secretary's suite, the entrances and exits from the convention hall where he will speak, the halls, even the air-conditioning ducts. He seemed to be a thorough man, and told Paul he was satisfied that everything was in apple-pie order. Beckwith said he would be returning tonight with the secretary, and two other Secret Service agents. Now there are six of you."

"As you say," Mack said, "Beckwith is a good man. But he's on the secretary's permanent detail and was not aware, when he was here yesterday, of a new development. We've had a report, from what we consider a reliable overseas source, that there may be an attempt to kidnap the secretary of state tonight."

"Here?" Taylor was incredulous. "At The Homestead? It seems an unlikely place."

"Under ordinary circumstances, it would be," Perry interjected, "but not now. With so many foreigners from so many different places, we can't take any chances."

"But I checked out this group," Taylor said. "The conference is sponsored by the Ford Foundation. That's hardly a subversive organization."

"Yes," Mack said. "But you must understand that there has been no investigation of the delegates; anyone, from any country, could sign up for the conference as long as they paid the fees. Frankly, we're afraid international terrorists might be sending the kidnappers here under the guise of legitimate delegates."

"Most of the guests I've talked to seem to be fine, educated people," Nelson said.

"Most terrorists," Mack said, "come from middle and upper class families, and most of them have college educations."

"I see." Taylor rose from his chair and went to the window, which looked out over a number of tennis courts. "We have fifteen tennis courts here, you know." Then he turned to Mack.

"All right, Frank. What can we do for you?"

"Have Mr. Nelson cooperate with us, without talking about it with others on your staff."

"Of course. Nor will I say anything to anyone else."

"We'll need a number of rooms," Mack said, "including one suite."

"That can be arranged."

"The suite will be our command center." Mack turned to Nelson. "Do you use television as part of your security system?"

"Goodness no. But we do have a complete closed-circuit setup for use at conventions."

"Can you have cameras cover the hall in which the conference is taking place?" Mack asked. "We would need to have the monitors installed in our suite."

"Yes. That will be simple," Nelson said.

"What is the conference schedule for the rest of the day?"

"Luncheon," Taylor said, looking at his watch, "is beginning now in the West Room. The conferees will gather again in the hall at two P.M. for a program of, I believe, two seminar presentations. They will be asked to clear the hall at five-thirty so that it can be prepared for the evening banquet. The dais for the secretary must be set up, the tables and chairs arranged, and a stage erected for the show which will precede the banquet."

"What sort of show?"

"The Young Columbians," Taylor said, "a fine group of twenty young people who sing and dance. You'll enjoy them."

"What's the time schedule?"

"The three bars open at seven. Guests are to be seated by eight for the show, which will last forty minutes. Then dinner, with the secretary beginning his speech about nine-thirty. He will stay the night, and return to Washington first thing tomorrow morning."

"One final arrangement," Mack requested. "I want you to have your security man see to it that seven of my men are given waiters' outfits, and are allowed to work with the regular waiters while dinner is being served."

"There might be a problem there," Taylor said. He cleared his throat, glanced at Albert Stevenson, then looked away from him quickly. "You see, all of our waiters are blacks."

Lucy's son spoke for the first time since they had entered Taylor's office. "That's why six of my black colleagues will be arriving shortly, to help me wait on tables. And I am thoroughly acquainted with your kitchen and serving procedures."

Taylor exclaimed, "My, what an exciting night for The Homestead!"

Mack opened the door and held it while Albert pushed his mother's wheelchair into the suite. Hyphenated-Jake came in behind them carrying an object wrapped in brown paper and the size and shape of an oil painting. Emilio, lugging Lucy's suitcase, followed as Clem pulled up the rear carrying two briefcases.

Frank and Perry were already standing before a long table which held four television monitors, each flickering with images from the conference hall located several hundred feet from the suite in another building. They turned to greet the visitors.

"Welcome to the front lines," Frank said.

"Mack," Lucy exclaimed, "what a fine place you got me."

"One of several bridal suites, Lucy."

"Mighty pretty," Clem said. He whispered to Emilio. "Did you ever hear the one about—"

"Please," Emilio interrupted him. "No more Jack Oakie jokes."

"Well, let's prepare for action," Lucy said. "Jake, will you prop that board up somewhere?"

Hyphenated-Jake removed the paper from Lucy's Gang of Twenty bulletin board. She had filled the quota after a final consultation with Butterfly, selecting those most likely to be on hand to assist Carlos in the abduction of the secretary of state. Most of the suspects were identified with accompanying photographs; the remainder only by an index card with biographical notes.

"And you two hang the rest of my rogues," Lucy instructed Clem and Emilio, who immediately began removing more photographs and cards from the briefcases—the "Probables" and "Possibles" in Lucy's selection—and set about hanging them on the walls with strips of masking tape.

"I have to get back to the fellows," Albert said.

"I'll be down shortly," Frank said, "and we'll have a skull session."

"Junior!"

Albert stopped abruptly.

"Yes, Mom?"

"Can't you do anything about those pants?"

Albert grinned sheepishly, and looked down at his feet. The pants of his waiter's uniform were six inches too short for his long legs, and the white jacket strained its buttons.

"Sorry, Mom. This is the biggest outfit they had." He grinned again, and went out of the suite.

Lucy propelled her wheelchair to the table where the television equipment was set up.

"How do all these gadgets work, Frank?"

"I have four cameras mounted in the hall, Lucy." Frank touched the edge of his spectacles, pleased that the others had turned and were listening to his explanation. "They cover, from one angle or another, the entire hall. And, they are remotely controlled from this cabinet. When you wish, you can activate the zoom lens which will give you a real close-up. Watch, I'll show you."

Frank turned a knob on the cabinet and the image on one of the monitors changed until the features of the delegates within its range in the conference hall were clear. One of the delegates was dozing, his head hung down.

"Don't change it!" Lucy leaned over and peered at the monitor. She stared at the image for several seconds. "The man who's sleeping there . . . why . . . why . . . Bingo! That's Eljido Huerta, the Uruguayan Tuparmaro who's been living in Paris for the past six years." Lucy turned, a triumphant smile on her face, and pointed to her Gang of Twenty. "There, the second photograph from the left in the top row. See if it's not the same man!"

Emilio inspected the photograph on the bulletin board, then

went to the television monitor. "No question," he announced. "It's the same guy!"

"Well done, Lucy," Mack said.

"Nineteen to go," Lucy said. Then, to Frank. "When we've identified as many as we can, how will it work tonight?"

"This walkie-talkie," Frank said. "I'll be downstairs with the others, and you communicate with me, with an indication of where Carlos's people are. I'll pass on the information, and Albert and his friends will take over from there."

"Will they all be sitting together?" Albert asked.

"Not a chance," Mack said. "They will be separated, in a widely dispersed pattern."

There was a polite knock on the door. Perry went to open it.

The man standing in the door appeared to be about fifty. He wore a bowler hat, a *pince-nez*, a formal collar, and a tweed suit which hung loosely on his extremely thin body. On his feet, he wore a pair of black rubber galoshes.

"Good afternoon. There was a note in my box which said I was to report to this room, and ask for Mack. It said that everything was to be on a first-name basis. I am John. May I come in?"

Mack went to the newcomer and shook his hand. "I'm Mack. Thanks for coming such a long way to help us."

"On the contrary," came the reply, "I should thank you. I've never been quite so excited in my life. And thank you for the first-class ticket. I became quite giddy from all the free champagne. And the flight from Washington was a delightful hop."

Mack introduced the transatlantic traveler, using only first names, to everyone in the room and explained that John would be working with them.

The lull after the introductions was broken by Lucy.

"John?"

"Madam?"

"John," Lucy said dryly, "why are you wearing galoshes?"

"Oh, dear." Mr. Rubbers looked down at his feet. "Forgive me." He sat abruptly on a sofa and began to remove them.

"Please excuse us," Mack said to Mr. Rubbers. "We have to prepare for tonight's work. I'll leave you with Lucy for the time being, and you can compare notes. Room service is very prompt here. Please do not hesitate to order any thing you want to eat or drink, including more champagne, if you like."

"I might well do that," Mr. Rubbers said.

"If you need anything, Lucy," Frank said, "you can call me on the walkie-talkie."

"Make yourself at home, John," Lucy said to Mr. Rubbers after the others had gone. She was instructing him on the use of the television equipment when there was a single, sharp rap on the door. Mr. Rubbers opened the door promptly.

"Good afternoon. I am Isaac."

Isaac was a short, stocky man who wore a dark suit, white shirt and thin black tie. He was completely bald.

"Come in, Isaac. I'm Lucy. And this is John."

Issac bowed his head, acknowleding the introductions.

"Can we order you anything? Something to eat or drink?" Lucy asked.

"Thank you, no." Isaac's English was precise, but heavily accented. "I am too tired to do anything but sit for a while. I have been flying for sixteen hours."

"Well, then," Lucy said, "you sit down and relax."

The three counterintelligence specialists were now seated —Mr. Rubbers, perched stiffly on a chair, his hands folded in his lap as if holding an imaginary cup of tea; Isaac slumped wearily on a sofa; and Lucy in her wheelchair.

"I must say," Mr. Rubbers commented, "this is the most thrilling day of my career. I suppose that both of you know what it means to be cooped up in a little office while the operations fellows travel around the world and enjoy the excitement."

"Yes." Isaac regarded Mr. Rubbers inquisitively. "Can you tell me where you are from?"

"Oh, no," Mr. Rubbers said. "I've been asked not to identify my service. Terribly sorry, old chap."

Isaac smiled. "I, too, have been instructed to avoid any mention of my service, but simply to help you if I can." He turned to Lucy. "But certainly our hostess can tell us what organization *she* represents?"

Lucy laughed. "Let's just say I'm from the Alabaman service. Now, let's get to work. We have another hour or so to check through the crowd of delegates. Then the room will be cleared out but they'll gather again for an hour of cocktails beginning at seven. During those two periods we must identify Carlos's entire gang. The American secretary of state will be arriving just about the time the show is over, about eight. We must be sure there are no terrorists left in that hall when he sits down to dinner. I've already identified one. Come here and look."

Lucy rolled her chair to the bulletin board, and the two men rose and followed her.

"That one," Lucy said, touching one of the photographs on the board. "Eljido Huerta. He's down in that hall right now."

"Extraordinary," Mr. Rubbers exclaimed. "Where did you ever get that photograph of him?"

"You might say he was on 'Candid Camera,' " Lucy said. "He kept wandering in and out of certain embassies around Europe and never realized how much attention was being paid to him."

"Huerta is the Tuparmaro who associated with Carlos in Paris?" asked Isaac.

"That's right," Lucy replied. "So now we have to identify nineteen more, if our information that Carlos is working with a group of twenty is correct."

"And how do we do that?" Isaac queried.

"By television," Lucy said, turning her wheelchair and propelling it to the table of technical equipment. The men followed.

"These four screens take in the entire hall," Lucy explained. "Each of these four dials corresponds to one of the screens, and will allow us to move in close for a positive identification. Watch."

As Lucy manipulated the controls the figure of Huerta grew larger. He was awake now, idly inspecting his fingernails.

Now Mr. Rubbers and Isaac were leaning over, peering at the television monitors.

Isaac put his finger on one of the screens. "Can we look

more carefully at this man?" Lucy adjusted the controls. "Ah! He is a Palestinian who often travels under the name of Badia." Isaac's face was grim. "He was at Munich."

"He's on my board of suspects," Lucy said, pleased.

"It's not necessary to tune in on this fellow," Mr. Rubbers said, pointing out a heavyset man in a light sports jacket. "That's Barton Wheeler."

"And this one," Isaac said, again placing his hand on the monitor. "Close in on him, please."

When the figure emerged into clear focus Isaac grunted with satisfaction. "I don't know his real name, but he has in the past used an Ecuadorian passport with the name of Antonio Dages Bouvier. He's probably a Colombian. But he's worked with Carlos for years."

"He's not on my board," Lucy said. "I thought he was one of the terrorists you people—" Lucy hesitated, "the Israelis captured at Entebbe."

"No," Isaac said. "Six terrorists were killed at the airport, but Bouvier escaped because he had gone into Kampala the day before."

"Well, we have four of them spotted. Not bad for a start," Lucy said. "I'm going to order something in the way of refreshment. John?"

"Tea, please," Mr. Rubbers said, looking at his watch.

"Just tea?"

"Tea, for me, means not only the liquid, but sandwiches, jellies and the like."

"Isaac?"

"A pot of black coffee. And can you arrange for all the registration cards of the delegates to be brought to us?"

"Sure," Lucy said.

"Carlos himself will be the most elusive of all. Undoubtedly he will be in disguise. There have been no pictures of him since the OPEC kidnapping in Vienna."

"And he wore a beard and a beret there," Lucy said.

"Yes," Issac said. "I doubt that any of us could be sure even if we were face to face with him now. It is said that his appearance has changed greatly, probably due to plastic sur-

223

gery." Isaac patted his coat pocket where his billfold was. "But I have with me a recent sample of his handwriting. Perhaps we can match it with one of the registration cards."

"I say," Mr. Rubbers exclaimed, "wouldn't that be splendid!"

It was six in the evening. There were fourteen men in the large storeroom where the food supplies for the kitchen of The Homestead were stocked. The shelves were filled with crates, canned foods, and the materials necessary to serve hundreds of people at a time. Some of the men stood. Others sat on potato sacks: Albert Stevenson and his six friends, all in waiters' costumes, as well as Emilio, Frank, Clem, Perry, and Hyphenated-Jake. The hotel security man stood beside Mack.

"Gentlemen, this is Paul Nelson, security chief here at the hotel. He's been very cooperative, and is standing by to help should any new problems arise."

Nelson held up a hand, like a guest at a civic club meeting acknowledging an introduction.

"The secretary of state should be taking off from Washington about now," Mack said. "We suspect that there are as many as twenty terrorists in the hotel, masquerading as delegates to the conference. We are trying to identify them now. They will all be carrying weapons. Nevertheless, we must see to it that they are all removed from the banquet hall before the secretary arrives, which should be after the show, a few minutes before nine, when dinner begins."

"Goddammit, Mack, this has gone far enough." Emilio's face was flushed with anger. "You've been playing your little games for too long. What if we don't manage to wrap up this gang? If even one terrorist is left in that crowd we can't allow the secretary of state to walk into the place! I just won't be a part of your crazy, dangerous plan."

Moments passed before Mack spoke.

"You're right, Emilio," Mack said. "I have been playing my cards close to my vest, but because it was necessary. We have a chance to capture Carlos and his entire band. Even so I wouldn't jeopardize the life of the secretary. I'm going to ask Perry to drive with me to the airport to meet the plane from

Washington. I'll brief the Secret Service detail on exactly what's going on here. We'll telephone you, Frank, and you can tell us whether you have been successful. If not, I'll convince the secretary to stay away from the hotel and return to Washington. In any event, the decision will be his, based on the recommendation of his Secret Service people."

"That sounds a little more sensible," Emilio said, mollified. "For the past few days I've been worried you were losing your grip."

Mack addressed Albert Stevenson. "The time to grab the terrorists will be during the show. You will have about forty minutes. It will be dark except for the spotlights on the performers. That's the time to pluck them out of the crowd and bring them back here to this room. Albert, do you or any of your buddies have guns on you?"

"I don't," Albert said. He turned to his football companions. "Do you?"

One of Albert's friends responded. "I've got my pappy's thirty-two."

"Don't try to use it," Mack said. "Unless you're an expert with weapons you'll just be in trouble."

"I'm no expert," was the reply, "but I'm no fool either." The man turned to Albert. "Al, what's with it with this dude? He wants us to go out in the dark and tackle all these people he admits are carrying guns. We might get hurt bad."

"You're all football players," Mack said. "Work in groups of two or three as you take the terrorists out of the action. When you move in on them, just be sure they don't have time to use their weapons. The trick will be to keep your eyes on their hands, just as you usually keep your eyes on the ball. If there's a problem, Clem, Emilio, and Jake will be behind you. They are each armed, and know how to use their guns."

Albert's friends looked at him. The big man hesitated, then said: "We'll do it the way the man says."

Then Albert turned to Mack.

"You say it will be dark out there during the show. How do we know who it is we're supposed to grab?"

"That's Frank's department," Mack said.

Frank Coughlin addressed the group.

"Lucy and her friends will identify the terrorists for us," Frank explained. "Emilio, Clem, and Jake will have the job of making it easy for you to spot them, even in the dark. Let me show you. Perry, come here and help me with a demonstration, will you?"

Perry, who had been sitting on a wooden crate, a bottle of beer in his hand, stood beside Frank.

"Now let's assume Perry is one of the terrorists identified by Lucy and company while he is standing with the other delegates during the cocktail hour. Either Clem, Jake, or Emilio will have the job of approaching him, and, on one pretext or another, placing a hand on his back. Perhaps by pretending to fall against him, or by touching him as they squeeze through the crowd. It doesn't matter, as long as they manage to put their hand on his back, like this."

Frank demonstrated by putting his hand on the back of Perry's jacket.

"How the hell," Albert asked, "is that going to help us find the people we're after out in the dark?"

"Because of this," Frank said. He picked up a box the size of a container for writing paper. "This is a substance called phosphor dust. During the cocktail hour about fifty guests who will not have attended the conference but want to hear the secretary of state will join the delegates. Three of those in attendance will be Emilio, Clem, and Jake. Before mixing with the crowd they will place their hands in this dust. Then they will seek out the terrorists identified by Lucy, and find a way to leave a handprint on the backs of the men's coats, or, perhaps the women's dresses. The dust is not visible in ordinary light."

"But," Frank continued, "each of you pretending to be a waiter will carry one of these." Frank opened another box which contained small, flat flashlights. "Each of these has a piece of Celluloid over the lens. That will expose the print on the back of each terrorist. In case things get wild, and there's some sort of general confusion, Paul, the hotel security officer, has arranged that I will operate one of the spot-

226

lights usually used for the show. It, too, will have the special filter which will make the handprints glow. Later, during the show, one way or another, you fellows bring out everyone marked by the handprint."

"Any other questions?" Mack asked. There were none. He turned to Paul Nelson. "I guess you know the local police?"

"Worked there for fourteen years," Nelson replied. "Chief's my cousin."

"Call him," Mack said, "and tell him to be down here with his deputies, by seven-thirty. Tell him to bring all the handcuffs he has at the station."

"It's basketball night on TV," Nelson said. "I don't know."

"Tell him he's about to be famous," Mack said, tersely. He turned to the others. "Good luck. And to you and your friends, Albert, thanks."

"The show begins in ten minutes, Lucy," Mack said. "How are you doing?" Mack, with Perry beside him, was standing behind Lucy's wheelchair. She and her new friends, Mr. Rubbers and Isaac, were scanning the television monitors. Mr. Rubbers held a glass of champagne, but his face was grim.

"Not well enough, Mack," Lucy said. "Between us we spotted fourteen of Carlos's crew—thirteen which were on the board, and another that Isaac recognized. We're bound to miss one or two, I suppose, but six is too many."

"What about Carlos himself?" Perry asked. "And Khalil?" Lucy nodded her head negatively.

"I really don't believe Carlos is in that crowd," Mr. Rubbers said. "I've seen perhaps two dozen photographs of Carlos taken in London, even a cinema filmstrip our fellows retrieved from the shop that developed home movies for the Ramirez family. I can't find anyone who even remotely resembles him in this group. If he's there he's done a masterful job of disguise."

"And Isaac has examined the registration card of each delegate," Lucy said, indicated a stack of cards on the table, "and can't find one with handwriting which might belong to Carlos."

"Is it possible that Carlos and the ones we've missed don't plan to appear at all now?" Isaac asked. "Perhaps he will wait until the banquet is finished, and then join the others to abduct your secretary from his room."

Before Mack could reply, Frank's voice came through the walkie-talkie from the storeroom near the hotel kitchen, and advised Lucy: "Two more to go, Lucy. Who's next?"

Isaac touched one of the television monitors, and handed Lucy a card from the stack of registration forms.

Lucy spoke into her walkie-talkie. "A young man, Frank. He's wearing a dull red jacket and blue pants. Dark skin and a thin mustache. He's registered under the name of Adnan Gursel, and he's standing in the southeast corner of the hall, talking with a woman wearing an Indian sari. He's a member of the Turkish People's Liberation Army."

"Okay," Frank said. "I'll send Clem out with his Chamber-of-Commerce-Welcome-to-Warm-Springs approach. That's been working well."

In a moment they could see Clem's figure appear on one of the screens. He made his way through the crowd, approaching a guest and extending his hand, then going on to another. Clem approached the Turk, whose face registered surprise when Clem reached to pump his hand, then, smiling broadly, slapped the terrorist on the back.

"Clem just branded Gursel, Frank," Lucy said into her walkie-talkie. "One more. There's a blond young woman already seated at the table just to the right of the speakers' platform. A Baader-Meinhof type. She's wearing a green dress and has a large brown purse on the table in front of her."

"Big enough," Mr. Rubbers added, "to contain a machine pistol."

"I'll send Hyphenated-Jake," Frank advised them. "I promised him the assignment if you came up with a woman."

They watched Hyphenated-Jake thread his way through the people drinking cocktails and walk directly to the woman. He leaned over toward her, as if to impart a confidence. She looked up, irritated, and shook her head.

"Jake is flirting with her," Mack said.

Then they observed as Hyphenated-Jake shrugged, his advances spurned, and placed his hand on the woman's back. The German girl stared at him angrily as he disappeared into the crowd.

"That's it," Lucy said, turning to Mack. "That takes care of the fourteen we've been able to identify. There's not much question about the identifications we've made together." Lucy looked first at Isaac and then Mr. Rubbers. "But we're still missing a half dozen."

"Including Carlos," Isaac said.

The lights in the conference hall blinked off and on, a signal that the delegates were to be seated for the stage show.

"The show's about to begin." It was Frank's voice from the walkie-talkie. "Do we go ahead?"

Mack leaned toward the walkie-talkie. "Yes, Frank. Begin to yank them out of the crowd after the performance begins. You're in charge. Perry and I are leaving now for the airport so that we'll be there before the secretary's plane lands. I'll telephone you from there to find out how it's gone."

"And you tell Junior and those boys to be careful," Lucy added.

"We'll be careful, Lucy. I'll expect your call, Mack. Over and out."

The lights were dimming as Mack and Perry prepared to leave. Isaac spoke to Mack.

"May I advise you to instruct your secretary of state to return to Washington? Carlos certainly plans to go through with his operation, or he would have never sent so many of his people here."

Mack said nothing.

"And," Mr. Rubbers said, standing and extending his hand, first to Mack and then to Perry, "may I thank you gentlemen for persuading my office to allow me to make this exciting excursion. I have spent almost thirty years in an office, staring out at the uninspired view of an old warehouse. It has been magnificent to be in the field."

Mr. Rubbers toasted them with his champagne; he was slightly tipsy.

"Well, you'll have a ringside view of the action now," Mack said, nodding toward the television screens. "Thanks for coming to help us." Then, turning to Perry. "Let's go."

The Young Columbians began their show, after an introduction welcoming the foreign guests and promising them they would hear America's favorite songs from Broadway. The attractive young singers and dancers, in vivid costumes and with frequent changes of pace, held the attention of their audience. Except for the shafts of light focusing on the performers, the hall was dark.

Frank provided Albert Stevenson with instructions for his first foray. "Begin at the back of the crowd," he said, "and then work your way through the audience. The first one is the small fellow at the table in the corner."

Albert and two of his football friends moved into the hall. He used his flashlight long enough to spot the terrorist; a handprint in the middle of the back of his jacket glowed orange. Albert approached him from behind, clasped a hand over his mouth, and, with his free arm, locked the man's neck with a crushing embrace. Albert's two assistants picked the victim up, and, without removing him from the chair, hustled their victim through the darkness and the swinging doors leading to the kitchen and the storeroom where Frank, Clem, Emilio, Hyphenated-Jake, and the local sheriff and his deputies waited.

Frank gave instructions to the small man who had carried his father's .32 on his mission to The Homestead. He went to the table where Barton Wheeler was seated.

"Mr. Justin Smith?" The question was in a whisper.

"Yes?" Barton Wheeler turned to answer the query.

"There's an international call for you in the front office."

"For me?"

"Yes sir. From London. The caller says it's an emergency. Just follow me."

The British terrorist walked behind the man in the white

waiter's coat. As he went through the door leading to the lobby two other white-jacketed waiters pounced on him.

Two of Albert's gridiron companions approached Eljido Huerta, the Uruguayan. After a flash of light revealed the luminous handprint on the back of his jacket, there was a sudden karate chop at the back of Huerta's neck, and his head fell forward on the table.

"What's this?" A man who had been sitting next to Huerta started to stand up with alarm.

"Shhhh!" The hiss was an admonishment. "Just part of the show, Mister. You'll see."

Eljido Huerta was whisked away to the storeroom.

The man who had escaped at Entebbe, the Colombian who had worked with Carlos in Europe, was surprised.

"A message for me?"

"Yes," Albert Stevenson whispered. "Carlos is here. He says there has been a change in the plan. You are to join him immediately in the men's room."

In the men's toilet the South American had his pistol halfway out of his shoulder holster before he was subdued by Emilio and Clem.

After checking another telltale handprint, one of Albert's companions beckoned to two of his friends. Then he grabbed with both his hands the man named Badia, who had been at Munich. There was a gurgling sound as he pressed his fingers into the Palestinian's windpipe. Badia slumped in his chair.

A woman turned in the darkness. "What *are* you doing?"

There were two simultaneous replies: "Too much to drink," and "Just part of the show, lady." The two waiters looked at each other, shrugged, and carried off the inert figure.

The singers and dancers on the stage went into a new routine, as the audience applauded.

Albert Stevenson and his squad continued to move through the darkness, their flashlights occasionally probing to find a glowing handprint. One by one they plucked the terrorists from the crowd.

"We take the next right turn for the airport," Perry said.

"I believe it's the left turn."

"Mack, what do you plan to say to the secretary's Secret Service detail? He really shouldn't go to the hotel."

"I'm not sure," Mack said, guiding the rented car around a hairpin bend on the mountain road. "We'll have to hear what Frank has to say when we telephone the hotel from the airport."

A sign announced a crossroad ahead.

"You should take a right," Perry said.

"No, it's to—"

The barrel end of the .44 Magnum Perry was holding against Mack's temple was cold.

"Stop the car, Mack," Perry said. "But don't take your hands off the wheel."

Mack slowed the car, then braked until it stopped.

"You've suspected for a long time," Perry said, "that I have been Carlos's penetration of your little operation, haven't you, Mack?"

"Yes," Mack said.

"You're wrong," Perry said. "I don't work for Carlos." Then he screamed *"Yo soy Carlos!"*

Perry smashed the barrel of the gun against the back of Mack's cranium. When Mack's head fell forward on the wheel, Perry hit him again, viciously, with the heavy gun.

Perry withdrew a plastic, pencil-shaped container from his pocket. He unscrewed the top and removed a hypodermic needle, thrust the point of the needle into Mack's neck, and pushed the plunger.

Perry got out of the car and went around to the driver's side. He opened the door and lifted Mack's body from under the steering wheel and to the other side of the front seat.

Perry slipped under the wheel, and closed the door. He paused before starting the car's engine, looked at Mack, mouthed a single word, *idiot*, before he drove away, turning to the right and speeding south, away from the airport.

9.

When Mack opened his eyes he was blinded by the glare of a bulb hanging directly above him. There was a throbbing pain at the back of his head. The light above him expanded and increased in intensity, then seemed to move in a sickening circle as Mack lost consciousness.

When he awoke again, he did not open his eyes. How long had it been since he had passed out—seconds, minutes, hours? Mack rolled his head away from the light. He opened his eyes; it was a moment before they focused. A few inches from his face he could see earth, dark soil streaked with clay, the surface dappled by spade marks. He looked up again, through squinting lids. He was underground, in some sort of pit. He could smell damp earth and another odor, familiar and intoxicating.

"Here, Mack," Perry said. "Hot coffee."

Mack lifted his feet slowly, and put them on the floor. The pain in his head was agonizing. He was sitting on a metal cot. His feet rested on unpainted planks.

"Have the coffee, Mack. There's brandy in it."

Mack turned. Perry was sitting on a stool. Between them was an iron grill, like the door of an animal's cage. Behind Perry a tunnel, dimly lit with unshaded bulbs, led to a turn a hundred feet away. At intervals the tunnel was shored against collapse by wooden beams.

Mack took the coffee Perry offered through the bars of the grill. He drank it and almost instantly felt the balm of the brandy in his chest.

Mack examined his underground cell. The earthen room was small, perhaps ten feet square. At each corner of the excavation heavy timbers supported two-by-four beams; the electric bulb

233

hung from one. In addition to the cot, the pit was furnished with a desk, a table holding a washbasin and water pitcher, a small electric heater and, in one corner, a portable toilet.

"Where are we?"

"You are in what is known as a *people's prison*," Perry said. "But only temporarily. The permanent inmate—the secretary of state—is being driven here now. When he arrives the game you and I have been playing will be finished. As you can see, there's hardly room for two."

"What about a cigarette, Perry?"

Perry lit a cigarette and passed it to Mack through the grill. Mack inhaled gratefully.

"You've thought for a long time that I've been reporting to Carlos, haven't you, Mack?"

Mack nodded.

"Do you remember my telling you in the car that I *am* Carlos."

"You are an American who once worked for the CIA," Mack said. "Carlos is a Venezuelan."

"He was," Perry said, "until I killed him in 1973 on the top of a mountain. Then I became Carlos."

"Why?" Mack asked. "How?"

"It began by accident," Perry said. "When the Agency sent me to Caracas to pitch Carlos, Lorca arranged the meeting by telling Carlos's father that I was a Canadian journalist, a socialist who would write a sympathetic story about his son. Carlos agreed, and selected the meeting site. He knew from childhood the trails down the mountain he could use if he found himself in a trap. Lorca went with me on the cable car to introduce Carlos. The only other people on the mountain were kids at the skating rink. Lorca watched them while Carlos and I talked. In the beginning he was pleasant, thinking I was going to put his name in headlines. But Carlos turned ugly when he realized I was from the Company, and was trying to recruit him. We had a fight. Carlos didn't have a gun, but I did. I killed him with three rounds from a thirty-two. I went back to the skating rink to tell Lorca. We decided to hide the body.

We dumped it into a crevice and covered him with branches and stones. As far as I know, the body has never been found.

"Before we buried Carlos, Lorca and I searched through his pockets, and found his passport and documents, and the key to his hotel room. The tag identified the hotel, and we went there to his room. When we opened the door there was a cable for Carlos on the rug; it had been slipped under the door by a bellboy. The message was from Moukarbal. It was mostly double talk, but the meaning was clear enough: a WOG team had located Boudia and assassinated him. Moukarbal was going into hiding, and Carlos was to return to Paris and take over the Commando Boudia. He was to avoid contact with Moukarbal, and anyone else he had worked with in the past. The name and address of his new contact, a man who had never met Carlos, was in the message. He would be the link to the PFLP, and support Carlos in reconstructing the Commando."

"And so you decided," Mack said, "that Perry Allison would become Carlos?"

"Like shit I did," Perry said. "Lorca decided I would become Carlos, and threatened me with blackmail if I didn't. I was ready to go back to Washington and tell Langley only that Carlos had said no to the pitch. Even if the Company had found out eventually that I had killed him they would have tried to hush it up. So I had no particular problems."

"But Lorca did?" Mack said.

"A pot full," Perry confirmed. "Carlos's father, who had set up the meeting, would be asking questions when Carlos failed to show up. He was a lawyer, with powerful connections, and he could have demanded a government investigation. Carlos had never violated Venezuelan laws, and in Europe he was just a support type who had never been involved in terrorist acts himself. If there had been a trial Lorca could have gone to jail as an accessory."

Mack snuffed out his cigarette. "Why didn't you just skip and leave Lorca holding the bag?"

"For two reasons," Perry said. "Lorca reminded me that because I was born in Maricaibo I was considered a Venezuelan,

235

despite the fact that both my parents were Americans. Even the Company wouldn't have had the clout to keep me from being extradicted in the case of a murder trial. Then he really put the screws to me. He threatened to give my name to Carlos's father. That would have been a death sentence. I was a pretty conspicuous jet setter at the time, and if Carlos's friends had learned that a CIA spook had gunned down one of their buddies, I would have been an easy target with a short life span.

"So, reluctantly, I became a terrorist," Perry continued. "The idea was that I would impersonate Carlos just for a while, a few months, and then Carlos would simply disappear—but in *Europe*, where neither Lorca nor I would be implicated. It was easy. We sent Carlos's father a message saying he had to return to Paris. I checked in with the COS and told him Carlos had turned down the pitch. I went back to Langley and then to my office in New York. I flew to Paris and knocked on the door of my new contact. No problem. I knew all about Carlos's background from reading his file. The Company had taught me to act like Carlos—the tradecraft, the terrorist methods, even how to handle the weapons. And, working for my father's oil trust, I had the cover to travel anywhere. It was a perfect setup. As Clem would say, it went smooth as snake shit."

Mack shook his head, but said nothing.

"And aside from being easy," Perry continued, "it was exciting as hell. It's on the record, Mack. Remember, I recommended that if anyone really wanted to recruit Carlos, the best bait would be the promise of a more thrilling life style. Carlos was dead when I wrote that, and so I suppose I was talking about myself. Later it amused me when Professor Baumgardner told me in Bonn of his conclusion that the Baader-Meinhof people had become terrorists because they were bored. During those first few weeks back in London I found myself enjoying the pretense of being Carlos. The excitement was habit-forming and I really became hooked when I realized I was better at it than he had ever been. Soon I was able to put together a new Commando Boudia in Paris and London. The time came when I had to do something to impress the kids

I had recruited. I read that Menachem Begin was visiting Edward Seiff at his home in London. I went there and almost succeeded in killing him. Then I tossed a bomb into the Hapoalin Bank."

"What about Moukarbal, Perry? According to the history books, Carlos killed him in 1975 in Paris."

"Moukarbal, the only man who could recognize that I was not the real Carlos, was arrested and became a police informant. Someone told him I was at a party in an apartment in the Rue Toullier in Paris. He took three police agents there. It was a unique opportunity. He was looking for a man long dead. I killed him and two of the detectives."

Mack winced.

"It bothers you? Killing people, Mack, is fun."

"And why the vendetta against CIA station chiefs? For fun?"

"I always figured there were two services with the smarts and capability to catch me. The Israelis and the Company. God knows I carried off enough operations against the Mossad. Then, I decided to shake up the Company, too. I introduced an element which was bound to add to its already faltering morale and efficiency—killing station chiefs. I had nothing to do with Dick Welch's assassination in Athens, but the furor which followed it gave me the idea that a *series* of dead chiefs would *really* shake up the Agency."

"Fred Bond?" Mack asked.

"Target of opportunity," Perry explained. "I saw a note in Lucy's papers indicating you were in Mexico, at the Maria Cristina. Even though I was checking in with Lucy every morning I found I could manage a flight to Mexico City and back without missing the roll call. I intended to kill you. Instead, Fred Bond opened the door of your hotel room. I had known him in the Agency, so he gave me the big hello and let me in the room."

"Everything you're telling me explains *how* you became Carlos," Mack said. "But *why*? Once you had created the impression that Carlos was still alive, why keep it up? Why take such incredible risks?"

"Money." Perry's voice was even. "Power."

"Money?" Mack asked. "The son of a millionaire?"

"Yes, Mack, as Carlos was." Perry poured more brandy into Mack's cup. "But I found a new kind of money. My money. Not the kind my old man used to dole out, like bunches of carrots at the end of a stick to keep me in line. Whenever he was unhappy with me he would mutter about rewriting his will. And not the kind of money that had to be examined by his tax people, grubby little guys who smirked when I tried to explain five hundred bucks I had really spent in a Paris whorehouse. No more Monopoly money for me, Mack. Bigger games, bigger money. One of Symser's companies paid me almost fifteen million in Argentina for the release of their manager. My share of the OPEC ransom alone was almost twenty million dollars."

"I don't understand, Perry. Unless you're crazy, you know they'll catch up with you. When you and I failed to show up at the airport, everyone must have realized that you were responsible. They'll be on your trail."

"They will be looking for Perry Allison," Perry said, "and he no longer exists. Only Carlos exists now. Once I decided to continue my life as Carlos, I started sending hush money to Lorca in Caracas. I could have killed him, but I was always afraid he would leave something behind, maybe in a safe-deposit box, revealing the true story. Then when you became so interested in him that we both went to Caracas, I knew I had to kill him. My German girls did a good job. And now I can't go back to being even a part-time Perry Allison, in case Lorca has left instructions for his son, or for the Venezuelan authorities."

Mack regarded Perry curiously. "You're not really a political crusader, Perry. And you didn't become an international criminal because you needed the money. Maybe you're just sick."

"Don't try to be a shrink," Perry said. "The fact is that I've become history's most successful and most famous practitioner of my particular trade. And soon I will be its most powerful. Can you imagine, Mack, what it will mean to have the secretary of state under my control?"

"What will you demand?" Mack enquired. "Ransom? Release of political prisoners?"

"Those are options, Mack, but they are only mundane second choices." Perry's voice was calm, edged with contempt. "Good enough for some, but not for Carlos. I'm about to embark on the most intriguing political adventure ever attempted by one man. I won't publicize the fact that the secretary is my prisoner. I won't make video tapes or anonymous telephone calls to the newspapers. The headlines will come later. My dialogue will be a covert one with Washington. They will have to explain the disappearance of the secretary of state some way, yet what will they be able to say? My demands, Mack, will come in increments. Reasonable, negotiable items that the president will be forced to accept in order to avoid personal responsibility for the secretary's death. Foreign policy, Mack. Policy shifts—a zig here, a zag there—shifts that could be gradually and plausibly explained. The possibilities are limitless. Do you realize the price certain governments will pay me as long as I can continue to humiliate Washington?"

Perry's eyes widened, and his voice became more strident. "It will work, Mack, if I play the game right. Washington will have no choice but to negotiate with me. I will manipulate history! Can you comprehend the magnitude of such pleasure, Mack?"

Mack asked himself if it was even remotely possible that Perry was right? He felt a chill in his body, as he recalled the usual ineptitude of any government forced to cope with unexpected threats.

"Washington would never give in to that kind of blackmail," Mack said.

"I believe Washington will," Perry said. "I can wait for weeks, even months. Meanwhile, no operation will be too risky for me. The secretary of state will be my insurance policy. Should I fail in an operation and be captured, who would not exchange me for the secretary of state?"

Perry paused and stared defiantly at Mack.

Mack pondered. He recalled that many years before, an intelligence veteran had warned him that the most difficult as-

239

pect of any complex intelligence operation was factoring in the element of human irrationality.

Mack shook his head. "You must be unbalanced, Perry, if you think your cronies will be able to abduct the secretary. When you and I failed to arrive at the airport your operation was doomed. The Secret Service would never have allowed the secretary to go to The Homestead."

"The Secret Service had no opportunity to make such a decision, Mack, thanks to your hardheaded stupidity. Lucy failed to find five of my people at the hotel. She couldn't because they never went there." Perry looked at his watch. "Instead they took over that little airport about three hours ago. They'll have done the job. Khalil, who was with me in Vienna, and four others, three men and a woman. They're the best in the business. The secretary will have been drugged, and is being driven here in an ambulance. If the schedule holds, he should be here any minute."

"It's not going to work," Mack said.

"It'll work," Perry said. "I learned something while you and I were playing our games these past few weeks, Mack. I was trying to use too many people. Twenty is too many for my kind of operation. It's too leaky, too many things can go wrong. I almost cancelled the whole thing a dozen times as it was, especially after you screwed up Schwarz's operation in Mexico. Then I realized, day before yesterday, that you still thought the plan was to capture the secretary at The Homestead and fly him away from the landing strip."

"So you've sacrificed the others, at the hotel?"

"Didn't have too much choice," Perry said. "Schwarz was my communication channel to them, and you put him out of business. Too bad. But they've served as decoys for my alternate plan, to trap the bird who will be living in this little nest. When he arrives, Mack, I'm going to kill you."

Perry pulled the .44 Magnum from his waist, and checked the action.

"We can't be too far from The Homestead," Mack said. "There'll be an all-points dragnet. They'll find you."

"No, Mack, they won't find me," Perry said. "They will be looking for me with planes and helicopters and direction finders but they won't find me, because I found your beacon."

Perry reached down, and from the floor near his stool picked up a black, metal box. Attached to it was an antenna, from which two wires trailed.

"I know you, Mack. And I know Frank and his cute little toys. I suspected he might have been tinkering with the rented car, and after I drugged you I stopped a few miles down the road and found your gadget."

"I'll admit I'm disappointed," Mack said. "But I still say you can't hide the secretary of state in this country without being found."

"But it will never occur to anyone to look for him here," Perry said. "Mack, where did I learn the tradecraft and the tricks of the business which allowed me not only to impersonate Carlos, but to outdo him?"

"With the Company," Mack said.

"Where with the Company?"

"Why, at the CIA training school. At The Farm."

"And who, Mack, would search for a missing secretary of state at The Farm? Because that's where we are."

Perry pointed straight up with his index finger.

"Don't forget that audacity is my trademark. We're under The Farm. All those clever young college graduates at school again to learn how to be spies, are just a few feet above us. Imagine their surprise when someday they learn that the American secretary of state, a troglodyte, was hidden in a cave under their feet."

"Brilliant," Mack said. "Audacious and brilliant. How did you manage it, Perry?"

"Khalil and his team dug the tunnel. It leads to a false wall, in a kitchen pantry, in a house just outside the perimeter of The Farm. Since the cover of The Farm was blown a half dozen years ago, the real estate developers have been crowding closer and closer, lobbying in Richmond for a share of those acres of forest full of deer and the ponds full of bass.

Khalil and the woman rented the house. So the secretary of state will be hidden here, at the end of the tunnel, for weeks, months, perhaps years. And it will never occur to anyone to look for him in a prison carved out of CIA's property."

There was a buzz from a box affixed to a timber in the tunnel. Perry listened. The buzz was repeated a second, third, and fourth time. Perry stood, smiling with satisfaction.

"Our visitor has arrived," Perry said. He put the Magnum in his belt. Crouching, so as not to bump his head, he went down the tunnel and disappeared.

Mack examined the lock on the door of his cage, then put his shoulder against the grillwork and pushed; it held firm. By stretching, Mack was able to reach through the grill far enough to grasp the brandy bottle. He drank. And waited.

Perry reappeared at the far end of the tunnel. He was pulling an ambulance cot in the dark. A man in a medical intern's white coat pushed the wheeled stretcher from behind. Mack had never seen this man before. He was tall, taller than Perry, and was forced to stoop low as he and Perry propelled the cot over the uneven earth floor of the tunnel. A white sheet completely covered the figure on the stretcher.

Perry and the man in the white jacket stopped at the iron grill.

"He may be drowsy," Perry said, "but who cares when you have such a distinguished guest?"

Perry flung the sheet aside, revealing the figure under it, and gasped.

"If you reach for the gun," Skip Wilson warned, "I'll put a bullet in your mouth!" She smiled prettily, aiming her pistol directly at Perry's face.

Perry whirled toward the man standing at the rear of the cot. He, too, pointed his gun at Perry.

"If she misses," the man in the white coat said, "I won't. You know me well enough, Carlos, to know that I don't miss."

"Traitor!" Perry drew back as if he had been struck. "You're a traitor!"

"Traitor to whom?" the tall man asked. "Perhaps to Carlos.

242

Perhaps to Khalil. But not to those who sent me to work with you."

"Who sent you? The Mossad?" Perry was almost apoplectic, his face flushed. "Who are you?"

"Call me Ishmael," the man said. He turned to Mack. "Half-brother to Isaac."

"What happened to the others?" Perry was frantic. "Where is Khalil?"

"Skip," Mack was speaking, "look in Perry's pockets for the key to this cage."

Skip patted Perry's pockets, found his keys, and opened the grill. Mack walked out and the man called Ishmael shoved Perry into the underground cell and slammed the grill shut.

"Proverbs," Ishmael said. "He who digs a pit will fall into it."

Perry slumped on the cot. For a moment he let his head fall, then he looked up at Mack.

"How, Mack?" Perry asked, his voice almost a whisper. "How did you beat me?"

"A little luck," Mack said, "and some good information." Mack searched in his pocket and found a crumpled pack of Gauloises; he extracted one and lit it.

"It was scarey when that telephone call from Carlos interrupted our first meeting," Mack went on. "From the beginning he knew what our intentions were, and he was so cocksure he challenged us by letting us know he knew. It meant there was a leak which threatened our operation, even our lives. Symser had to be ruled out right away; he didn't know enough to be useful to Carlos. After a while the possibility that Carlos had penetrated the Agency had to be ruled out as well, because neither Skip nor anyone else knew the total picture of our operations sufficiently to pass on to the Agency the kind of knowledge Carlos was receiving. It had to be one of us.

"Then," Mack continued, "Fred Bond was murdered in my hotel room in Mexico City. Fred was an able officer and had learned to survive in dark alleys—too much of a pro to be surprised in a small room by a stranger. He must have known and trusted the man who put two ounces of lead in his head.

That's when I first suspected that one of us was not only working for Carlos, but killing for him."

Mack dropped the cigarette on the plank floor of the underground room and ground it under his heel. He glanced at Skip: she was wearing the Haitian amulet.

"And then, Perry, we flushed out an elephant—something you knew that you didn't know we knew. After the brouhaha at the Villa Hermosa you believed Frank had tried to open Schwarz's safe and failed. He didn't fail. So we knew the background of Operation *Hogar* and that Carlos had been making regular deposits, ten thousand dollars a month, to someone in Caracas. Lucy identified them only as 'the Humboldt payments.' She didn't understand what that meant, but I had a notion it might be connected with you, Perry. Alexander Humboldt was the German naturalist who spent years studying the flora and fauna of Venezuela, and exploring the sources of the Orinoco River. A hotel in Caracas was named for him —the empty hotel on top of the mountain where you met Carlos in 1973. That's when I decided we should visit Venezuela. When we were leaving on the plane you claimed you were frightened. I was the one who was shaken up, because it was then I became convinced that you were not only working for Carlos, but that you might be impersonating him. All because I was lucky enough to have chatted with a Uruguayan waiter weeks before, the night I had dinner with Skip in Washington. The ring of that accent was still in my mind while I listened to you and the taxi driver chattering in Caracas, Perry. I recognized belatedly that the man claiming on the telephone in a Uruguayan accent to be Carlos, couldn't be. Probably one of your Tuparmaro buddies, Perry, reading from a script you wrote for him before you left New York to join us that night in Washington.

"There was another disturbing development in Venezuela," Mack continued. "When we met Lorca I began the discussion by asking him if we knew why we were there. He answered that he knew he wanted to talk about Carlos. That bothered me. Because a half hour before you told me that, in arranging the meeting, you mentioned to Lorca only that we wanted to

244

talk about an urgent matter. Did he assume we wanted to discuss Carlos? Or did you *warn* him?"

The man called Ishmael listened attentively, a bemused smile on his face. Perry said nothing.

"When we returned from Caracas," Mack said, "I lied to everyone about Carlos's plans." He paused, glancing at Skip. "Well, I deceived *almost* everyone. And I promised you that I would notify the FBI that Carlos might attempt to fly out of the country from the emergency airstrip near Clifton Forge. But when I did talk to the Bureau, I told them everything, and asked that the information be passed on the the Secret Service and the Agency."

Perry's voice was small. "And then you tricked me into believing that you really expected me to try to kidnap the secretary at The Homestead, when you knew Khalil would be waiting for him at the airport!"

"And it worked, Perry," Mack said, "because you were arrogantly stupid. Stupid enough to think that I would lay the life of the secretary of state on the line. He's sleeping tonight in his home in Georgetown. The plane that arrived at the airport carried Skip and a group of antiterrorist commandos, the special unit which has been training for years at Fort Carson in Colorado, just as the Israelis had a team for Entebbe, and the Germans one for Mogadishu."

Mack turned to Skip. "What happened at the airport?"

"Our friend was there," Skip glanced at the man called Ishmael, "and four others. Two men and a woman were arrested. But when the plane door opened and Khalil realized he had been trapped he began firing with a machine pistol. There were other shots from other guns." Skip paused, and looked at Ishmael. "Khalil was killed. The bullets entered the back of his head."

Perry screamed at Ishmael: "Traitor! You killed him!"

"Khalil was the victim of the wrath of God," Ishmael said. "Perhaps, in the confusion, it might have been my gun which was God's instrument. It pleases me that he is dead." He paused, then continued in a low voice, staring at Perry. "I had a friend. He was an athlete, a platform diver. When he thrust his body into space and arched his back it was like watching the flight of a bird. He was just past his twenty-first birthday when he died at Munich. Khalil was at Munich, too."

Perry glanced at Mack. "They would never have found us, except for this traitor. I discovered your ridiculous beacon—"

"We would have found you," Skip interrupted. "In fact we found you several days ago. We knew of this underground prison, and the Company's been watching it since you began digging the tunnel."

"How?" Mack asked. He was honestly surprised.

"From the seismographs," Skip said. "They're placed at intervals around the school. They let us know if someone is digging even enough to slip under the fence. Perry's excavation set the needles quivering. We've known about this place from the beginning."

"Where are the others?" Mack asked.

"Upstairs," Skip said. "With the local police and a delegation from the FBI."

"Perhaps," Ishmael said, "it is time for the lady to leave."

"Why the lady?" Mack asked.

"Perhaps she would prefer not to be a witness when you kill this man."

"No," Mack said. "I won't kill him."

"Very well." Ishmael shrugged. "Both of you may go. I will do it." He flipped the safety on the machine pistol.

Perry backed into a corner of the earth cell.

"No," Mack repeated. "We cannot murder him."

"But we must." Ishmael was incredulous. "Don't you realize that as long as he lives as a prisoner, Carlos will provide the motivation for countless acts of terrorism around the world? Planes will be hijacked. Government officials will be kidnapped so that terrorists can demand the release of their hero, Carlos? Don't you see that, alive, he will not likely remain a prisoner, but will be free again to murder and take hostages?"

"I understand," Mack said. "And you're right. But we can't kill him."

"But we must! You are being illogical. It took me five years to work myself into a position of confidence with Khalil so

246

that I could kill him and this man. My service would never have instructed me to cooperate with you if we had suspected you would allow him to remain alive. He must be executed!"

Mack knew the Israeli was *right*.

When Mack spoke aloud to the man called Ishmael his voice was strained and his face tight. "I know your rules, but we can't kill him. Some other place, some other time, but not here. If you find yourself with him on the Sinai be my guest. I'll help if I'm with you. *But not here!*"

Skip realized that she had never before heard Mack shout.

Mack opened the door to the cage. He lifted the gun he had taken from Perry. "Let's go—*Carlitos.*"

Skip led the way through the tunnel, Perry behind her, followed by Mack and Ishmael. At the turn they ascended a ramp of planks, went through the pantry, and into the kitchen.

Clem turned as they entered. He was standing at the range, stirring a large skillet of simmering eggs; a ham, partially sliced, was on the sideboard near him. For a moment it was quiet as Frank, Hyphenated-Jake, and Emilio glared at Perry.

Finally Clem spoke. "We haven't eaten for a long time. Everybody's welcome but you, Allison. You ain't invited. There's some fellers waiting for you outside."

Perry lunged forward. With one arm he encircled Skip's neck, crushing her body against his; with his free hand he grabbed the butcher knife Clem had been using to slice the ham.

Emilio sprang forward, and both Mack and Ishmael had their guns at the ready, but it was too late. Perry was holding Skip in front of his body, the knife at her throat.

"She dies if anyone tries to stop me!" Perry warned. His eyes were dilated and violent.

Ishmael stepped forward. His gun was still held high.

"Wait!" Mack commanded.

"I warned you," Ishmael said. "Sooner or later an escaped terrorist will hold hostages again. One woman is not important."

"He's right." Skip's voice was even. "Come get this bastard!"

"Don't let them, Mack. I'll kill her!" Perry dropped the knife

247

to Skip's bosom. The tip of the knife penetrated her sweater between her breasts. A dark stain emerged and widened on the cashmere near the Haitian amulet.

"We are going to do what he says," Mack said.

"That's better," Perry hissed. "Go outside, Mack, and tell them we're coming out. I want a car ready, engine running, with the right-hand door open. Go!"

Mack walked out of the kitchen, through the living room, and opened the front door. He shaded his eyes with one hand: five cars beamed their headlights on the house. Red and yellow lights rotated from two police cars.

"Who's in charge out there?" Mack shouted.

"I'm Williams from the Bureau," was the response. "This is federal."

"Allison's holding a knife on the CIA woman. Back up one of the cars, and have it facing the driveway. Leave the engine running, and the door on the right open."

"No, McLendon. That I can't do."

"Do it, Williams. He'll kill her if you don't."

After a moment there was a grudging response. "All right."

There was the sound of an engine starting. One of the cars backed, turned, then stopped. The driver left the engine running and the right-hand door open.

Perry pushed Skip out the door, clasped her close to his body, and moved her to the car. He shoved her through the front seat, the knife still at her chest, until she was under the steering wheel.

Perry turned and yelled at Mack. "It's up to you now, Mack. If I see anyone following us your woman gets the knife!" He turned to Skip. "Let's go, bitch spy. Head for the highway!"

Skip stepped hard on the accelerator. The car's wheels spun momentarily, caught, then sped forward as Skip drove the car into the nearest tree. There was the sound of crunching metal and breaking glass.

"Cover Skip!" Mack shouted. "I'll get Perry!"

Emilio and Hyphenated-Jake rushed to the driver's side of the smashed vehicle and wrenched open the door to pull her from the car. Mack ran to the other side, but Perry had moved

quickly to escape into the trees. There was the sound of underbrush being crushed beneath his feet as he thrashed through
a thicket in the darkness.

"Take this, Mack!" Frank handed Mack one of the flashlights
they had used in flushing Carlos's gang from the crowd at
The Homestead.

"Tell the others not to use their lights," Mack said. "I'm
going after him."

Mack plunged into the woods. Ahead, he could hear Perry
moving, branches and twigs snapping. Mack flicked on the
flashlight: it produced no illumination but, for a moment, he
could see an orange glow through the trees.

"Perry?" It was quiet. "Perry, I'm coming after you. Do
you hear me?"

Again there was the sound of Perry attempting to escape
through the bushes and trees. Now Mack could clearly discern
the glowing hand print Perry did not realize marked him.

"Perry? Remember at the hotel when Frank was demon-
strating how the phosphor dust was to be placed? He was
branding you then, Perry. I'm coming after you and I can
find you."

Mack could hear Perry cursing in the darkness. The orange
glow disappeared, then came into view again, as Perry desperately ripped off his coat to be rid of the telltale brand.
Now Mack crashed through the underbrush and leapt toward
the light.

Beside the crashed car, Emilio and Clem knelt next to
Skip.

"Are you all right?" Hyphenated-Jake asked.

"Shaky, but I'm okay," Skip said. "Where are they?"

"They are fighting," said the man called Ishmael. "They are
trying to kill each other in the forest."

The FBI man grasped Frank by the elbow. "Let's go in there
and help McLendon."

"Don't," Frank said. "Let him do it alone."

The group stood at the edge of the forest, listening to the
grunts and groans of the two men who were battling in the
dark like blinded gladiators.

Then it was silent. Skip turned to Frank. He put his arm around her shoulder as they waited.

"Frank?" It was Mack's voice.

"Yes, Mack."

"Turn on the lights. We're coming out."

Light flooded the forest.

Perry lurched out of the darkness. His body was heaving from exhaustion; he stumbled drunkenly. He was holding both hands to his head, as if to shut out some deafening thunder. He dropped to his knees, his head falling forward. He was whimpering.

Mack came out of the trees. In one hand he held the butcher's knife.

"I want you to remember me, Carlos," Mack said.

"Jesus!" exclaimed Hyphenated-Jake. "Mack has notched both of his ears!"

Perry held his hands tightly to his head, blood streaming through his fingers.

"Family quarrel?" the intern asked. "You both look pretty battered."

"Nothing like that," Mack said.

"Is this man your husband?"

"No," Skip said. She was sitting on an emergency room medical bed, a sheet wrapped around her shoulders. The intern was preparing to stitch the wound in her breast. He glanced, disapprovingly, at Mack.

"If this had been a gunshot wound I would have had to advise the police. You'll have to move the . . . whatever that is."

Skip smiled, looked at Mack, then swung the Haitian amulet behind her neck.

"How many stitches, doctor?" Mack asked.

"Two, maybe three. It's superficial. I'll prescribe something in case there's pain, but aspirin will probably do it."

"I feel fine," Skip said. She sat erect as the intern inserted the fishhook needle. Skip's breasts were taut.

When Mack and Skip finally emerged from the hospital and

drove off in the rented car there was a suspicion of dawn in the east.

"I'll turn in the car at the Washington airport," Mack said. "Then we'll have some breakfast."

"I'm hungry," Skip said.

They did not speak for a few minutes. Then Mack said, "You were great back there. And I'll admit I was relieved to see Ishmael. When Perry told me he had found Frank's beacon I was afraid you would never find me. I didn't know they had seismographs around The Farm."

"I don't know that they do," Skip said dryly. "I just didn't want that little bastard to think he had outwitted the Company. Not a bad idea—I think I'll put it in the suggestion box."

At Richmond, Mack turned off to the Washington highway.

"Where will you be spending Christmas, Skip?"

"I might visit an aunt in New England. You?"

"Tom is with his mother in Europe for the holidays."

It was quiet for several minutes. Then Skip asked, "Mack, why did Perry become Carlos?"

"He told me it happened accidentally. He was drawn into it by circumstance, and then he enjoyed the money and being important. But more than anything, he claimed it was the excitement of a new and thrilling life style."

"Do you believe that?"

"Could be," Mack said. "When Patty Hearst was kidnapped, the family called in a psychiatrist named Hacker. The first thing he did was warn them that Patty might react to her captor's viewpoint. He was right. Overnight the innocent, loving daughter of a multimillionaire changed into America's most wanted criminal. That was just at the time Perry was becoming a terrorist, too. Patty—Tania. Perry—Carlos."

"I'm not sure I buy that," Skip said. She thought for a moment. "For my money, Perry was a spoiled, selfish, son of a bitch, and would have been one, rich or poor. It was all even more pronounced having been born and raised among the oil barons. Essentially, he was a coward, out to take care of himself at the expense of everyone else. In the beginning being Carlos was easy and convenient, but then he got sucked in more and more deeply. At some point the game he was playing began to have an attraction all its own, which tended to take some of the blush off the increasing risk."

Neither Mack nor Skip spoke for a long time. Then she moved over in the seat, against Mack, and put her head on his shoulder. She closed her eyes.

"Skip?"

She opened her eyes and looked up.

"Before we turn in the car we could pick up some traveling clothes, go to the airport, and buy two tickets to Haiti."

Janet Wilson did not speak. Finally she said, "Wake me, Mack, before we get there." She closed her eyes again.

Mack turned off the headlights. The sky was bright and clear, and he had traveled the highway many times. He knew where it led. What he didn't know was their final destination.